Praise for Cathy Pegau and her Charlotte Brody mysteries!

BORROWING DEATH

"Entertaining."
—*Publishers Weekly*

"A great mixture of history, mystery and a little bit
of romance. The characters and setting are well-written
and readers will be waiting impatiently for the next
installment to come out."
—*Suspense Magazine*

"It's a real delight to return to the fully realized world
of Pegau's 20th-century Cordova, and the new
central mystery is compelling."
—*Fairbanks Daily News-Miner*

MURDER ON THE LAST FRONTIER

"An excellent start to her promising
new Charlotte Brody series."
—*Mystery Scene*

"The setting of Cordova in the 1920s is as
interesting as the story itself."
—*RT Book Reviews*

"*Murder on the Last Frontier* does everything
right, sucking readers in and refusing to let go until the end."
—*Fairbanks Daily News-Miner*

Books by Cathy Pegau

MURDER ON THE LAST FRONTIER

BORROWING DEATH

MURDER ON LOCATION

Published by Kensington Publishing Corporation

MURDER ON LOCATION

CATHY PEGAU

KENSINGTON BOOKS
www.kensingtonbooks.com

KENSINGTON BOOKS are published by

Kensington Publishing Corp.
119 West 40th Street
New York, NY 10018

All Kensington titles, imprints, and distributed lines are available at special quantity discounts for bulk purchases for sales promotion, premiums, fund-raising, educational, or institutional use.

Special book excerpts or customized printings can also be created to fit specific needs. For details, write or phone the office of the Kensington Sales Manager: Kensington Publishing Corp., 119 West 40th Street, New York, NY 10018. Attn. Sales Department. Phone: 1-800-221-2647.

Kensington and the K logo Reg. U.S. Pat. & TM Off.

eISBN-13: 978-1-4967-0059-9
eISBN-10: 1-4967-0059-7
First Kensington Electronic Edition: March 2017

ISBN-13: 978-1-4967-0058-2
ISBN-10: 1-4967-0058-9
First Kensington Trade Paperback Printing: March 2017

10 9 8 7 6 5 4 3 2 1

Printed in the United States of America

To the People of Cordova

past, present, and future

Acknowledgments

Since Charlotte made her first appearance, I've received both praise (for which I humbly thank you!) and criticism over her ideas and actions. "Too modern a woman of the time," they said. I bit my tongue and sat on my hands to keep myself from firing off an irritated "Read a little history!" response.

One of my favorite quotes is by Laurel Thatcher Ulrich: "Well-behaved women seldom make history." Women have always made an impact on the world, we just don't hear as much about them. And it certainly takes a particular sort of woman to grab the attention of most historians. Are they all ill-behaved? No, but those are the ones who stick in our minds. And by "ill-behaved" I mean women who do not conform to the social mores of their time, not necessarily bad people.

I admire those women because they had the guts to stand up for things they believed in, to take charge of their own lives despite the attempts of society to make them sit down and do what they "should" be doing. To heck with that.

Thank you, ladies, for inspiring me and other women. You've shaped us and our world, and we hope to do the same. So I'll amend Ulrich's quote: Well-behaved women seldom make history . . . or the future.

MURDER ON LOCATION

Chapter 1

The SS *Fairbanks* made its approach to the Cordova ocean harbor, belching black smoke that quickly dissipated on the icy breeze. Anticipation from the crowd waiting on the dock was as thick as the aroma of tar, tide, and the exhaust from the line of idling automobiles. Sunlight glinted off the gray-green water and the bright white of the hull of the ship still one hundred yards away.

Charlotte Brody smiled at the memory of coming to Alaska on a similar vessel just six months ago. Still a "cheechako" in the eyes of the locals, she was settling into her new home. Plans to return east come spring—only a week or so away, supposedly—had been indefinitely postponed.

The steamer's air horn blew a greeting as it approached, and the largest gathering of Cordovans Charlotte had ever seen in one place cheered in response, waving hats and hands.

"Isn't this exciting?" a woman standing beside Charlotte asked no one in particular. Smiling and starry-eyed, the woman brandished a rolled-up movie magazine like a member of the Signal Corps conveying messages to troops.

Charlotte didn't quite share her or the crowd's enthusiasm. Half the population must have turned out for the *Fairbanks*'s arrival. Who knew Cordova, home to some of the most practical people she'd ever met, would become positively giddy over a film crew coming to town?

Then again, given the cold, dark quiet of the winter they had just been through, the arrival of such unusual persons gave the town a boost to its torpid mood. Despite the calendar claiming it was mid-March, the more vitalizing days of the coming season were still a month or so away.

A frozen, salty gust blew in off the water, confirming suspicions of that date. Charlotte shivered within her heavy coat and the trousers she wore. It was also a few tens of degrees from what she knew as spring.

Maybe more like two months away.

If she hadn't been assigned to cover the event, Charlotte would have happily stayed in her warm little house and avoided the whole thing. Or most of the fanfare and over-the-top events, at any rate. Andrew Toliver, owner of the *Cordova Daily Times* and her boss, would have done it himself, but a fall on a slippery step had broken his foot. Being the only other writer on the paper, it fell to Charlotte to cover the most exciting thing to happen to Cordova since the railroad.

Toliver insisted she chronicle the visit by the Californians, painting Cordova in as positive a light as she could. He was sure the articles would be picked up by other newspapers, particularly those in areas where filmmaking was growing, and put the booming town in the minds of the rest of the country, if not the world.

Charlotte flexed her fingers within her mittens in an attempt to get them warm enough to use her pad and pencil when it came time to take notes. She would do her job and do it well, for the sake of the paper and for the town she now called home. The cast and crew would be in Cordova for two weeks. Maybe she'd get caught up in the excitement.

God, I hope so, Charlotte thought as she watched the *Fairbanks* maneuver into position alongside the dock.

While she could admit interest in watching films—they were a great way to entertain or educate—she didn't understand the growing popularity of the actors to the point that ordinary people seemed to put them above others. Many had excellent talents, and some poignant films had been made, but she saw no reason to elevate actors to an idealistic or romanticized status. There were plenty of other people doing real work who deserved acknowledgment and recognition.

Bells rang aboard ship. Several uniformed members of the *Fairbanks* crew threw thick lines over the rails to the longshoremen on the dock. Once the steamer was fastened and the engines throttled down to a low rumble, the gangplank was lowered and secured. Conversations in the crowd became random cheers and whistles, yet no one on the dock moved closer to the vessel. Charlotte noted a number of men facing the crowd now, standing at regular intervals and giving warning glares to any who dared to pass.

Security for the Californians? What did they think was going to happen in Cordova?

After several minutes, a mustached man in a tweed cap and khaki trench coat, with a motion-picture camera balanced on his shoulder, carefully limped down the gangplank. He set the long legs of the tripod on the dock. He made a few adjustments to the box, aimed the lens toward the top of the gangplank, and checked the viewfinder.

The cameraman cupped his hand around his mouth. "Ready to roll!"

He turned his cap around, bent to look through the viewfinder, and began cranking.

A man in his forties strode across the deck and stopped at the top of the gangplank. He wore a bowler hat, a thick white scarf around his neck, and a long black coat. The people on the dock began clapping and cheering. Who was he?

Behind him, a group of men and women gathered in a semi-circle. All were bundled against the cold and not recognizable. A few waved to the people on the dock, much to the delight of several onlookers by the sound of their exclamations.

Smiling, the man in front raised a megaphone and spoke to the attentive audience. "Thank you. Thank you, my friends." His voice boomed from the cone. "It's so wonderful to be back here in Cordova." He swept his hand in a gesture to encompass everything before him. "The most beautiful city in the Alaska Territory."

Cheers and whistles exploded from the dock dwellers, temporarily deafening Charlotte.

"Hey, Wally, you owe me a sawbuck!" someone shouted from the crowd.

Everyone laughed, including the man on the ship.

"And I'll pay it back, I promise," he said, still smiling. "Because with the help of all you fine folks and *North to Fortune*, we're gonna put Cordova on every map and on every mind in the country."

This man could run for mayor.

"For those of you who don't know me, my name is Wallace Meade."

The name was familiar to Charlotte, thanks to Andrew Toliver, and now she had a face to go with it. Wallace Meade owned several properties in Cordova and was generous to local organizations. Meade also had business interests in other towns throughout the territory, including a gold mine in Fairbanks and a tract of land near Juneau where he ran a lumber mill.

Meade had been down in the States for months, Charlotte had learned, busy in California and New York drumming up interest for the up-and-coming film industry to look north. According to Toliver, Meade had finally managed to engage the crew he needed to produce what was supposedly going to be a "truer than life" depiction of Alaska.

Whatever that meant.

"I know the good people of Cordova," Meade continued, "and I've assured the cast and crew that you're the friendliest bunch north of Seattle." The crowd cheered again, and Meade's smile broadened. "So let me introduce a few of these folks to you." He gestured for a tall, thin man to step forward. The man wore a long fur coat, with his scarf pulled up over his nose and mouth. "This here is Stanley Welsh, director of such notable films as *A Place in Their Hearts* and *Granger's Last Stand*. Stanley?"

Charlotte had heard of the films but hadn't seen either of them. One was a murder mystery and the other something about battles during the Civil War.

People cheered, and Welsh took the megaphone from Meade. He tugged his scarf down, revealing his clean-shaven face and narrow features. "Hello, Cordova!" Welsh waited for the noise to die down. "We are so very happy to be here and appreciate your fine welcome on a cold day."

Charlotte thought she detected something of an accent in the man's speech but couldn't place it. Eastern European, perhaps?

"When Mr. Meade told us about your lovely town and showed us pictures, I knew right away it would be perfect for our film, *North to Fortune*. Some wanted us to wait a few more months until it warmed up, but I insisted my cast experience the real Alaska, cold and all. Authenticity, you know!"

"Only if you fixed the story!" a man shouted from behind the crowd.

Several people turned to see who had interrupted the director. No one stepped forward, and Welsh ignored the comment.

What was that all about?

"We will be here in Cordova for approximately two weeks," Welsh continued, "filming exterior shots of the mountains, glaciers, and lake. Our cast and crew are the best and ready for anything. I think some of you are familiar with our lead players."

Welsh smiled as a younger man stepped forward, doffed his

hat, and waved it at the crowd. His dark hair fluttered with the sea breeze.

A woman shouted, "I love you, Peter!"

"Yes," Welsh said, "Peter York will be playing Lawrence, our hero. And Roslyn Sanford is our leading lady, playing the part of Dorothy." A petite woman came up beside York and waved. She could have been anyone; she was so bundled in furs it was difficult to see her face. "We're all terribly pleased to be here, but we should let everyone get off the boat now. Thank you."

Welsh and Meade shook hands, holding the position as a still photographer on the dock took a picture. The photographer gave the men a thumbs-up gesture and the two released hands. Meade took the megaphone from Welsh.

"Tonight, we'll present a few brief scenes from the film and have some other thrilling performances at the Empress Theater," Meade said into the megaphone. "Eight o'clock curtain. Be sure to get your tickets."

"I have mine," the rosy-cheeked woman beside Charlotte said, flapping the movie magazine. "Goodness, that Peter York is a handsome devil, isn't he?"

"I suppose," Charlotte said, mostly to herself, as she jotted notes.

"In his last movie, he played a sheik prince." The woman sighed dramatically, and Charlotte wondered if she'd have to catch her should she faint. "So handsome."

The crowd parted as the cast and crew descended the gangplank, creating a narrow lane for the visitors to reach their awaiting cars. Cordova didn't have enough taxis to take them all, of course. The vehicles belonged to private citizens, hired for the sole purpose of transporting these particular VIPs. The audience would have to find their own way back to town.

Meade led the way, followed by Welsh and a statuesque woman holding his arm. Behind them, Peter York escorted Roslyn Sanford. At least a dozen more well-dressed people followed, obviously not Cordovans by the way they stared up at the surrounding mountains in wide-eyed wonder. A tall, be-spectacled young woman gazed intently at her new environs as if absorbing every detail.

A few of the men broke away from the California group and moved directly to the longshoremen. One man gestured toward the ship, a crane, and then to two waiting flatbed trucks. The shore man nodded, his cigar bobbing up and down as he chewed on the stub.

Shuffling across the slick dock with shoulders hunched against the cold, the visitors piled into the cars. The Cordovans followed as close as the security men would allow, some shouting requests for autographs, others their declarations of love.

Good gravy.

"Miss Brody?" Mr. Jenkins, the Alaska Steamship Company agent, came up beside her, grinning broadly.

Charlotte took his extended hand and shook it. "Good afternoon. Quite the excitement today."

"Yes, indeed," he said, gazing out at the crowd. "We haven't had this sort of brouhaha for some time." Jenkins focused on her again. "Mr. Meade was wondering if you would accompany him and the others to the hotel for an interview."

Charlotte stared at the agent. "Me? How does Mr. Meade know about me?"

Jenkins shook his head, shrugging. "He asked if there were any newsmen about. I told him I thought I saw you in the crowd. He asked me to fetch you."

The back of Charlotte's neck tightened. "Fetch?"

Perhaps she was overreacting, but she was a grown woman, a professional journalist, not something to be retrieved. And Mr. Jenkins wasn't a dog. She would not be at the beck and call of Wallace Meade, no matter what sort of do-gooder he was in the community.

"Um, I'm sure I misheard him," Jenkins said, eyes large with distress as he noticed her frown. "Yes, my apologies, I'm sure I did. Would you follow me, Miss Brody? Please?"

She should say no. She should tell Mr. Jenkins to tell Mr. Meade to take a flying leap. But she didn't want to put Mr. Jenkins in the middle of anything, and she shouldn't judge Meade without facing the man himself. Perhaps he was just tired after a long voyage.

Allowing the benefit of the doubt, for now, Charlotte forced a smile. "Lead the way, Mr. Jenkins."

Relief eased the tension lines from his narrow face. "Thank you. Over here."

He gestured toward the line of automobiles and started to make a path through the crowd. The onlookers reluctantly moved aside as Jenkins tapped shoulders and requested passage. When they finally reached the edge of the group facing the vehicles, Charlotte noted the men keeping the Cordovans from mobbing the visitors had closed ranks. Jenkins told the nearest one that he was escorting Charlotte at Mr. Meade's request.

The man gave Charlotte a quick once-over, then pointed a thumb toward the vehicle at the front of the line, a new deep green 1920 Oakland touring car that Charlotte recognized as belonging to Clive Wilkes. His Studebaker had given up the ghost in December. The passenger side front door opened and Wallace Meade stepped out. The bespectacled young woman Charlotte had seen earlier sat beside the driver. She gave Charlotte a shy smile.

"Mr. Meade," Jenkins said, "this is Miss Charlotte Brody of the *Cordova Daily Times*. Miss Brody, Mr. Meade."

Meade stuck out his right hand. "Nice to meet you, little lady. Andrew Toliver speaks highly of you."

Little lady? Gritting her teeth, Charlotte offered a firm grip to counter the barely there pressure many men provided when shaking hands with a woman. "He's often spoken of you too, Mr. Meade."

Meade's dark eyes narrowed, then glinted with amusement when he realized she hadn't necessarily paid him a compliment.

"Indeed. Please, join us for the ride back to town." He opened the rear door. Director Stanley Welsh and the woman he'd escorted down the gangplank sat on the leather bench seat. "Stanley, Carmen, this is Miss Brody from the local paper. Miss Brody, Stanley and Carmen Welsh, and that's their daughter Cicely up front."

"Pleased to meet you," Charlotte said, shaking the hands of each of the elder Welshes and smiling at Cicely, who peered over the front seat.

Mr. Welsh slid closer to the opposite side of the car, pressing himself against the other door. Mrs. Welsh made room for her.

Charlotte climbed in beside the Welshes, notebook and pencil in hand. Once she was seated, Meade closed the door and returned to his place in front. It was close quarters in the car, considering all their bulky outerwear, but not uncomfortable. Still, Charlotte was glad it was a short ride into town.

"Let's go," Meade said to the driver. He then turned to address the back seat. Poor Cicely Welsh. She was squashed to the driver's shoulder, angling her head to keep Meade from talking into her face. Meade seemed oblivious. "Toliver cabled me to say he was laid up with a broken foot, but that you'd be spot-on ideal for the job of writing up articles for the next few weeks."

Spot-on ideal? Charlotte was amused with Toliver's fib. He knew she wasn't exactly thrilled with the assignment. But knowing Meade's success was due in no small part to his ability to soft-soap folks to get what he wanted, maybe it wasn't Toliver's wording at all.

"I don't know about ideal, Mr. Meade," she said. "I certainly enjoy going to the theater, but I'm not well-versed in the film business."

Stanley Welsh smiled. "Probably all the better for us."

Wincing suddenly, Welsh turned his head toward the window and coughed into a fold of his scarf.

"Are you okay, Papa?" Cicely asked, her brow drawn with

concern. Welsh waved her off, the coughing less intense. Cicely frowned, keeping an eye on her father.

"Film is a marvelous world," Meade said as Welsh recovered from his bout. "Full of so much potential and growing every day. Why, I expect moving pictures will smother live theater in a few short years—"

"That would be a sad day," Carmen Welsh interjected. "There should be both."

Silently agreeing, Charlotte jotted down their exchange in shorthand, willing to let the conversation play out rather than interfere with questions for the moment.

"I should say so, my dear." Stanley Welsh patted his wife's arm. Charlotte couldn't tell if it was in true support or as pacification in front of a stranger. And a reporter, to boot. "Carmen was a stage actress from the time she was a tot. What I think Wallace means is that as wonderful as live shows are, the ability to distribute film around the world will enable scores more to enjoy a story. Get the media to the masses."

"Exactly," Meade said. "Especially up here. It's cheaper to send reels of film than casts and crews for live shows. And by the same token, why shouldn't the natural beauty of Alaska be shared around the world?" He twisted farther in his seat to better focus on Charlotte. "That's why I traveled from studio to studio, director to director, looking for someone who'd appreciate the natural wonder of the territory."

"And that's when you found Mr. Welsh?" Charlotte asked.

"Indeed." Meade beamed at the director. "Stanley talked to Roslyn about coming in, since she's such a crowd-pleaser, and Cicely here wrote a bang-up scenario."

Charlotte had read the credits titles on some films, happily noting how many women were involved in productions. "*North to Fortune* is your story, Miss Welsh? How wonderful. Have you written many?"

Cicely's cheeks pinked. "A few. Roslyn is under contract with the studio, but she's popular enough now to choose her films.

I've written three other scenarios at her insistence. We work well together."

"Roslyn has the heart of the audiences and the ear of the studio head," Welsh said, chuckling. "If she requests a certain director or writer, then it will be done if it means getting her to agree to do a picture. Not to mention Cicely is quite talented."

"I'm pleased to see women with so much say in the industry," Charlotte said. "Have any of you been to Alaska before, besides Mr. Meade, I mean?"

"No, none of us have." Cicely gazed out the windscreen. "It's as beautiful as Mr. Meade said. I read up as best I could while writing the story and figured we could change things as needed to remain accurate. Right, Papa?"

"Of course, of course." Welsh waved a hand in dismissal, as if they'd had that discussion in the past. "But we also want an exciting story that grabs the audience." He clenched a fist and raised it in enthusiasm. "Action! Adventure! Heroic deeds! That's what sells."

Carmen covered her husband's fist and lowered it. "Don't get overexcited, dear. Along with that, we want characters who people can rally behind and believable plots."

Welsh pecked his wife on the cheek. "That as well."

"You see, Miss Brody," Meade said, "there's a lot involved with making a film on location. The production company was initially reluctant to help fund the trip, but Stanley and I convinced them authenticity was key."

"Absolutely," Charlotte said.

"We want this film to be made with the full support of the town," Meade continued. "Can we count on you to help with that?"

Charlotte made a gesture in the direction of the dock behind them. "You saw the crowd, Mr. Meade. I'm quite sure you have it already."

Meade grinned. "Yes, and it was a glorious reception. But the entire town won't be out with us when we do location shots. At least I hope not." He chuckled at his own words. "Which means, anything reported back to them, and subsequently picked up by other papers in the States, can potentially influence the success of this film or future projects brought up here."

Ah, so that was it. Meade wanted to make sure the *Times* painted things in a positive light. Charlotte couldn't blame him, of course, but she wasn't his publicist, she was a journalist.

"Do you anticipate any problems?" she asked.

"There's always some sort of difficulty or another on a film," Meade said.

"I'm not quite sure I understand what you're getting at, Mr. Meade. Do you mean the man who shouted about fixing the story?"

Meade and Welsh exchanged looks that Charlotte could only interpret as a brief, silent argument. Carmen quirked a slender eyebrow at her husband, and Cicely seemed as confused as Charlotte. Finally, Welsh appeared to give up, shaking his head and glancing out the window.

Meade focused on Charlotte over the seat. "A month or so ago, just after we announced our intent to come up here and revealed the basic story of *North to Fortune,* I received a letter."

Charlotte's curiosity stirred. "What sort of letter?"

"Someone had disclosed the plot details of the film to the local Native group, and it found the ear of some lawyer. There seem to be concerns that the portrayal of Natives may be undignified," Meade said.

Cicely's mouth dropped open. "Mr. Meade, you never mentioned that to me. As the scenarist, I want to make sure—"

"We took care of it, Cicely," Welsh said, his voice hard. "I told Wallace not to bother you with it."

"Not to bother me?" Cicely turned around as best she could without impeding the driver. Her face was red with anger. "If my story isn't accurate, or someone finds it insulting, I need to know."

"It was just some blowhard." Welsh gave a dismissive shake

of his head. "Everyone gets these sorts of letters. If we abided by every fool who got their feelings hurt, we'd never get a film made. Don't put that in your article, if you please, Miss Brody."

Charlotte had stopped taking notes, but she certainly took note of Welsh's attitude. "Who wrote the letter?"

Everyone but the driver looked to Wallace Meade. Did they not realize the man behind the wheel had ears and a mouth? Or was he being paid enough to keep mum?

"It was signed by the President of the Alaska Eyak Council, Jonas Smith, and the lawyer out of Juneau, Caleb Burrows," Meade said. "I know the men by reputation only, and they're no fools, Welsh, I told you that. Wrote back to assure them the film would be truthful."

Charlotte recognized Smith's name and the AEC, a small but growing group of Natives in Cordova who stood for fair treatment and rights on their own lands.

"Considering how Native Americans in the States are treated in film as well as in real life," Charlotte said, "you can't blame the AEC for their concern."

Stanley Welsh frowned at her. "We know the Alaskan Indians are nothing like that. *North to Fortune* will depict them as the simple, peaceful people they are. Everyone will admire how they survive in such hostile conditions with such primitive tools and ways. Why, in the scene where the Native saves Peter's character, the noble savage becomes the hero. For a short time, at least. And Peter teaches him to be civilized in return."

Charlotte cringed. "Mr. Welsh, Native Alaskans are certainly not uncivilized, nor are they savages of any sort. It's ludicrous to suggest otherwise."

"And far from primitive, Papa," Cicely cut in. The frown lines between her eyes deepened. "I read up on a noted anthropologist's works and spoke to an Alaska actor about life up here. I put some of it in the scenario. What scene are you talking about? I never wrote anything like that."

Again, Welsh offered a dismissive wave. "I thought the story needed a little more action. We'll talk about it later. I believe we're at the hotel. More fans—Oh."

Charlotte peered out the window as the car rolled to a stop in front of the Windsor, Cordova's most prestigious hotel. The four-story building dominated Second Street, promising luxury and comfort. A group of a dozen or so people bundled against the cold stood on the wooden walk near the double doors. Several in the crowd held signs that read, UNFAIR TO NATIVES and WE ARE A PEOPLE, NOT A PLOT.

Meade glared out the driver's window. "Damnation."

Chapter 2

The driver set the brake and hopped out, then opened the rear door for Stanley Welsh. Welsh levered himself out of the car and offered his hand first to Carmen and then to Charlotte. On the other side of the vehicle, Meade assisted Cicely.

A black Buick pulled up behind them along the walkway and the doors opened. Peter York and Roslyn Sanford emerged, along with another petite young woman. Peter smiled at the group on the walk, then, reading the signs, realized they weren't the adoring fans who had been waiting at the dock. With a nervous nod in their direction, he made his way over to Carmen and Stanley Welsh. Roslyn also appeared to be thrown off by the presence of the silent group. She joined the lead car's occupants, standing between Cicely and Meade.

All of them ignored the protesters on the walk, who made no effort to directly confront the Californians. Charlotte noted the AEC members murmuring to one another and glancing at two men in dark coats and hats, as if waiting for direction or for something to happen.

Though Meade and the Welshes seemed disturbed by their

appearance, Charlotte was looking forward to questioning the Alaska Eyak Council. While she didn't want to create a feud in the pages of the *Times,* printing opinions and points of view other than those of the masses was her favorite aspect of being a journalist. By the messages on the signs and the contents of the letter Meade and Welsh had received, she had a feeling any direct conflict would be a doozy.

"Bang-up beauty of a landscape, isn't it?" Peter said, rubbing his bare hands together. "I hail from Minnesota. Haven't felt this cold in ages."

The other young woman made a face between her fur hat and collar. "It's like hell, it is. I thought I saw a penguin back there."

"Wrong side of the world, dear," Roslyn said, sliding her hands inside her sable muff.

Meade frowned and cleared his throat. "Peter, Roslyn, Paige, this is Miss Brody of the *Cordova Daily Times.* She'll be tagging along and writing about our stay here." His words were obviously a warning to Paige to shut her mouth, at least in public. "Miss Brody, I'd like to introduce our leads Peter York and Roslyn Sanford, and this is Paige Carmichael."

Handshakes and congenial smiles came from Peter and Roslyn, but Paige was too honest or not well-versed enough in public relations to hide her displeasure at their location.

"Is it always this cold?" she groused, giving an exaggerated shiver.

"I don't know," Charlotte replied. "This is my first winter here."

From the corner of her eye, Charlotte saw one of the protesters step forward. She recognized him as the leader of the AEC.

"Mr. Welsh? Mr. Meade? I'm Jonas Smith, president of the Alaska Eyak Council." The cadence of his speech and slight accent was familiar to Charlotte these days. Smith turned and gestured. A tall man in a long wool coat and fedora came forward as well. "This is Caleb Burrows. We'd like to know if you received our second letter and have considered our position on the matter of Native portrayal in your film?"

Meade's smile was tense. "Mr. Smith, your concerns have been taken into consideration. If you'll excuse us—"

"That sounds like lawyer talk," Caleb Burrows said. He smiled as well, his dark eyes shining. Perhaps a few years older than Charlotte, he appeared to be Native Alaskan by his features. "We want to be assured the Eyak people aren't insulted or depicted in a derogatory way, Mr. Meade. I don't think that's too much to ask."

"Don't be ridiculous," Stanley Welsh said, coming forward. Both Cicely and Carmen Welsh tried to stop him by physically grasping his coat sleeves, but to no avail. "Of course it isn't going to be insulting. Why, once this film is released, everyone will know of the simplistic, noble, and peaceful peoples of Alaska. They'll want to come up here and meet real Alaska Indians. You'll be able to stand on any street corner and have your picture taken, charge as much as a dollar, I'd wager, and make lots of money."

Cicely Welsh's eyes widened behind her spectacles and her face paled. "Papa, please."

Jonas Smith's expression darkened with rage. "We are not some sort of sideshow for people to gawk at."

"He didn't mean it that way, Mr. Smith," Cicely said, futilely attempting to pull her father away from the man. "The scenes will be fixed. I promise—"

"I'm the director," Welsh said, speaking over his daughter. "I will say what scenes are to be changed." Carmen took hold of his other arm, but he shook her off. "No one tells me how to make my film."

He fell into a coughing fit that changed Cicely's and Carmen's looks of embarrassed horror to that of concern. Welsh reached into an inside pocket of his coat and withdrew a small brown bottle. Removing the cap, he took a healthy swallow, and then coughed into his sleeve.

Meade finally stepped forward, patting Welsh on the back. In assistance to his coughing or as some sort of indication of a job well done? Maybe Meade wasn't as upset about negative publicity as he claimed.

"Let's take this off the street like civilized men, shall we, Mr. Burrows?" Meade reached out and grasped the other man's right hand, smiling all the while. Burrows and Smith both glared at him. "Mr. Welsh and I will be in touch with you soon." Releasing the lawyer, he turned away and gestured for the crew to head toward the Windsor. "Why don't we go check in?"

The Welsh women and the actors glanced nervously between Meade and the AEC members as they made their way into the hotel. Stanley Welsh muttered between coughing fits, but allowed himself to be led inside.

"We won't be put off, Mr. Meade," Burrows said. "I can guarantee you that."

"I'm sure we'll come to a satisfactory agreement, sir." Meade touched Charlotte's arm. "Miss Brody, I think we'll freshen up and relax a little for now. You'll be at the theater tonight, won't you?" His smile was tense and didn't reach his eyes. "I'd be very happy to give you a personal interview and access to the cast after the show. I'll give security your name so you can come backstage."

Charlotte hadn't been keen on going, but of course now she was too curious about the interaction with the AEC to treat the assignment as a piece of fluff or page filler. "Oh, I shall be there, Mr. Meade. You can count on it."

The members of the AEC spoke quietly among themselves as the film people disappeared inside the Windsor. Caleb Burrows and Jonas Smith conferred in low, urgent tones, but not so low that Charlotte couldn't hear them.

"They have some nerve dismissing us like that," Smith said,

his face dark with anger. "Do they think this is some sort of joke?"

Burrows laid his gloved hand on Smith's shoulder. "If they do, we'll set them straight. Let them think we're easily mollified, Jonas. We'll be the patient ones, and when we meet with Meade and Welsh they'll know in no uncertain terms that we mean business."

"Mr. Burrows? Mr. Smith?" Charlotte stepped closer to the two men. "Can I get a quote for the *Times*?"

They exchanged looks, then Burrows patted Smith's shoulder. "I'll handle this, Jonas. Let's meet back at your house in a couple of hours, give everyone a chance to have supper before the gathering at the theater later."

So they planned on attending the show. This was certainly becoming more of a story than Charlotte had assumed. Why hadn't any of the AEC's letters or protests been in the local paper?

Smith nodded to the other man, shook his hand, and tipped his hat to Charlotte. "Miss Brody."

He moved off to talk to the others in their shared language. Though she couldn't understand what he said, she noted his calming tone and the nominal reduction of the anger in the members' eyes.

"I'm afraid we haven't been properly introduced," Burrows said, removing his hat despite the chill in the air and offering his right hand. His black hair was fashionably cut, and his smile showed even, white teeth. "Caleb Burrows, at your service."

Charlotte shook his hand, appreciating that he held hers firmly, not as if she were too delicate to touch. "Charlotte Brody of the *Cordova Daily Times*. Tell me, Mr. Burrows, how did you get involved with this situation and the AEC?"

Burrows set his hat on his head and clasped his hands behind his back when they released. "Jonas heard about the film being produced and was concerned when it described disturbing scenes of Alaska Natives perpetrating crimes for the sake of making us the villains, or worse, painting us as savages needing to be tamed. A mutual friend recommended Jonas contact me. Together, we drafted the first letter to Meade and Welsh."

"Did either of them respond?" Charlotte asked. She was taking notes as fast as her chilled hands allowed.

"They did." Burrows's dark brows knit. "But it was typical of Meade's roundabout way of saying a lot without saying much at all. Not unlike a lawyer," he said with a grin.

Charlotte smiled. "I understand Mr. Meade has held several positions and practiced a number of professions, but I don't think lawyer is one of them. The double-talk must come naturally."

Burrows gave a boisterous laugh, drawing the attention of the few passersby. "I can't deny the advantage of natural talent."

"So Meade and Welsh replied, but in effect did nothing to address Mr. Smith's and the AEC's concerns?" Charlotte said.

"No, they did not, as far as we could tell." Burrows shook his head as if disappointed in the Californians. "I traveled here, and with the input of the AEC, we drafted a second letter three weeks ago."

Charlotte recalled what Meade and Welsh had said in the car on the way to town. There was no mention of a second letter by them. "That second letter was more than a request to change the Native representation of *North to Fortune*?"

Burrows nodded once. "It was. Defamation is a serious matter. We want the film to show the Native people in a more realistic light. If they didn't agree to that stipulation, we indicated we'd take legal action and make any and every effort to stop the filming."

"What sort of efforts?" Charlotte asked. How far would Burrows and the AEC go?

The attorney smiled again, but it was a predatory expression. "As I said, Miss Brody, whatever it takes."

Charlotte held her notebook and pencil a little higher. "Can I quote you on that?"

"I wouldn't have said it otherwise."

"Why wasn't any of this in the *Times*, Mr. Burrows?" There had been nothing but eager anticipation of the film company's arrival for several weeks and not a word about the AEC's displeasure.

Burrows lifted his hat and slicked back his hair, a thoughtful expression on his face. "Part of the reason was the fear of backlash from folks here if the film people decided not to come up. In case you hadn't noticed, Miss Brody, there have been some awful things done to and said about Native people in these parts."

Though most white Cordovans seemed to get along with their Native neighbors, there were still conflicts. Charlotte had heard the all-too-casual remarks demeaning Native, Filipino, and Black members of the community. She'd also learned of incidents through conversations with Andrew Toliver, Deputy James Eddington, and her brother Michael's new assistant Mary Weaver, who was an Eyak. Michael had treated several of the participants after fights. The altercations had been physical, with injuries or sometimes vandalism occurring on both sides, but none had been fatal. So far.

"The AEC isn't against the filming itself," Burrows continued, "and there is some economic potential for all of Cordova. We just want fair treatment. If achieving that could be accomplished quietly, then there was no reason to make a spectacle of it."

"You don't think Meade and Welsh are going to work with you, do you?"

"All I know, Miss Brody, is that the more people pretend you aren't there, or aren't significant, the more likely something unpleasant will occur." Burrows gave her a knowing smile. "Legally unpleasant, of course."

"Of course," Charlotte said. "What was Meade and Welsh's response to your second letter?"

Burrows's gaze narrowed, the smile faltering. "Response? There was no response. That's part of the reason why we gathered here today. We wanted to let them know we wouldn't be ignored."

Meade had said he'd replied to the letter. Had he lied?

"Perhaps the response was lost in the mail or something," Charlotte suggested.

"Perhaps," Burrows said, conceding to the possibility, "but what's done is done. The AEC wants nothing more than *North to Fortune* to be accurate. Will anything come of a defamation suit? I doubt it. We just want to be heard. There's no need to start a to-do in the pages of your newspaper, but we won't stand to be ignored either."

"Understandable, Mr. Burrows. I'll do my best to make sure both sides are objectively presented." That was her job, after all, even if she did sneak her personal opinion into the pages of the *Times* now and again.

Burrows gave her a wary look, but it soon transformed into a charming smile. "I appreciate that, Miss Brody. It would be a pleasure to sit down and talk about this in depth, perhaps over dinner some time. Unfortunately, I have some work to do before this evening. If you'll excuse me."

He tipped his hat, then turned on his heel, his long strides taking him down the Second Street walkway as if he owned the town.

Charlotte watched him for a minute before heading in the opposite direction, toward the *Times* office. Mr. Toliver would be there, finishing the setting of the Linotype for tomorrow's edition. If she was fast enough, she could put in a short piece about the arrival of the film crew and, perhaps, a hint of the controversy with the AEC. Nothing too in-depth; she still needed Meade and Welsh's side for that. But there would definitely be mention of the group waiting at the Windsor.

It bothered Charlotte that neither Smith nor Burrows had come to the *Times* with their concerns and letters. Were prejudices in Cordova that strong? Fears of reprisal that deep?

After stopping at the café to pick up ham sandwiches for herself and Mr. Toliver for a late lunch, Charlotte entered the *Times* office just as the corpulent Andrew Toliver emerged from the Linotype and printing room. He wore an ink-stained apron to protect his waistcoat and trousers. The sleeves of his pristine white shirt were protected with black stockings. Toliver leaned on the cane in his left hand while he closed the door. His left foot was encased in a thick plaster cast that started mid-shin and ended at his toes.

"Miss Brody, how'd it go?" he asked, hobbling over to his desk and settling into the leather chair there. He leaned the cane against the wall.

Charlotte hung up her coat and hat, and unwound the scarf from her neck. "Very well. I rode back to town with the director and producer."

Toliver's eyes glinted. "Excellent. I'm sure you have some wonderful bits to share with Cordova."

Charlotte took the wrapped sandwiches from her coat pocket and brought them to the desk. Closer to the press room, the familiar odors of ink, hot lead, and paper greeted her as she sat in one of the straight-back chairs on the opposite side from Toliver. "Perhaps. They were very happy to be here, and very impressed with the turnout at the docks."

Toliver chuckled as he accepted a sandwich from her with gratitude. "I'd wager half the town was there."

"At least," Charlotte said. "I'd never seen so many in one place since coming here. But that's not what's so interesting."

His mouth full of ham, mustard, and thick bread, Toliver could only raise his eyebrows in question.

"Apparently they've received letters from the Alaska Eyak Council and their lawyer, a Mr. Caleb Burrows, regarding the way Alaska Natives are to be shown in the film." Charlotte watched Toliver for his reaction. "I was curious why the AEC hadn't contacted the paper."

Toliver stopped chewing and stared at her. Charlotte held his gaze. Had he been aware of the AEC's concerns?

He swallowed, took a large handkerchief from his pocket, and daubed his mouth and face before answering. "I knew Smith and Burrows were contacting them, but it wasn't our place to publish those concerns without their permission."

So it had been a matter of avoiding public confrontation at the behest of Smith and Burrows. Nothing printed, despite the many pieces published since the filming was announced.

"They have legitimate concerns," Charlotte said.

"Of course they do, but why shine a light on a problem if you can manage to address it without creating an incident? Smith and the Eyak people didn't want to make local waves. They understand the value of being good neighbors."

Charlotte crossed her arms. "You mean even if a defamation lawsuit is summarily dismissed, if it causes the production to be canceled or moved to another location, the AEC would catch hell. And who knows what some fool might do in retaliation."

Toliver rested his forearms on the desk and steepled his fingers. She could tell he was trying to be diplomatic in his response. It was just the two of them; there was no need to hold back. "I'm saying, there are more than a few folks in this town hoping for a boost to the local economy with the arrival of the film people. Potentially some long-term increases if, as Meade believes, Alaska can become not only a destination for filming but perhaps tourism, as well as for its natural resources."

"At what cost?" Charlotte rose and paced the short width of the office area, her irritation needing some sort of physical outlet. "Allow the world at large to believe falsehoods about an entire population just to put a few dollars in the till? Surely Cordovans can understand their Native neighbors' feelings on such a matter."

"I believe most can," Toliver said, "but again, I wasn't the one who requested to keep the letters of concern quiet."

Charlotte sat heavily in her chair. She wasn't so naïve to think there were no prejudices in Alaska. As a white woman, she saw glimpses of racist attitudes, though she'd never felt the brunt of them. But it was there, eating away at society like gangrene. She didn't want to ignore it, but she didn't want to instigate anything that would hurt people either.

"Follow the story," Toliver continued, "but don't print anything the AEC isn't comfortable with sharing. Remember, we have a responsibility to all our readers."

As much as Charlotte wanted to argue that fair treatment needed to be enacted no matter what, she'd take her cues from the wishes of the AEC. There were differences between New York and a small town like Cordova as far as what was printed and what wasn't, or at least *how* it was printed. Social issues and sensitivities required delicate handling. Everything was more personal. That didn't mean she could or would disregard wrongdoings, no matter who was involved.

"Plenty of people passed by the Windsor and saw the AEC talking to Meade and Welsh. I have to write up something," she said as she picked up a pad of paper and a pen from the desk. "And Caleb Burrows gave me permission to quote him."

Toliver frowned. "Caleb Burrows is fond of seeing his name in print. He may be working with the AEC, but he has a reputation as a pot stirrer and grandstander. Be careful with him."

Charlotte considered the charming attorney. Some journalists would have happily quoted every word that fell from his lips. Luckily, she'd long ago steeled herself against the thrall of handsome men who said what they thought you wanted to hear. "I will be, and I'll promise to be vague and neutral for now. Burrows and the AEC will be at the show tonight. We won't be able to pretend anymore if something happens."

The news man sighed and shook his head. "No, we won't."

Charlotte leaned across the desk and laid a light hand on his arm. "We can't get into trouble for reporting factual events, Andrew. We'll handle it carefully. It's just too important to ignore."

She rarely called him by his given name, but they'd been working together for six months and had formed a relationship beyond that of employer-employee. He was becoming more of a friend, which was both comforting and fraught with other difficulties. Charlotte found it easier to defy authority figures like bosses.

He patted her hand and smiled. "Agreed. Now eat your sandwich and get that piece written. Henry will be in after he's finished at the café to help with printing. You, my dear, have your work cut out for you."

Chapter 3

Charlotte slid the wire post of her earring through the hole in her left lobe. The gold teardrops dangling from her ears glittered in the lamplight. She'd piled her blond hair on her head and added touches of rouge to her cheeks.

"Rebecca, are you ready? Deputy Eddington will be here any minute."

Something thumped on the other side of the bedroom wall.

"Almost," the girl called out. "I can't find my other shoe."

Smiling and shaking her head, Charlotte rose and smoothed the skirt of the shimmery gold dress. The long silk sleeves would do little to ward off the chill of the theater, and the deep V of the neckline was certainly more revealing than her usual garb of heavy wool skirts or trousers when the temperature dropped. Alaskans were more practical than prissy, but like most Cordovans, she enjoyed the opportunity to dress up on occasion. As a combination reception and theatrical event, many of the local financial backers of the film would be there, probably in black tie and holding front row center seats during the performances.

It was doubtful that Jonas Smith or others in the AEC had financially supported the film, so Charlotte was anxious to see what they'd do at the theater if the AEC didn't receive a satisfactory response from Meade and Welsh.

In her stockinged feet, Charlotte went to the next room and stood in the open doorway. Rebecca noisily rooted around in her closet. Clothing littered the floor and bed. Several sturdy pairs of shoes were strewn across the floor as well. "I'm not sure how you manage to find anything in here."

Charlotte wasn't much better at keeping her closet organized and found it somewhat hypocritical to berate Becca for the same fault. In the last three months, things between them had changed from the awkward stage of getting to know one another and navigating the unfortunate situation of Becca's brother Ben, to the pleasant routine of living together.

Technically, Charlotte was Becca's guardian, having promised Ben she'd make sure Becca stayed in school. When the girl opted to stay with Charlotte rather than her estranged extended family, Charlotte was both flattered and anxious. She wasn't one for taking on a parenting role, far from it, but she was sure she could see to Becca's needs. Over time, their relationship had become more than that of guardian and ward. They enjoyed a friendship, a sense of sisterhood and comradery in their shared love of reading and writing.

"I know," Becca said from within the closet, her muffled voice full of worry as she thrust one shoe out for Charlotte to see. "Esther leant me her best Mary Janes and I can't find the match."

Just as Charlotte stepped into the room to help, a triumphant "Aha!" sounded and Becca emerged from the closet. Her previously combed and braided hair had become loose, and her skirt and blouse were decidedly less starched. She sat on the floor and strapped on the shiny black shoes.

"Hurry and comb your hair before you come down. We don't want to be late for the opening act."

She started to move into the hall, when Becca said, "Or whatever the AEC plans to do."

Charlotte turned around, unable to hide the surprise on her face. "What do you know about the AEC and what they'll do?"

"My father was a member," she said. "He and Esther's father talked about the meetings in front of us when we were little. Esther goes to some of the meetings with her family now. She told me about the problems with the film. They're mad." She lifted her chin, defiance in her eyes. "We're mad."

Becca's late father had been Native, as was her school friend Esther. Becca had been raised mostly by her white mother, without much contact with her father's side of the family. She and Charlotte never really discussed her Native roots. Maybe it was time to do so.

"You should be mad," Charlotte said. "I'm just learning that the Eyak people are less than thrilled with the storyline of *North to Fortune*. It's likely the AEC will be present tonight. Why didn't you tell me about the AEC and their feelings about the film?"

Becca's cheeks darkened. "Esther said they were going to try not to make a big fuss if they could help it, but if the film people didn't agree to change things the AEC would respond. I had to promise not to tell you because—"

She dropped her gaze to the floor.

"Not to tell me because I work for the paper or because I'm white?" Charlotte asked. Maybe she shouldn't put Becca in such a position, but Charlotte couldn't deny the pang of hurt in her chest.

"It's not that," Becca said, raising her eyes. "Being white, I mean. Esther is my best friend, and she was worried that if it got out she'd get into trouble."

Charlotte stepped in front of Becca and grasped her hands. "Keeping promises is important."

"But I should have told you," the girl said, a pained expression wrinkling her brow.

"You have the right to keep your own counsel." She gave Becca's fingers a gentle squeeze. "I trust you to use your judgment, but I want you to know that you can trust me too. If you tell me something in confidence, it goes no further than us. All right?"

"Unless someone might get hurt."

Charlotte nodded. "Exactly. We don't want that. We'll talk about what we can do, should that ever be the situation. I won't go running to put it in the paper."

"Or to tell Deputy Eddington?" Becca asked.

"Only if it's something he needs to know."

Charlotte felt a twinge at the vague reply. She'd had her share of skirting the edge of the law, even crossing the line. James Eddington had given her hell over it, going so far as to lock her up for a day. But he was known to bend the rules a little himself, now and again.

Becca smiled, hopefully in acknowledgment that Charlotte was there for her first and foremost. "I'll tell you things if I need to."

"Good." Charlotte pecked her on the cheek. "Oops, I almost forgot my bag." She hurried back into her room and found the clutch purse on the vanity. Tossing in her compact and lipstick, she glanced at the tabletop to see if she'd need anything else.

"Your notebook." Becca walked over to the bed where Charlotte had dumped her satchel. She fished out the small bound book and a pencil. "Since you'll be working and all."

A rapid, three-beat knock followed by a double knock came from the front door.

Charlotte's heart jumped at the familiar sound. "That's James. Can you go let him in? I'll be right there."

Becca headed downstairs while Charlotte checked her makeup and hair. Alaskans seemed to enjoy having a reason to dress up, and no one gave you a sideways look if you didn't, for most occasions, but tonight was different. Chances were good most everyone would want to impress the visitors from the States. Impressing the man escorting you wasn't a bad idea either.

Charlotte grabbed her shoes from the closet but didn't put them on. She'd wear her boots to the theater and carry her fancier footwear. Another practice she'd gotten used to in the last six months. Carefully holding up the skirt of her gown to keep from tripping, she descended the stairs.

James and Becca were chatting at the foot of the stairs. Or rather, Becca chatted and James smiled and nodded at her excited banter. He glanced up at Charlotte. Their eyes locked and his smile broadened, showing the dimple in his left cheek. Charlotte's stomach fluttered. In his black suit and waistcoat, his dark hair slicked back except for a stubborn lock that draped over one of his blue eyes, James Eddington was the picture of Alaskan masculinity, even with his somewhat crooked, thrice-broken nose. Maybe because of it.

Over the last few months, they'd spent more and more time together. Lunches, dinners, chats at one of their offices, a show or a dance. Charlotte enjoyed every moment, and while some men would have expected more than their hand-holding or brief kisses, James, true to his Southern gentleman roots, allowed her to dictate the limits of their relationship. Charlotte was no prude—far from it—but the specter of a past relationship and the aftermath kept her wary. She wasn't afraid James would do anything untoward; she was worried she might.

He extended his hand to her. She grasped it as she continued down and stopped on the last step, putting them at eye level. Gazes still locked, James lifted her hand and pressed his lips to the back of her fingers. A distinct zing traveled across her skin, up her arm, and into her chest. Her breath hitched. James always had an effect on her, but the touch of his lips, the look in his eyes, seemed that much more intense tonight.

"You look incredible, Miss Brody," he said.

"You don't look so bad yourself, Deputy." Charlotte descended the last step, her hand still in his. "New tie?"

"Just bought it today. Fletcher's was doing a brisk business."

Charlotte laughed. The men's clothing store might see a nice increase in sales while the Californians were around. Alaskans might not concern themselves with up-to-the-moment fashions, but it never hurt to be in step now and again.

"Shall we go?" James gestured toward the door.

"Let us get our coats and boots." She reluctantly released his hand and started toward the closet to gather her outerwear.

"Just the coats, ladies," he said, coming up behind her. "I have a car."

Charlotte faced him, coat and shoes in hand. "A car? Since when?"

James took her coat and held it out for her; then he did the same for Becca. "Since I figured trudging through the snowy street in fancy clothes wouldn't be appreciated."

She strapped on her shoes. The heels were higher than her everyday shoes, but she still had to look up to meet his gaze.

"Perfect," he said, taking her hand again. He started to lean forward, as if to kiss her, then his eyes darted to Becca. Hastily straightening, he gestured toward the door again.

Outside, the evening had turned quite chilly. Stars twinkled and a half-moon offered a soft glow of light, but a bank of clouds obscured the sky over the bay. They might be in for some wet weather.

James held her hand on the icy steps, guiding her down to an older Model T parked on the street.

"Where'd you get this?" Charlotte asked as he opened the passenger door.

"Bought it off Clive. He's been fixing up, then selling vehicles when he isn't running the taxi service."

Becca got in, eyes wide as she took in the interior and slid toward the middle of the bench seat. "I've never been in a car before."

"It's been a while for me too. Hope I remember how to drive," James said, and Becca laughed.

Charlotte sat beside Becca and made sure her coat and skirt were away from the door. "Well, don't expect me to do it. I've never driven before."

"Really?" He seemed truly surprised. "I'd have thought a forward-thinking, worldly woman like yourself would have jumped at the chance."

Charlotte shook her head. "Nope, I'm partial to public transportation. Give me a street car any day."

"I don't think Cordova's quite there yet," he said.

James secured the door, then hurried around the front of the car. He turned the crank once—twice—three times. The engine popped and grumbled a few seconds before starting. Rubbing his hands together, he got in and adjusted the throttle on the steering column. The uneven popping and growling sounds smoothed out. "She runs a little rough but seems to be reliable."

Charlotte couldn't help but grin at the excited, boyish look on his face as he checked the mechanisms. "She's lovely."

James laughed and patted the dashboard. "In the dark, yes. I might have to pretty up a few things if we're going to use her on a regular basis."

"What do you have planned?" Charlotte asked. They had been seeing quite a bit of each other, which was wonderful, but there weren't so many roads in Cordova that motorized transportation was required.

"You'll see come spring," he said, giving Becca a conspiratorial wink. Becca winked back. What were those two up to? James sat back, pushed in pedals with his feet, and set the gear. "Here we go. You may want to hold on to something."

The Model T jumped forward, down the hill toward town. Charlotte took a small measure of pride in the fact she only gasped as she grabbed the dashboard and didn't yelp.

James found a spot to park the car across from the Empress Theater. The marquee was lit with the names of the major players in *North to Fortune,* as well as the producer and director, Meade and Welsh. Charlotte saw a good number of people in line, but didn't immediately recognize anyone, bundled as they were. Were any of the AEC people there?

James came around and opened the door. He held her hand as she got out and stepped onto the slick walkway, then did the same for Becca. Charlotte and Becca each took one of James's arms and they crossed the street. The line into the theater was moving along, albeit slowly. Excited conversation and bursts of laughter provided an almost holiday-like atmosphere. Having live entertainment wasn't unheard of, even out here, but the significance of the headliners was unusual.

"I'm supposed to meet with Mr. Meade after the show to interview him," Charlotte said.

"Maybe you can use your press pass and get special seats," Becca suggested, her eyes bright with hope.

"I doubt that would do much good, other than annoy people." Charlotte shook her head. "I'm not about to push ahead of anyone here. We'll get in soon enough."

They walked to the end of the line, greeting others and taking their place. Charlotte made small talk with Mrs. McGruder, the grocery store owner, and Mrs. Sullivan, her former landlady, who were ahead of them. She often saw both older women, either while shopping or running errands around town. Charlotte still felt a pang of guilt for the fire that had damaged Mrs. Sullivan's rooming house, but the woman didn't hold any ill feelings about the terrible incident.

The happy chatter around them became murmurs of discontent bordering on anger. Charlotte glanced up as she listened to Mrs. Sullivan talking about her sons' latest exploits. Under the lights of the marquee and the streetlamp, she noticed a small group of people had gathered to the side of the theater entrance.

Some wore traditional furs while a couple had red cloaks with elaborate designs of ravens or eagles on the back. Many carried signs like the ones Charlotte had seen earlier in the day at the Windsor. However, unlike earlier, this group wasn't silent. One softly beat on a skin drum while the others began to sing. Though she didn't understand the words, Charlotte found the song quite beautiful and mesmerizing.

The people standing in line seemed interested, smiling at the performance even as they pretended not to see the signs. Others ignored them. Mostly.

"What the hell are they doing?" a man somewhere ahead of Charlotte, James, and Becca asked. "No one wants to hear that."

Becca frowned in the man's direction. Charlotte took up the girl's hand and gave it a small squeeze. She looked at James. The deputy scanned the line, eyes narrowed as he peered over the heads of the people in front of them.

Someone near the man hissed a warning to pipe down, but he wasn't done.

"What's unfair? They don't know what the hell they're talking about." His voice grew louder. "Hey! Go home. We don't want you here, ya damn—"

He was abruptly cut off by an order to shut his mouth.

Most of the Eyaks kept singing, though surely they had a sense of what the man intended to say. One of the young men turned toward the heckler, his dark eyes blazing, his fists balled at his sides. The woman closest to him touched his arm and said something to him. He responded through clenched teeth, staring at the man in line.

"What the hell are you lookin' at, boy?"

"Stay here," James said to Charlotte and Becca.

His long legs took him to the offender in a few strides. Leaning out from her place in line, Charlotte could see James talking to a tall man dressed in what appeared to be a beaver coat that went to his knees and a matching hat. The deputy put himself between the man and the Eyaks, close so the troublemaker had to focus on him. James kept his voice low, but his intention was perfectly clear: Shut your mouth.

The beaver-clad man started to argue with James, pointing at the Eyaks. His voice rose, and James poked him in the chest, his gaze intent. The man's face changed from flushed and angry when he was harassing the protestors to narrow-eyed and lips pressed in a thin line. At least his attitude was directed at James now.

After another few words of, Charlotte assumed, warning, James glanced at the Eyaks, who were still singing. The young man in the group looked at James, but when James nodded to him, he turned away.

James gave the beaver-wearing man a final word of warning and returned to Charlotte and Becca. If he hadn't been there, Charlotte was sure a fight would have erupted. Had the AEC considered that when they'd planned their demonstration? The young Eyak kept glancing at the line as he sang, his hands opening and closing at his sides. He had been ready to confront the white man in line, which would have possibly set off a brawl.

Charlotte nudged Becca and raised an eyebrow when the girl looked at her. Becca shrugged and shook her head. No, she hadn't known what the AEC was planning for the evening. If she suspected someone might purposely instigate a big fight, Charlotte was sure Becca would have said something.

Charlotte still felt the underlying tension as the Eyak continued singing and the line of people moved forward into the theater. After showing their tickets, they followed the throng into the ornately decorated lobby. If the attendees' renewed laughter and chatter was any indication, the incident outside seemed all but forgotten by the time Charlotte, James, and Becca passed between the interior double doors and into the theater proper. How easy it was for some to dismiss the impacts upon and feelings of others.

The walls of the Empress were painted a deep maroon above dark wainscoting. In the pit before the stage, members of the Cordova Orchestra played a jaunty tune while folks found their seats or greeted one another.

"Let's step over here for a moment," Charlotte said, tugging lightly on James's arm. "I want to take a few notes."

She fished inside her purse for her notebook and pencil, wanting to jot down her impressions of the close call outside before she forgot details. "I won't be long; then we can find our places."

The three hundred seats were filling quickly with people dressed in their finest, the majority of men in black tie and the women in gowns or cocktail dresses. The grandeur of the clothing far outweighed the humble setting of wooden seats and benches set up on the tiered floor. Many attendees carefully folded their coats and laid them down as cushioning.

On the floor to the right and left of the stage, cameras had been set up to capture the event. Stanley Welsh spoke with the same gentleman who had filmed their arrival at the dock. The director gestured toward the stage, and the cameraman nodded, adding his own motions to the conversation. Welsh clapped him on the back, then crossed in front of the stage to speak to the other cameraman.

Charlotte noticed Wallace Meade standing with a group of three older men near the stage. One of them was the beaver-coat-wearing man from outside. It didn't surprise Charlotte that Meade was chummy with Cordova's more well-to-do businessmen. He had worked a number of jobs as a young man, shrewdly investing his wages and starting his own businesses that turned significant profits. As one of Alaska's most successful entrepreneurs, he enjoyed a certain prestige among others of his ilk as well as the more "common man."

Meade smiled and laughed with the men, but his gaze darted around the room as he spoke. His focus locked on the wide doorway beside Charlotte, Becca, and James. Following Meade's line of sight, she saw Caleb Burrows and Jonas Smith had just walked into the theater.

"This should be interesting," Charlotte said.

James's brows met over his crooked nose. "Let's hope not."

Charlotte had to agree that one incident an evening was enough.

Burrows had his hair slicked back, and his suit was impeccable. A Native woman accompanied him, her long black hair in a perfectly sleek chignon, her dark blue gown clinging to her bosom and hips. Smith held the arm of his wife, Emma, a short, plump woman in deep pink.

Cicely Welsh arrived from the lobby and smiled at the Smiths, Burrows, and his companion. "I'm so glad you were able to make it. I reserved seats for you down near the front."

Frowning, Meade hurried up the aisle to the newly arrived group. He started to say something, then caught Charlotte's eye and abruptly cut himself off. "You should have let me know you were coming. I wouldn't have wanted to miss greeting everyone properly."

Burrows held out his right hand, grinning. "And so you haven't." He gestured toward the woman he accompanied. "Miss Violet Langler, vice president of the Council. You know Mr. Smith. This is his wife, Emma."

Meade made all the appropriate, pleasant noises and handshakes of greeting, though Charlotte could see anxiety in the lines around his eyes and mouth. He was not happy at having AEC representatives here tonight. However, the event was open to the public, so he had no cause to protest. He should have expected them, Charlotte thought, especially after their encounter at the Windsor.

"I apologize for not getting back to you gentlemen earlier today," Meade said. "Mr. Welsh has been working out details for the glacier site filming."

Cicely shook her head. "Stanley is asking for some dangerous stunts. He wants poor Roslyn to climb into a crevasse."

"I'm sure he wouldn't put Roslyn in any real danger," Meade said. "It would do us no good to have our star injured, would it?"

Burrows gave Meade a significant look. "I admire a man who looks out for his people."

"Of course." Meade arched an eyebrow at him. "Wouldn't want lawyers all over us."

Burrows laughed, as did the others. A certain amount of tension seemed to leave the group, but Charlotte had the feeling it was merely social niceties being met. Given the right circumstances—and less of an audience—she imagined Burrows and Meade might have had a more spirited conversation.

Stanley Welsh strolled up the aisle from the stage. He nodded and smiled along the way until he reached Meade's side; then a frown furrowed his brow. "Wallace, that damn stage manager you hired doesn't know what he's doing. I swear, if that stupid N—" He cut himself off as he realized who was standing with them. His frown deepened for an instant, then a more neutral expression smoothed out the lines on his face. "Burrows."

"Welsh." The lawyer's previous good cheer had evaporated. "You remember Mr. Smith. This is his wife, Emma, and Miss Langler."

Welsh nodded to the others. "A pleasure to meet you." He turned his attention back to Meade. "About that stage manager, Wallace."

Meade rolled his eyes and shrugged, smiling. The work of a producer was never done, the gesture said. "Sorry, folks, I'd better see what's what. Please, allow me to show you to your seats."

He motioned toward the side rows, near the back.

"I have seats for them closer to the front," Cicely said. "Center section. There should be placards in place."

Meade's smile tightened. "Of course. This way, ladies and gentlemen."

The Smiths, Burrows, and Miss Langler followed the producer down the aisle.

Welsh watched them for a moment, then turned and glared at Cicely. "Where's Roslyn?"

"She should be here soon," the scenarist said. "She ran to the ladies' wear store for new stockings."

Welsh's cheeks darkened with anger. "She should have gone earlier. Don't you women have enough stockings between you? You share everything else, for God's sake."

He stepped closer and spoke into his daughter's ear, one hand gripping her upper arm. Charlotte couldn't hear what he was saying, but Cicely's expression spoke volumes.

She paled as she glanced around them. Catching Charlotte's eye, her face pinked. Cicely moved away from her father. "There's no call for that. I'll be backstage."

She strode down the aisle, head high and back stiff.

Welsh scowled and muttered something under his breath as he followed her.

"Do you know what that was about?" James asked.

Charlotte glanced up at him as he scanned the crowd. Occupational hazard, she knew. Whether he was on duty or not, he was *always* on duty. It didn't surprise her that he had taken in the exchange between the Welshes without seeming to be paying them much attention.

"I have an idea." Charlotte looped her arm through his. "And yes, I plan on asking about it." She touched Becca's shoulder, urging her to go down the aisle. "Let's find our seats."

Charlotte had to admit that the company did a bang-up job of keeping the audience entertained. Not only did they perform some short bits of *North to Fortune,* but several of the cast and crew members sang, danced, or played instruments. Wallace Meade was in his glory as host, building the excitement or drama of the snippet of a scene they were about to see, or extolling the multiple talents of the company.

All the while, the cameramen cranked on, capturing each performance, only taking time out between acts to put fresh film in the cameras.

At the end of the show, the performers took their bows to enthusiastic applause, and Meade thanked everyone for coming. He reminded the audience that once *North to Fortune* was complete, there would be special showings in Cordova, Anchorage, and Juneau. The crowd cheered, and the curtain closed. The orchestra struck up a lively tune to accompany folks as they sought the exits.

Some attendees tried to make their way to the stage, but a few of the same security men who had been at the dock earlier—or at least they seemed to be the same solid, serious men—barred passage.

"How are you supposed to get backstage to interview Mr. Meade and the others?" Becca asked. She seemed disappointed that her chance to meet the company would be thwarted.

"Don't worry," Charlotte said, holding James's arm and Becca's hand. "We have an in."

The three of them edged their way down the aisle, against the flow of people headed out. A large man with his arms crossed stood before the stairs that led backstage.

"Excuse me, I'm Charlotte Brody, with the *Cordova Daily Times.* Mr. Meade is expecting me."

The man gave her, James, and Becca the once-over. "Says you. Beat it."

Charlotte felt James stiffen. He moved the lapel of his coat aside to reveal his silver deputy marshal's badge. "Not being terribly polite, are you? Why don't you get Mr. Meade and we'll make sure no one goes back there for you, all right?"

The security guard didn't move for a few moments, and Charlotte wondered if he was going to make a big deal of it. Perhaps deciding it wasn't worth the effort, he headed backstage.

"What would you have done if he refused?" Becca asked.

James shrugged. "Not much I could have done, really. Sometimes it's all in the attitude. Implying you have authority even without stating as much can get folks to do things your way."

"Abusing your position, Deputy?" Charlotte asked, laughing. James wasn't an unbending straight arrow when it came to the law, she'd learned, and interpretation of the law could be hazy up here. However, she'd never seen him use his position to his personal advantage.

"I like to think of it as a side benefit." He smiled at her. "Though maybe that's why Henry gives me a free cup of coffee at the café most mornings."

"That's Henry for you," Becca said. She had worked at the café for a short time before coming to stay with Charlotte and was friends with the young man. "Mr. Conway doesn't mind the coffee, but Henry had to pay for the piece of pie he gave to a girl he's sweet on."

Charlotte and James exchanged amused looks.

"You know a boy really likes you when he gives you pie," she said.

"Noted," James replied with a nod.

The security man came back through the doorway. "Mr. Meade vouched for you."

"Thank you." Charlotte led the way up the stairs, followed by Becca and then James.

Backstage, it was a mix of controlled chaos and languid dawdling. The crew was packing away equipment and costumes while the *Fortune* cast gathered off to the side. Standing nearby, Caleb Burrows, Miss Langler, the Smiths, and Cicely Welsh chatted with a cast member, a man who appeared to be

Native. Cicely smiled nervously while the man spoke. Hoping he'd assure the AEC that all was well with the *Fortune* script?

"Miss Brody," Meade called from the other side of the stage. "So glad you could join us. And who are your friends?"

Charlotte introduced James and Becca. James was pleasant, but Meade's status in Cordova as a businessman and developer likely didn't impress James any more or less than that of a railroad or cannery worker. He tended to treat everyone with the same amount of respect—or suspicion—no matter their social standing.

Becca was polite as well; however, her attention was mostly taken by the group of actors and the activity around her.

"What did you think of the show?" Meade asked, pleased with himself.

"Very impressive. You have a talented group," Charlotte said. "That one young man, Billy something, was quite funny. Is he in the film?"

Meade seemed puzzled for a moment, then recognition dawned. "Oh, yes. Billy, the red-haired chap. No, he's not in the film. One of Markham's men. A good kid."

"You didn't have any real Natives onstage for the scenes that were played," Becca said, fixing her dark eyes on the man. "Aren't you going to use some?"

Meade blinked at her, then gave Charlotte a look that seemed to ask if she was going to control her young friend. Charlotte waited silently for Meade to respond.

He smiled indulgently at Becca. "Well, little lady, there's Fred Bannon right over there. He's Native."

Becca glanced at the man speaking with Cicely and the AEC representatives. "I don't think he is, or at least not from Alaska."

Meade's smile tightened. "Not a lot of Alaska Native actors to choose from in California, my dear."

"But if all they're doing is moving around in the background, like he did onstage, you don't really need actors." Becca shrugged. "My friends and I could do that much. At least we look like we belong here."

"That's a bang-up idea, young lady," Stanley Welsh said as he and Carmen came up to them. "I'll hire you to give the film that much more authenticity. The AEC and Cicely will like that. Come on out with us on location."

Becca's eyes widened. "Really?" She looked at Charlotte. "Can I?"

Charlotte was taken aback by the request. And of course she'd need to give Becca permission to do such a thing; Charlotte was her guardian. "What about school?"

"I'm doing all right," Becca said. She grasped Charlotte's hands in both of hers. "Please? I promise I'll get my work done as soon as we get back. Cross my heart."

Becca made the binding gesture over her chest, her eyes pleading.

Wallace Meade's face reddened. "See here, Welsh, we don't need to hire children. We have plenty of people—"

"Nonsense," Welsh said, waving him off. "A dollar or two a day won't matter, and it will get Cicely and those AEC people off our backs." He turned to the other group standing backstage and raised his voice. "Cicely, we're bringing in a few local Natives to make the film more authentic. We'll see who we can round up for a day or so. What do you say to that?"

Burrows and his companions stared at Welsh. Cicely watched for their reaction, but when nothing more than stunned silence filled the space, she cleared her throat and said, "That's great, Papa. I'm sure it will add a lot to the film."

The lawyer strode over to Welsh. Behind him, Cicely paled.

"While this is a fine gesture, Mr. Welsh," Burrows said, "it won't make up for the scenes where Natives are poorly depicted."

"I told you we'll take care of that," Welsh said through gritted teeth. "There's no need for this . . . this . . . harassment."

"Harassment?" Burrows's brow furrowed. "Forgive me if I don't believe you, sir."

"What more do you want, Burrows?"

"Someone from the AEC should go out on location with the company," the lawyer said. While Meade and Welsh stared at him, mouths open, Burrows warmed up to the idea. "Yes, I think that would be a tremendous help in assuring the Natives in your film are correctly portrayed. I'd be happy to oversee the filming, and would provide accommodations for myself, of course."

Meade shook his head. "I don't think that's wise."

Burrows's chin rose, dark eyes blazing. "What are you afraid of, Meade? That I'll prove your 'authentic' film is nothing but balderdash and lies?"

"Now see here." Welsh took a step toward the lawyer, his face red. "You people should be thrilled for the opportunity."

James eased Charlotte's arm from his. Focused on the three men, he gently urged Charlotte and Becca to back away. Feeling the tension in the air, Charlotte followed his silent instruction, hoping it was a precaution that would amount to naught.

"Thrilled?" Burrows's eyes widened in disbelief. "About what?"

"Gentlemen, gentlemen." Meade held up his hands in a placating manner. "I'm sure we can come to an agreement."

"You haven't made much of an effort on that front yet," Burrows countered. "Allow us to be on-site to consult and, yes, correct mistakes."

"Ridiculous." Welsh raised a hand to make some sort of gesture.

Quick as a snake, Burrows snatched his wrist and twisted Welsh's arm behind him. Welsh gasped with surprise. Carmen stepped back, hand to her heart, her mouth a silent O of shock.

Charlotte put a protective arm up in front of Becca and moved away as well. It was one thing to witness an altercation, another to be at the receiving end of an errant blow.

James immediately came forward to grasp Burrows's shoulder and forearm. He and Burrows were of similar height and build. If anyone could physically subdue the lawyer, it would be James.

"Easy there, mister," James said in a calming manner, yet there was steel in the words. "Let's not do anything hasty."

"You saw. He was going to strike me," Burrows said to James. "He raised his hand."

"I did no such thing," Welsh claimed, pain etched on his face. "I was merely gesturing."

James slid his hand down to the lawyer's wrist. His other hand grasped the material of Burrows's coat. "Let 'im go and we'll settle this."

"Good God, man, let him go." Meade started toward the lawyer, but stopped, perhaps thinking better of getting in the middle of the altercation.

Burrows slowly released Welsh's arm. James eased his grip on Burrows, and both of them moved away from Welsh. "If that's the case," Burrows said, "then I apologize."

Welsh and Carmen gingerly rubbed his affected shoulder, the two of them watching Burrows as if he was about to go after Welsh again. "Of course that's the case," Welsh said. "I'm not a violent man."

"Neither am I." Burrows stuck his right hand out toward the director. "I'm afraid I've violated the first rule of being a gentleman by letting my emotions get the better of me. My sincere apologies, Mr. Welsh."

Welsh eyed the offered hand warily, but then took it. "Apology accepted."

Burrows pumped his hand, grinning, half-apologetic, half-calculating. "I'd still like to come out to the site with the company. I promise to behave."

Meade's mouth dropped open. "Are you mad? I have absolutely—"

Welsh held up his free hand, cutting off the producer, and

grinned. "I like a man with balls, Burrows. Come on out, and bring another of your chaps with you if you'd like."

"Stanley, we can't—"

"Of course we can, Wallace." Welsh clapped both men on their shoulders. "It'll all be fine and dandy now. You remember to come too, little lady," he said to Becca. After giving a final slap to each man's shoulder, he took Carmen's arm. "Let's head back to the room, my dear. The others are talking about visiting a few of the local establishments, but I'm afraid I'm not up to the gallivanting of my youth. Oh, and remind me to visit the bank in the morning, will you?"

"Yes, dear," Carmen said in a bewildered tone. "Good evening, all."

The sudden turnaround of Welsh's attitude stunned Charlotte. He wasn't a man easily swayed. What was going on in his head? Maybe she'd find out when they were on-site.

When they were out of earshot, Meade addressed Burrows. "This is unnecessary."

Back in control of himself, Burrows smoothed back his hair. "On the contrary, Mr. Meade. I'd think that in order to avoid bad press you'd make allowances for so simple a thing as having an observer or two on location."

The lawyer nodded to James, Charlotte, and Becca. "My apologies to you as well. Good evening."

He rejoined his companions and the four of them headed out through a side exit.

James spoke to Meade. "I can come out as well, if you feel it's necessary."

Meade pulled a crisp white handkerchief from his pocket and daubed his face. "No, it'll be fine, Deputy. Miss Brody, I'd appreciate you not giving this encounter much play in your newspaper."

Charlotte fought her natural inclination to tell the man he had no right to dictate what was in the pages of the *Times* and instead attempted to be diplomatic. "Just about everyone backstage saw and heard the whole thing, Mr. Meade. There's little I could say that won't be in every brothel and gaming hall by the end of the evening, as well as the cafés and barbershops by tomorrow. But I will mitigate what I can to avoid any embarrassment on all parts."

Meade's jaw muscles bunched and his mouth pressed into a hard line, willing her to rescind. Charlotte held his gaze, prepared to stare him down until the floor sweeper came through, if need be. Finally, Meade broke eye contact and shook his head. She managed to conceal her grin of victory. He didn't seem too pleased that she hadn't readily accepted his direction. Wallace Meade was used to having his way in Cordova.

"Fine, Miss Brody," he said with growling resignation. "Write what you will. It's not like it can hurt this damned production any more than everything else has." With that, he stomped away like a child denied a favorite treat.

"What did he mean by that?" Becca asked.

Charlotte took her arm and shrugged. "I guess the movie business isn't all fantasy and frivolity. Are you sure you want to do this, Becca?"

"I am," the girl said without hesitation. "It's like acting in one of the plays at school, isn't it? And I probably won't have much to remember."

Charlotte didn't want to bring up the probability that Welsh was using her as window dressing, but she didn't want Becca to be exploited either. "You realize he invited you to appease the AEC."

Becca smiled. "Oh, I know. The AEC had talked about trying to get real Alaska Natives in the film and now there will be some."

"They planned this?" Charlotte didn't hide her surprise at the possible scheme.

"Golly, no," Becca said. "It was something to bring up to Mr. Welsh and Mr. Meade. I just got lucky."

How involved was Becca in the AEC's meetings and decisions? As a child, she shouldn't have much of a say, nor should she be used by them. But if Becca had stepped in on her own, Charlotte wondered if she should be more mindful of the girl's involvement with the group.

"We'll talk to Miss Atkins tomorrow," Charlotte said. "But I don't want to hear any complaints about doing schoolwork."

Becca's smile widened. "Not a peep, I swear."

Chapter 4

Two days later, Charlotte and Rebecca arrived at the Main Street train station, bags in hand and still somewhat sleepy at seven in the morning. The sun hadn't risen yet and a cold breeze came off the bay. They stood out of the way as they watched several men from the film crew hustling to get equipment aboard the waiting train's freight car.

The tang of burning coal hung in the air, and the platform vibrated with the rumble of the idling steam engine. The train usually had several passenger cars for the three-hour trip to the glacier site, and the continued trek for folks destined for Chitina and McCarthy, towns closer to the Kennecott Copper Mine two hundred miles away. For this special charter there was only a single passenger car, a freight car, and two empty ore cars that would eventually return to Cordova with tons of copper ore to be shipped south.

"Where is everybody?" Rebecca asked with a yawn.

"On their way, I hope. Though I doubt the conductor would leave without them. I understand Mr. Meade paid extra to have the train leave at the company's convenience."

Charlotte had spent the day before following the company

around as they prepared for the excursion out to Childs Glacier. Most of the camp had been set up over the last week, Mr. Meade and Mr. Welsh having contacted local men and merchants beforehand with plans and wired funds. "Rustic but comfortable" was the term the gentlemen had used.

They'd had several small buildings erected for storage and a generator for lights and equipment. Heavy canvas tents with raised floors and kerosene heaters would house the company for the week they were on location. Charlotte and Rebecca would share a tent, and she was assured the accommodations would be just as cozy as her own home.

Shivering in her heavy mackinaw, wool trousers, and thick stockings, Charlotte would believe that when she saw it.

"Here they come," Becca said, nodding toward the string of cars approaching the platform.

The Windsor was barely two blocks from the station and they had to be driven? How did they expect to survive a week near a glacier under "rustic" conditions? Charlotte was still relatively new to Alaska, but even before she arrived she'd had no delusions regarding the weather.

The cars stopped under the lights near the platform and doors opened. Film people and drivers emerged from all four doors of each vehicle, hauling out bags or going to the trunks to retrieve luggage. Stanley Welsh hefted a small bag and began coughing. Beside him, his wife, Carmen, put a hand on his back and spoke into his ear. Still coughing, Welsh shook his head and waved her off.

I'd wager she was trying to get him to call off the trip. It didn't surprise Charlotte that Welsh refused. He didn't seem like the sort to let a cough stop him from doing much. The Californians ascended the short set of stairs leading from the street to the train platform.

"I'll tell the conductor we're about ready," Wallace Meade said.

The others stopped near Charlotte and Becca, offering quiet greetings.

"I'm guessing they don't have coffee service on this train," Paige said glumly.

"The regular train is usually outfitted with a dining car," Charlotte said. She hadn't ridden the train to Childs Glacier or beyond, only had heard about the tours and amenities offered. "But I don't think Mr. Meade contracted for that."

Peter York draped an arm around his costar's shoulder. "The hotel was kind enough to pack a thermos or two of coffee and some pastries. Chin up, Paige. Think of it as an adventure."

Paige gave him an unladylike snort. "I'd be more inclined to go along with these crazy ideas of Stanley's if he'd make it worth my while."

Peter and Roslyn exchanged looks over the young actress's head. He jostled Paige's shoulder in a friendly, big brother sort of way. "Aw, it's just for a week. It'll be great fun. Like camping. You'll see."

Paige flipped her coat collar up. "I grew up in the Bronx. Not a lotta camping on 138th Street."

Hunkering in her coat and frowning, it was obvious how Paige felt about their Alaska adventure. She offered little more than a mumbled greeting when Stanley, Carmen, and Cicely Welsh joined them. Beneath the platform light, the director appeared drawn and sallow.

"Are you all right, Mr. Welsh?" Charlotte asked. "My brother, Michael, is one of the town doctors. I could ask him to see you before we depart, if you'd like."

Under the circumstances, she was sure Michael wouldn't mind being called out so early.

Cicely got a hopeful look in her eyes, but as he had with his wife during his coughing fit at the car, Welsh waved off Charlotte's suggestion. "I'm fine, but thank you for the offer, young lady. Just a touch too cold for these warm-weather lungs."

"Papa—"

Welsh shot his daughter a glare. "I'm fine, Cicely."

Cicely clearly didn't believe her father. Neither did Charlotte. Shaking her head, Cicely turned away from her parents and joined Roslyn, Peter, and Paige as they discussed accommodations on the glacier.

Yips and barks carried up the street. Dave Scott, who usually worked for Brite-White Laundry, drove his sled and dogs toward the station, the six animals trotting with heads and tails high. Dave directed them around the back of the building. They emerged on the far side of the platform, allowing for easier access to the freight car behind the passenger car, where they would ride.

"Whoa," Dave called when they were in a safe spot, just beyond the men at the end of the platform loading the film company's cargo. The dogs drew to a halt, panting. Dave set an anchor in the snow, pounding it with the heel of his boot, then checked on the dogs and the content of the loaded sled before consulting the crew.

Wallace Meade came through the door from inside the building and crossed the platform to talk to the men loading the freight. One of the dogs began barking. Dave hushed him, but to no avail. Meade had to practically yell over the noise for his men to hear him.

When he had finished giving instructions, he joined the Welshes, Charlotte, and Becca. "Ready to go?"

"We are." Charlotte nodded toward the end of the platform. "I think Mr. Burrows and his companion have just arrived."

A car had parked near the station. Caleb Burrows and a young man got out, each toting a rucksack and bedroll. Meade and Welsh were allowing them to stay in one of the tents, but they were on their own for bedding. Burrows wasn't wearing his typical dapper suit and expensive coat. Instead, he wore a military-style pea coat, wide-brimmed hat, and wool pants. The man with him, also a Native Alaskan, was similarly dressed. Burrows reached through the open window and shook the driver's hand; then he and the younger man headed to the platform.

Meade grimaced. "Wonderful." His expression immediately changed to something less sullen. "Wonderful," he repeated loudly, with much more enthusiasm, and clapped his hands together. "All right, ladies and gentlemen. The conductor said we can get on whenever we're ready. All aboard!"

The cast and crew shuffled toward the passenger car. Charlotte and Becca followed several steps behind, allowing everyone time to climb aboard. As they waited for the others to enter the passenger car, Caleb Burrows and his companion joined them.

"Good morning, Miss Brody," Burrows said, touching the brim of his hat. He turned his smile to Becca. "Miss Derenov."

Becca's cheeks flushed, but she met his eye. "Good morning."

Charlotte mentally gave the girl a pat on the back. From the time they'd met, Becca rarely showed so much as a hint of timidity. She was polite and respectful, but in no way demure. Her forthrightness made her seem older than her twelve years. No, thirteen, as she'd had a birthday last month.

Goodness, she was more of a young woman now, wasn't she?

"This is my assistant, Miles Smith." Burrows nodded toward the young man beside him. "Miles, this is Miss Brody of the *Cordova Daily Times* and Miss Derenov."

Miles doffed his hat but didn't offer a handshake. Charlotte recognized him as the young man from the theater the other night. He appeared to be in his early twenties, not much younger than Charlotte herself, with jet-black hair cut in a similar style to Burrows.

"Are you studying to be a lawyer, Mr. Smith?" Charlotte asked.

Miles glanced at Burrows as if seeking permission. Burrows gave him a barely perceptible nod. "Thinking about it," he said. "But for now I'm just helping out."

"You're Jonas and Emma's son, aren't you?" Becca said.

Charlotte gave Miles Smith a closer look. He did have Jonas Smith's facial features, now that she considered the two men.

Miles narrowed his gaze, doing the same with Becca as Charlotte had with him. "You're Ben's kid sister."

It made sense that Miles Smith and Becca's older brother, Ben, would know each other. They'd probably gone through school together.

Color infused Becca's cheeks, as it often did when the conversation turned to Ben. "That's right. Come on, Charlotte. Let's get seats before the good ones are taken."

She tugged on Charlotte's arm. Charlotte gave the men a brief smile and accompanied Becca onto the train. They navigated the narrow aisle between two rows of padded bench seats as the others stashed bags and decided who would sit nearest whom. Cicely and Roslyn had claimed one bench. Across the aisle, the elder Welshes were getting comfortable. Paige sat behind them, arms crossed as she glared at the back of Stanley's head.

Paige is really quite unhappy here, Charlotte thought as Peter hurried out of the aisle to allow her and Becca to pass. He threw himself onto the seat behind Roslyn and Cicely, and began chatting about the trip out to the glacier. Apparently the desk man at the Windsor had given him an entire brochure's worth of information that morning.

Becca led Charlotte to an empty seat. The girl set her bag and herself down. She said nothing while Charlotte slid her own bag under the seat in front of them and sat.

Poor kid. As bold as she could be, when it came to talking about her brother, Becca closed in on herself. Charlotte knew better than to say anything. She'd give Becca the chance to sort out her feelings. If she didn't come around by the time they were at the glacier site, then Charlotte would try to get her to talk.

Burrows and Miles had followed them into the car. Most of the crew ignored the men, save for Cicely, Roslyn, and Peter, who greeted them politely. They sat behind Charlotte and Becca.

Cameraman Roger Markham came up from the rear of the car, limping but moving with purpose, a sheaf of papers in hand. His khaki coat was unbuttoned, his cap tilted back on his head.

"Damn it, Stanley, what are you thinking?" He sat in the seat in front of the Welshes, startling Meade who had just sat down there alone moments before, and turned to face them. Markham thrust the papers at Welsh. "I told you, we can't do the shot like this. Unless you have a boat and a crane, it ain't happening."

"The boat will meet us there," Welsh said placidly. "We'll figure out something with the aerial shots, Markham. Wish I'd've thought of getting an airplane up here."

Markham's eyes widened in disbelief; then he closed them, muttering something that may have been a prayer. Or a curse. Whichever it was, it seemed to calm him, somewhat. He rose without another word and returned to the back of the car where other men on the crew were smoking cigarettes and shaking their heads.

The train whistle blew and the song of howling dogs came from the freight car where the canines and their handler were riding. Were they excited or voicing their discontent at not running the route?

"All aboard!" the conductor called from the platform. "All aboard for Childs Glacier, Chitina, and McCarthy, and all points in between."

Charlotte smiled. As far as she knew, there weren't many official "points" in between, and the cars would be empty as the train continued on from the glacier to Chitina.

The train lurched, the engine roared, and with a screech of metal wheels on metal rails, the cast, crew, and observers for *North to Fortune* headed east.

The CR&NW followed Eyak Lake, between two mountain ranges that bordered Cordova. They passed the Native village where a few children waved at the train and passengers while the adults continued on with the business of the day. The tracks crossed the Eyak River, about five miles from Cordova. The mountains to the south were replaced by copses of spruce, willow, and alder. The snow-covered mountains receded a relatively short distance to the north as the landscape gave way to river flats.

"Beautiful," Charlotte heard one of the women say.

She had to agree, and mentally kicked herself for not taking a trip earlier. James had tried to describe the area to her, but it was more picturesque than she had imagined.

Telegraph and telephone lines hung between poles that paralleled the rails. Curls of smoke rose from the chimney of a cabin near the tracks at Eight Mile. Farther away, several homesteads were marked by the sight of wood smoke on the south side of the tracks.

What a lonely place to live, Charlotte mused. Though if one was looking for seclusion, she supposed Alaska was the best spot for it. Cordova was remote enough for her.

"My auntie lived out here when she was a girl," Becca said, staring out at the snow- and tree-filled landscape.

The aunt she referred to was a distant relative of Becca's father; Charlotte knew little more than that of Becca's family. She wasn't sure Becca had spent much time with her father's family, but perhaps her parents had visited. "How did she and the others get to town?"

Becca shrugged. "By boat, along the river and across the lake. They had to move when the railroad came."

Becca still had some relatives in and around Cordova. Some sort of family disagreement had caused a rift a number of years before, though Becca didn't seem to know the details. Or perhaps she wasn't willing to share. That was fine by Charlotte. A person deserved their privacy. If Becca wished to tell her what she knew, she would, in her own time.

When Becca had needed somewhere to live, Charlotte had suggested contacting those relatives, though she had also offered a place to Becca. Becca had chosen to stay with Charlotte, and Charlotte was thrilled to have her. If and when Becca was ready, Charlotte would do all she could to help Becca reconnect with her relatives.

Roger Markham's voice rose from the front of the car where he was, once again, sitting with the Welshes. "The boys and I went over it for the millionth time. It'll be near impossible to get that shot without someone getting hurt. There's no way, Stanley. No way."

Cicely, Roslyn, and the others all had their attention on the men. Cicely's shoulders were stiff, her lips pinched. Roslyn leaned toward her to whisper something. Whatever she said did little to appease the scenarist.

"This is a pivotal scene," Welsh argued. He was not as calm as when Markham had brought up the same issue at the station. "Dorothy needs to escape the villain in a fashion that requires heroic rescue from Lawrence. Floating down the river among icebergs is it."

"We can't put Roslyn or Pete in such peril for real, Stanley." Cicely shook her head. "I'll rewrite—"

"No," Welsh said firmly. Neither he nor anyone else seemed surprised his daughter had used his given name. Perhaps that was a Hollywoodland or California thing. "It stays. Make it work, Markham, or I'll find someone who can."

He rose, mopping his brow with a handkerchief, and ambled up the aisle to the front of the car. He yanked open the door between cars. A gust of frigid air blew in. Welsh jerked the door closed and stood on the narrow platform, his back to them.

"He just needs a moment," Carmen said to no one in particular.

For a man who had complained that the northern air was too cold for his Southern lungs, Charlotte wondered how he could stand to be out there in the icy wind.

Markham headed to the back of the car, his face thunderous. "That man's gonna get someone killed. I won't have it. I won't."

He sat with the other crewmen and again reviewed the pages of the scenario.

"Seems like Mr. Welsh is having some troubles." Caleb Burrows spoke just loud enough to go no farther than Charlotte and Becca's ears. The attorney was leaning back in his seat with his arms crossed over his chest and his eyes closed. His companion, Miles, maintained a stoic expression as he looked out the window. "Might do him some good to listen to others now and again."

"I think most of us would benefit from that virtue," Charlotte said.

Eyes still closed, Burrows smiled. "Touché, Miss Brody."

Charlotte patted Becca's knee. "I'm going to do a little more interviewing. Be right back."

Synchronizing her steps with the sway of the train, Charlotte made her way to the seat occupied by Peter York, behind Cicely and Roslyn.

"Do you mind if I ask you a few more questions?" she asked when the trio realized she was there. "Our readers will want to know every little bit about the filming and how you're finding Cordova and Alaska."

They exchanged looks, then Peter grinned and scooted closer to the window. "That would be grand. Always happy to give the press and the people as much as they want. Have a seat."

Charlotte fished her notebook and pencil from her coat pocket and sat beside him. The two women half-turned to give her their attention. Across the aisle, Paige Carmichael shifted in her seat. "Please join in, Miss Carmichael. You have a number of fans here, particularly of the young male variety."

Paige grinned, the first real smile Charlotte had seen on the young actress's face since they'd arrived. She moved closer.

"You mentioned earlier you were from the Bronx," Charlotte said to draw her in. "What made you want to go to California and get into films?"

For the next half hour, Charlotte asked the actors innocuous questions about their backgrounds and how they came to Hollywoodland. They enjoyed sharing their stories and Charlotte was grateful for her ability to take shorthand. Cicely Welsh, however, was less forthcoming. Perhaps being someone who stayed behind the scenes suited her more reserved personality.

Early on in the interview, Welch returned to his seat, his face bright red from the cold, and his eyes sunken in.

He really doesn't look well, Charlotte noted as she jotted down Peter's response to where he'd grown up. Maybe she should have contacted Michael while they were still in town.

Charlotte steered the conversation to the current film. That brought Cicely into the exchange. It was Roslyn who had insisted that Cicely write the scenario.

"She's the best in the business," Roslyn said, smiling at the other woman. Cicely blushed and smiled back. It was obvious the two were good friends as well as colleagues.

Charlotte's next question was probably going to silence the lot of them, but she had been itching to ask it since they'd crossed the Eyak River. "And the scene Mr. Welsh wants that Mr. Markham is worried about. How is that going to work out?"

As predicted, the actors and scenarist fell silent, expressions of guilt and consternation lining their faces.

"I'll tell you how it'll turn out, young lady," Stanley Welsh said louder than necessary from his seat in front of and to the right of Charlotte. He was half turned around, gaze fixed on the back of the car, on Markham and his crew. "It's a never-before-seen action sequence that will be talked about for years to come. I have every confidence that our cast and crew will succeed."

"And the safety issue Mr. Markham is concerned about?" Charlotte asked.

Irritation flashed across his narrow face before Welsh brought his direct gaze to her. "No one will get so much as a scratch."

A snort of frustration or disbelief came from the rear of the car, pulling everyone's attention there, but it was difficult to say who'd made the noise. Welsh and Markham seemed to be in some sort of staring contest, neither willing to back down. Charlotte was glad she didn't have to work with either of the two stubborn filmmakers.

After a few moments, both men broke eye contact. Markham started speaking quietly to one of his men, the red-haired comedian Billy. Welsh turned around to face the front again. Carmen Welsh leaned closer to her husband, whispering fiercely into his ear.

"I'm sure we'll all be fine," Roslyn said, but the tight smile on her face belied her projected cheerfulness. Was she concerned about the stunt or trying to smooth over the tension? "We'll be safe as babes in our mothers' arms."

The other actors nodded and murmured halfhearted agreement. Cicely Welsh glared across the aisle at her father, then stared out the window at the late-winter wonderland.

With that, the interviews were essentially over for the time being, and Charlotte returned to her seat beside Becca.

"Do you think it'll be dangerous, Charlotte?" the girl asked softly. She was supposed to be in a few scenes with Roslyn and Peter. Was the intended iceberg scene one of them?

Charlotte noticed the internal struggle on Becca's face. "I know you want to be in the film, but if it's too dangerous I'm going to have to put the kibosh on it. You understand."

Becca nodded. "I don't mind taking some chances, but people die in minutes in the cold water."

Charlotte encircled Becca's shoulders with one arm and pulled her close. "No one's going to die."

* * *

The train slowed as it approached the steel and concrete truss bridge crossing the Copper River at Miles Lake, giving the passengers a good long view of the face of Childs Glacier to the northwest. Everyone gazed out the windows in awe as icebergs that looked to be the size of motorcars bobbed along in the current.

The blue-white face of the massive glacier and the swirling, ice-filled gray-green river made Charlotte shiver. Welsh wanted to put Roslyn Sanford on one of those floating hunks of ice? Charlotte watched one crash into another, the two spinning and dipping in the freezing water. Madness. No wonder Markham and Cicely were so concerned.

Once it crossed the bridge, the train came to a gradual stop before a small platform and a two-story station house. Everyone gathered their personal belongings and disembarked. The chatter grew more excited outside, where the bracing cold and frozen landscape had their full impact.

"All right, folks," Roger Markham said when the company had assembled on the platform. "We have a ton of gear to move over to the site. So grab a bag or a box and come back for more. All hands on deck."

Most began moving toward the freight car that was being unloaded.

As Charlotte passed her, Paige asked, "Does he mean everyone?"

"That's usually what 'all' means, dear," Roslyn Sanford replied in a nicer tone than the others were likely thinking.

Charlotte and Rebecca joined the others in hauling boxes of food and other necessities for their stay at the base of the glacier. Even Wallace Meade and Stanley Welsh lent their hands and backs. Meade's younger years as a stevedore weren't as far behind him as Charlotte assumed.

Roughly one hundred yards from the platform, a tent city

had been erected as well as a few small wooden shacks in a clearing surrounded by frost-covered willows and alder.

"Impressive setup," Charlotte said.

Peter York, hefting a wooden box, fell into step beside her. "Stanley doesn't fool around when he wants what he wants. Cost a pretty penny, according to Mr. Meade, but worth it to keep us all snug as a bug, Stanley said. We're only out here for a week, though I'd stay longer than that if I could."

The actor's easygoing attitude was quite different from what Charlotte had expected from the idea of pampered movie folk. Then again, Peter's background suggested a more rural upbringing than some of the others.

The entire company did their part in moving freight to the site, including the dog team. Their excited yips and barks added to the cacophony of shouts from Markham, as he directed this crate here or that one to go there, and a man named Smitty, who was in charge of meals and cooking, as well as the general supplies for the company. Heavier or bulkier items were carefully placed on the dog sled and taken to the appropriate tent or shack.

Charlotte and Becca were assigned to a heavy canvas tent with several wool blankets strung along the walls to help keep it warm. The tent was also furnished with a raised, rough wood floor and a kerosene heater. Two sturdy cots had two wool blankets each folded atop thick mattresses. A small table between the cots held a lantern and a box of matches.

"This won't be so bad," Becca said, tossing her bag on the floor near one of the cots. "I went camping with Esther and her family where all we had over our heads was a lean-to made from a tarp."

"In the winter?" Charlotte asked as she fiddled with the kerosene heater to get it started.

"Well, no," the girl admitted, "but even summers can be chilly and damp."

Charlotte held her hands out toward the heater. The space would warm up soon enough. "Let's make up the beds, then head to the mess tent. Lunch should be ready soon."

There was no place to unpack their belongings, so it looked like they'd be living out of their bags for the week. As they made their beds, Charlotte was happy to discover hot-water bottles among the linens. Whoever was in charge of arranging amenities for the location filming had done a fine job in considering their comfort. She made a mental note to chat with Smitty to get an idea of what it took to outfit a film company on location like this.

The cast and crew gathered in the large canvas mess tent for a hearty lunch of beef barley soup, ham or chicken sandwiches, coffee, and hot chocolate. Charlotte and Becca stood in line among the chatting crew. Charlotte asked Smitty if she could talk to him at some point.

"When I can catch a breath, you bet, missy," the burly man said as he plated food and called out to his assistants to brew more coffee.

Charlotte and Becca collected their silverware and faced the seating area of the tent. Caleb Burrows and Miles Smith sat at the end of a table, separate from the others.

"Should we go sit with them?" Becca asked quietly.

"If you'd like." Charlotte hadn't had the chance to talk to Burrows in depth, but she didn't want to suggest to the visitors that she was taking sides either.

They approached the gentlemen. "May we join you?" Charlotte asked.

The two men rose, Burrows smiling in welcome and Miles's expression typically unreadable. "Please do," the lawyer said.

Charlotte sat beside Burrows and Becca beside Miles. Both young people stared down at their food while they tucked in. It surprised her that Becca, usually confident and self-assured, was behaving so in front of the young man. Though Charlotte recalled similar reactions to boys at that age, she had a feeling Becca was thinking about her brother.

"How are you finding your accommodations, Mr. Burrows?" Charlotte asked.

Burrows nodded as he chewed a bite of sandwich. He swallowed, then said, "Not bad at all. It's been a while since I've slept without solid walls around me, but it'll do."

"When was that, during the war?"

Burrows quirked an eyebrow at her. "Yes. How'd you know?"

Charlotte gestured toward his coat. "You're wearing army-issue coat and boots. I doubt a man like yourself would have purchased or procured such items as an affectation or merely for their sense of fashion. And that move you put on Mr. Welsh the other night indicates some level of training."

Burrows laughed. "Very observant of you, Miss Brody. Yes, I was in the army. I put my law career on hold and joined up."

"Where you ended up sleeping in tents rather than in the Judge Advocate's office?"

"Would it surprise you to know I wanted to be with the enlisted men?" He sounded defensive as well as half-amused.

Charlotte considered the lawyer. "Not at all, Mr. Burrows. You seem like a man who prefers to have a hand in matters, not watch from the safety of a desk."

Burrows's expression shifted for a moment. She couldn't tell, exactly, what it meant, but he nodded once. "I do what I can for causes I believe in. I think we're cut from a similar cloth in that respect, Miss Brody."

"Oh?"

"I've read some of your articles for the *Times*. You aren't shy about sharing your opinion on certain subjects. And your pieces in the Eastern newspapers are even more obviously in support of social equity." Burrows's dark eyes stayed on her as he sipped his coffee.

Did he think she'd be embarrassed by such praise, or the fact that he knew her work? Hardly.

"Which is why," she said, "I want you and the AEC to realize the *Times* wishes to publish a full and comprehensive story on what's happening here, with *North to Fortune*, as well as any other issues affecting the Native population."

Miles Smith snorted derisively. "Not that any of the white readers care."

"That's not true," Becca said, her head coming up. "Dr. Brody, Deputy Eddington, Miss Atkins, there are plenty others who care too."

"Not enough," the young man said. "You don't see any Eyak on the city council, do you?"

Burrows held up a hand. "There's a lot to be done, for sure, Miles, and we'll get there."

"What's the point of getting these people"—Miles gestured to the mess tent occupants, his voice rising—"to tell the truth if our own neighbors don't see us as equals?"

The conversation in the tent had gone quiet, all eyes on Miles.

"It's a start," Becca said.

Miles's mouth pressed into a thin line. He let his glare travel the tent. Several people looked away. His gaze fell on the table where Stanley Welsh and Wallace Meade ate their meals. "It better be."

Miles rose, his food only half finished, and stalked to the table where dirty dishes were to be stacked. He set down his tray and left the tent. For a moment, no one spoke, then quiet conversation began again.

"He's a passionate young man," Burrows said. "It's hard to see your people treated poorly on their own land."

"I hope the movie people have agreed to the changes to your satisfaction," Charlotte said.

Burrows grinned. "My satisfaction would have an all-Native

cast as the heroes and the white people the villains. A little closer to reality, don't you think?"

Charlotte's research—ridiculously and overwhelmingly as told by white Americans or Russians—on the settlement of Alaska by the Russians and the subsequent purchase by the United States yielded accounts that stated interactions with the Natives were mutually beneficial, or that the Natives put up a fight and needed to be controlled. She suspected the Natives' side of the story wasn't nearly so pat, nor as favorable to the whites.

"Unfortunately. Though I think everyone has the opportunity and impetus to be hero or villain, depending on circumstances."

"That's very diplomatic of you, Miss Brody." Burrows wiped his hands and mouth with a cloth napkin. "As a woman fighting for equal voting rights, I'm sure you can understand the feeling of oppression by the current powers that be. Where's the difference between you wanting that recognition and a Black or Native woman wanting the same? Where's the wrong in my people wanting fair treatment, let alone rights to ancient lands that have been 'discovered' and now claimed by whites?"

There was, of course, no counterargument to what he said, because it was the truth.

After excusing himself, the lawyer rose from his seat and disposed of his tray. He approached Meade and Welsh, stopping to speak to them. "I'll see you gentlemen in Mr. Meade's tent after lunch."

With that, he departed, head high and back straight.

"Sounds like they haven't worked out all the problems," Charlotte said quietly.

Becca returned her attention to her soup bowl but didn't seem to be eating much. "I don't expect they will."

Charlotte felt a pang of misery for the girl. Being half Native, she felt the push and pull from both sides. Whites more often than not considered her Native and some Natives considered her white. Becca was proud of both sides of her heritage, had loved both her parents. That she'd been compelled to defend and represent both was no surprise, and Charlotte would do her best to support her.

Chapter 5

After lunch, Stanley Welsh decided to take advantage of the light that was left to film a few test scenes. The cast streamed in and out of the costume tent in preparation. Then they walked out onto the ice, their fur garments covering them from head to foot.

Lucky them, Charlotte thought as she stood behind Welsh, shivering. Caleb Burrows and Miles Smith watched as well, arms crossed, and Miles wearing his familiar scowl. She couldn't blame the young man for being angry. He'd probably seen more than his share of racial bias, probably heard all too often that he wasn't on the same level as a white man.

Having Caleb Burrows there to show Miles—to show all of them—that prejudices were not going to prevent him from doing what was right would go a long way in the relationship between Natives and whites. At least Charlotte hoped so.

Welsh called out instructions to the actors through his megaphone. Minor players, such as Becca and a few others, stood where they were told and moved as directed. Cicely furiously noted Welch's adjustments without reaction most of the time.

Now and again, Charlotte caught her frowning or shaking her head at her father's changes to the story.

Charlotte kept her hands deep in her pockets. She would have to take her own notes later, because it was damn sure too cold to take her mittens off and write.

"I want Roslyn and Peter in this shot. He'll save her when she falls into the crevasse," Welsh shouted into the cone. "Yes, just like that, Peter. Watch yourselves. When we do it tomorrow, we'll get Roslyn down there nice and safely. Paige, step back. You're in the frame. We'll get to your scenes later."

Paige huffed and moved away from Peter and Roslyn. "Later. That's all I hear from you, Stanley. Later this and later that."

Welsh lowered the megaphone from his mouth, his voice deceptively soft. "Later or not at all. Your choice." Ignoring Paige's glare, he reached into the inside pocket of his coat and withdrew the brown bottle Charlotte had seen him with at the Windsor Hotel. He uncorked it and took a deep swig.

After returning the bottle to its place, he raised the white cone again. "All right, let's bring the helpful Natives in. Good. Good. When we film tomorrow, Lewis, you'll be the first on the scene, discover Roslyn down there, then run off to get Peter and the others."

Though Charlotte had learned it was unusual for such extensive rehearsals and test shots, she understood Welsh was a stickler for perfection. Snow and ice made lighting tricky, he had explained. Having the cast run through the scenes to incorporate different camera angles and movement would give them several options for the final cut.

Markham hoisted his camera onto his shoulder and awkwardly cranked while another man held the tripod's legs to help with balance. Together, they followed the action of the players to the edge of a crevasse. Once that scene was filmed, the company moved on to another area where the dog team would whisk Peter and Roslyn away over the field of ice.

Dave the dog handler, Peter, and Roslyn consulted on the technique required to get her into the sled and how to command the dogs. When Dave was in charge, all went smoothly, and with a single word the dogs dashed across the ice and into the sunset. Dave brought the team around and had Peter stand on the footboards. Peter loosened the snow hook used as an anchor, grunting something with the effort, and the dogs bolted. He tumbled backward. Dogs, sled, and leading lady shot off without him. The lightly loaded sled bounced across the ice, Roslyn lifting up from her reclined position. She whooped, though whether it was out of excitement, surprise, or fear was difficult to say.

"Whoa! Whoa! Whoa!" Dave's command to the excited canines seemed to go unheeded, much to the alarm of the onlookers. Finally, the team came to a halt a couple hundred feet up the glacier. The black-and-white husky in front turned and looked about, as if puzzled.

Everyone rushed over, calling out dangerous areas, as Roslyn gingerly eased herself out of the sled.

Cicely got to her first, placing her hands on her friend's shoulders and checking her over. "Are you all right?"

Roslyn, her cheeks pale but her eyes wide, smiled. "Of course. My goodness, what a ride!" She turned to Dave, who had taken hold of the dogs' line. "Can we do that again?"

Dave seemed as puzzled as his dog, but then smiled. "Anytime you like, ma'am."

"Gosh, I'm sorry, Roslyn," Peter said, and he hurried to her side. "I let the anchor thing off too soon. You could have been hurt."

Dave snorted. "Not bloody likely. The dogs have more good sense than most people I know. They can avoid crevasses and weak spots better than any human."

Once everyone was assured no harm had come to Roslyn, Welsh called it a day. He reminded them of the cast and crew meeting after supper, and that wandering off-site was not a good idea.

As they all headed back toward the tents and shacks, Charlotte caught up with Becca. "What did you think?"

Becca shrugged. "A lot of standing around. But it was interesting."

"I'm sure it'll be a lot more fun and interesting tomorrow," Charlotte said. "Come on, let's get warmed up."

Charlotte and Becca stayed at the crew meeting after supper long enough to learn when Becca was due to report the following morning. A general wake-up call would ring through the camp, and breakfast would be hot porridge and coffee. After everyone ate, filming would begin to get the best light.

Tall poles adorned with bare lightbulbs were spaced throughout the site, illuminating pathways between the several rows of sleep tents, the main mess tent, and the wooden shacks that housed props, costumes, supplies, and the privies. The distinct roar-hum of a generator came from one of the sheds.

It was a luxury to have light and not rely upon lanterns or flashlights except within the tents, though Wallace Meade had reminded everyone that the generator was to be shut off by eleven p.m. Anyone traversing the camp afterward had best take a lantern or flashlight.

Charlotte made sure she and Becca carried their flashlights as a precaution, but it was still early enough that the lights were on when they went to use the lavatory before bed. Becca finished her ablutions first and returned to their sleeping tent.

Emerging from the roughly appointed but clean facility some ten minutes later, Charlotte was about to turn right, toward the front of the mess tent, when she heard low voices around the back.

"I don't think—"

"Nonsense," another interrupted. "You know as well as I do—" His voice dropped to a volume too low for Charlotte to make out more than intense whispering.

By the clipped accent, it sounded like Stanley Welsh. Whom was he speaking to?

Charlotte stepped closer to the wall of the mess tent and made her way toward the men, for she was sure it was another man. Taking care not to trip over the stakes or guide wires, she peeked around the canvas corner. Near the waste bins, barely discernable in the light coming from a bare bulb, Stanley Welsh stood close to Caleb Burrows. It was difficult to read their expressions. Welsh's grasp on Burrows's shoulder while he patted the man's chest with his other hand was also difficult to interpret.

"Just between us, eh?" Welsh said. He patted Burrows's chest once more and strode away, toward the sleeping tents on the other side of the mess.

Burrows stood there for a few moments, his back to Charlotte. His left arm was bent, as if he had his hand on his chest, where Welsh had touched him. With a heavy sigh and a shake of his head, Burrows followed Welsh's path toward the sleep tents, disappearing into the darkness as he moved out of the soft glow from the bare bulb.

What was that all about? Were the two men finally coming to some sort of agreement? Burrows didn't seem as happy about it as she thought he might.

Charlotte retraced her steps, staying in the provided light, and went back to the tent she shared with Becca. As they readied for bed, they heard others heading to their own tents, footsteps crunching on the frozen ground, conversations ranging from quiet exchanges to boisterous and animated. The canvas walls did little to muffle the sound or the cold, and Charlotte was grateful for the heater. Once Becca was settled in bed, Charlotte bid her good night and turned down the lantern.

The sounds of the campsite, while not terribly loud, continued for some time, making it difficult to fall asleep straight away. Laughter and music came from the far side of the site. Music? Who had hauled a Victrola all the way out here? And while Prohibition was in effect, she was pretty sure at least a couple of bottles had been brought along. Perhaps the cast and crew had decided to celebrate with a pre-filming party.

Charlotte closed her eyes and snuggled down among her blankets. Just as she was dropping off, two people passed, women by the sound of it, whispering furiously.

"He's being completely unreasonable," one of them said.

"Are you surprised?" the other responded. "There's no way he'd accept. . . ."

The voices and footsteps crunching on the old snow faded, allowing Charlotte to attempt to sleep. Periodic bursts of laughter or shouting became background noise.

Almost like living in New York again, Charlotte mused as she drifted off. She'd become used to the quiet of Cordova nights.

A shout and a muffled crash jarred Charlotte out of sleep. She sat up in the chilly, dark tent, listening, blinking to clear her head. What time was it? How long had she been asleep? More raised voices, but she couldn't tell what they were saying. An argument of some sort, that was easy enough to discern. But between whom?

"Becca," Charlotte whispered, testing to see if the girl had been awakened.

When Becca didn't respond, Charlotte peeled back the layers of blankets and set her stocking-covered feet on the floor. Cold radiated through the thin wood planks. She pulled one of the blankets off the bed and wrapped it around herself. Padding over to the tent door, she untied the flap and poked her head out. The cold breeze brought her fully awake and quickly numbed her nose and cheeks. The lights on the poles were dark.

Flickering light overhead caught her eye. A swath of green ribbon-like light moved against the star-studded night sky. The aurora borealis, the northern lights. Charlotte took in the beauty above. She'd never seen the aurora before coming to Alaska. Stunning was the word that came to mind. Simply stunning.

Another clatter from the same direction of the voices drew her attention from the light display, but there were no other unusual sounds. No one else seemed to be moving about, and the voices had stopped. The glacial wind coming off the ice field ruffled canvas. Wood thumped on wood. Probably an unsecured door of one of the makeshift shacks banging against its frame.

On the outskirts of the campsite, not too far from Charlotte and Becca's tent, several of the dogs whined or gave low howls. A sharp bark cut through the night air, then another.

"Shaddup, Byron!" Dave yelled. His tent was right beside the dog pen, on the outer edge of the camp.

Everything stilled once again.

With a last glance up at the undulating green aurora, Charlotte ducked back inside, secured the tent flap, and rubbed her frozen cheeks until they warmed. Just someone stumbling about and the dogs being restless, she reckoned.

Charlotte climbed back into bed. Getting comfortable once again, she listened for more disturbances. Nothing, and after long minutes of near silence, she fell asleep.

The clang of metal on metal rang through camp.

"Let's go, people," Smitty, the chief cook and supply officer shouted. "Breakfast is ready, and if you ain't in the mess in ten minutes you'll get cold porridge."

Clang clang clang.

How could it be morning already, Charlotte wondered as she swung her legs off the bed.

"Becca, time to get up." She fumbled for the matches on the small table, struck one, and lit the lantern. The lump that was Becca in the other bed didn't move. "Let's go, kiddo."

"Five minutes," came the muffled reply.

Charlotte couldn't blame her for wanting to sleep longer or stay warm, but they were out here for a reason.

"Okay, but if your breakfast is cold, don't say I didn't try. And you don't want to be late when it comes time for filming."

She had expected a more enthusiastic response, but Becca rolled over and slowly untangled herself from the bedclothes.

"It's earlier than you get me up for school," the girl grumbled.

Angling her pendant watch toward the light, Charlotte checked the time. Just after seven o'clock. "Not really. Come on. Up and at 'em."

Becca reluctantly got out of bed. The chill in the tent, despite the kerosene heater running, spurred them to dress quickly. Bundled in coats, scarves, hats, and boots, they tied the tent door closed behind them, attended to their lavatory needs, and then hurried to the mess tent.

Inside the large canvas and wood structure, the coal stove was surrounded by sleepy crew members sipping coffee. Others were seated at the long tables, eating their oatmeal, or were standing in line for breakfast. Charlotte and Becca joined the end of the quick-moving line, and once they had their food and coffee, found seats with Roslyn Sanford and Cicely Welsh. Cicely had dark circles under her eyes that her spectacles seemed to exaggerate. A purple-black bruise marred her left cheek.

"You look a bit tired, Miss Welsh," Charlotte said. "And that bruise. Everything all right?"

Cicely barely glanced up from her bowl as she gingerly touched her face. "It's fine. Up late doing a few revisions. Stanley had better like these."

Charlotte realized Cicely called her father by his given name when she was at odds with him. Was she aware of it, actively separating their relationships?

"I'm afraid the bruise is my fault," Roslyn said sheepishly. "Ceelee and I were going over some scenes and we got a bit . . .

boisterous." She scanned the tent. "Where *is* Stanley? He's not one to sleep late."

Cicely's head came up and she looked around as well. "No, he isn't. Mother isn't here either, but she's probably still sleeping. And where's Mr. Meade?"

As if he'd been given a cue, Wallace Meade strode into the mess tent, smiling and greeting everyone. "Good morning, all. Good morning. Great day for making a great film, eh?"

He cut in front of the last few people standing in line and took a cup of coffee offered by the assistant cook. The cook said something to Meade, who shook his head and turned away. Glancing around the room, his gaze fell on the table where Charlotte, Becca, Roslyn, and Cicely were sitting. His face brightened and he strode over.

"Good morning, ladies. Mind if I sit down?" He was already in the process of doing just that. Meade set his hat on the table beside his cup but kept his gloves on. It was rather chilly in the mess tent. "Where's your father, Cicely? He'd said he wanted to get a few shots of the sun rising over the mountains."

"I know, but he isn't here yet. I'll go see if he's in his tent." She rose and started toward the door.

Carmen Welsh, her hair hastily pinned up and a beige and blue blanket over her coat, nearly ran into her daughter as she came in. "Oh, Cicely dear, is your father here? He usually wakes me so we can breakfast together."

Cicely's brow furrowed. "No, I thought he might still be in bed."

Carmen shook her head. "He isn't in the lavatory tent either. I had one of the men check."

"He wouldn't have gone out onto the site already," Cicely said. "Not before breakfast. Not alone. Roger and the cameramen are all in here."

"Where could he have gone?" Carmen sounded worried. She looked around the tent as if Welsh had somehow been overlooked. "Paige isn't here either."

"That stupid little . . ." Roslyn muttered just loud enough for Charlotte to have heard her. She caught the actress's attention, eyebrows raised in query. Roslyn looked away, cheeks flushed.

Was there something between Paige and Welsh?

"He can't have gone far, Mother," Cicely said.

Carmen wrung her hands. "He wasn't feeling well last night, so he took an extra dose of medicine. You know how that makes him sometimes."

Cicely moved past her mother and out of the tent. Carmen followed, along with several others willing to join in the search. Charlotte rose and quickly caught up to the women.

"Does his medicine make him disoriented?" Charlotte asked. Was that what he'd taken from his coat pocket during rehearsals?

Carmen nodded, a fretful expression on her face. "If he's taken too much. What if he became confused when he went to the lavatory or something before bed?"

"Did you see him take any?" Charlotte asked. The cold rolling in off the glacier made her face numb.

"No, I was asleep before he returned last night."

Roslyn caught up with them. "Paige hasn't seen him. Nor has anyone else I ran into."

Periodic calls of his name yielded no response. Welsh wasn't in any of the tents or sheds.

"Over here!" Dave the dog handler called from the dog pen. Everyone hurried over, feet crunching on the snow and ice.

Some of the dogs were whining and howling at all the excitement. The pen itself was nothing but a few posts and some wire, more of a suggestion for the animals that this was their place rather than any real means to contain them. Or perhaps it was meant to keep overly curious people at a distance. Dave had said some of his team could be touchy about strangers. As they all approached, the dogs became more vocal.

"There are scrape marks and boot prints in the crusty snow

up through here," Dave said over the barks and mumbled growls. "You can see where someone was walking until they got onto the harder ice."

"Could those have been from yesterday?" Charlotte asked.

Dave shook his head, squinting toward the glacier. "Don't think so. Most everyone went through the middle of camp to get to the shoot site. Me and the dogs are over here to stay out of the way."

Charlotte glanced backed toward the main area of tents and buildings. The snow had been trampled flat up until about where the dog pen and Dave's tent stood. Looking down, she noticed a tuft of fabric caught on the nail of one of the corner posts. The post leaned into the pen at a slight angle. Charlotte loosened the strands and studied them for a moment. Were they important? She put them in her pocket for the time being.

While she was crouched down, she saw one of the dogs had its foot on something smooth and black. "Dave, what does he have there?" she asked, pointing to the animal.

Dave climbed over the wire fence and approached the dog. "Whaddaya got there, Shelley girl?" Another dog, a big hairy brute, went over to check as well. "Outta the way, Byron."

Byron and Shelley? It seemed that Dave the dog handler was a fan of the Romantic poets.

He reached under Shelley's paw and removed what looked like a shoe. Shelley whined at the loss. Byron wagged his tail and danced about, as if Dave was about to play fetch.

"A leather slipper," Dave said, walking over to them.

"Oh, goodness." Carmen Welsh's voice shook. "That looks like Stanley's."

Concern gripped Charlotte, and she exchanged worried looks with the others gathered. What was Stanley's slipper doing in the dog pen?

A thick layer of straw had been strewn inside the pen for the dogs to lie on. Along the front and side of the pen, some straw had escaped to the outside, but it appeared that a wide path had been swept clean of the stalks. The swath of cleared snow with vague footprint indentations followed the pen for a few feet then angled off toward the ice field and disappeared.

Concern changed to fear. Welsh wouldn't have gone out there, would he? After admonishing the company yesterday about trekking alone?

"This way," Charlotte said, swallowing hard, hoping she was wrong. "Spread out and be careful of crevasses."

Wallace Meade stepped in front of her, his hand up to stop her. "Stanley wouldn't have been out here after dark. He knew better."

"Medicine does funny things to people," Caleb Burrows said from beside him.

Meade shot the lawyer a glare as he lowered his hand.

Charlotte shook her head at the men. This was no time for their antics. Scanning the rough ice underfoot, she kept to as straight a line as possible while searching the ice and packed snow for some indication of a sure route. No such luck.

"You'd've thought one of them Native boys would have picked up the trail," a man said. "Him go thatta way." Someone else chuckled.

Despite the urgency to continue forward, Charlotte stopped, turned, and addressed the men beside her. "That's enough. Keep your ridiculous, racist comments to yourself. We don't tolerate that sort of talk here."

She'd heard even worse comments in town, but the Californians didn't need to know that, and Charlotte certainly didn't want to hear their awful words. Not that they had cause to listen to her, but she'd found that if one called out a bully, particularly one who made remarks anonymously, they were often too cowardly to challenge you.

Satisfied there would be no more comments, at least in her presence, she continued in the direction the swept path suggested. Here and there, the ice was cleared of loose bits, indicating something had perhaps been dragged along the glacier like a broom.

"We're getting close to a few dangerous areas," Roger Markham said from her other side. "Watch your step."

Dangerous areas. The crew had noted edges and crevasses the day before. Most weren't too wide or deep, but there was that one Welsh wanted to lower Roslyn into. . . . The warnings to take care and stay away from the edge rang in her head.

"Wait." Charlotte stopped once again. She found Cicely and Carmen down the line. They both wore puzzled expressions. "Stay here," Charlotte told them, then returned to Markham's side. "Mr. Markham, will you come with me, please?"

His expression was also one of uncertainty, but as he made his way toward Charlotte, he seemed to read her face and intention. "Damnation. All right. Stay here, people. Let's go, Miss Brody."

Together, Charlotte and Markham carefully walked toward the crevasse. The ice had been scuffed and broken the day before as the company rehearsed and blocked their scenes. There were no obvious drag marks like those in front of the dog pen or coming from that less used direction along the ice. But as she and Markham approached the crevasse, something in Charlotte's stomach clenched. They stopped and peered over the edge.

"Son of a bitch," Markham muttered.

Ten feet down, inside the wide crack in the ice, Stanley Welsh stared up at them.

Chapter 6

The first thought that struck Charlotte was that Welsh's body was not the worst she'd seen as far as condition. No, that honor went to Darcy Dugan, and Charlotte was grimly relieved not to have seen Lyle Fiske's burned remains as a comparison. She shuddered at the six-month-old memory of Darcy's murder. That had been a particularly brutal crime. This situation was different. At least it seemed to be. Welsh appeared to have slipped or fallen into the crevasse, possibly breaking his neck or freezing to death.

A wave of sadness for Cicely and Carmen filled her chest. Charlotte turned to the two women. They, along with the others, started forward.

Charlotte held up her hands. "Stop. Don't anyone come any closer." She focused on Cicely and Carmen. "I'm sorry. Mr. Welsh is down there."

"Papa!"

"Stanley?"

Both women once again moved forward. Charlotte stepped toward them. "No, don't. Please. You . . . you don't want to see him like this."

Cicely stopped, her dark eyes wide and her fair face drained of color except for the livid bruise on her cheek. Beside her, Roslyn Sanford embraced the scenarist, her expression just as stricken. Carmen Welsh clutched the wool blanket tightly around herself. Her eyes rolled back in her head and, with a gasp, she fainted. The man behind her was quick to catch the poor woman before she struck the ice.

"Please, everyone," Charlotte said. "Go back to the mess tent. We need to get the coroner and marshal up here as soon as possible."

"What for?" Markham asked.

Charlotte turned back to the cameraman and, keeping her voice down, said, "Because they'll want to determine what happened. In order to do that, they'll need to see Mr. Welsh where he was found. And ask questions. We can't let anyone leave."

Chances were, Stanley Welsh had become disoriented by his medication and wandered off. Mother Nature was particularly unforgiving up here.

But what if he hadn't? Charlotte was sure she was overreacting, but better they let the professionals figure it out.

Markham frowned at her for a moment, then addressed the cluster of confused and worried people. "All right, you heard the lady. Let's get back to the mess. According to the schedule we were given, the train'll be by in a little while. We'll have someone go back to town to tell the authorities."

"We can't just leave him down there." Cicely Welsh wasn't quite hysterical, but there was definite sorrow and shock in her voice. Roslyn's arm tightened around her.

Carmen was being carried back down the ice to the camp, leaving Cicely to speak for the family. Charlotte sympathized with the young woman.

"Please, Cicely," Charlotte said, coming up to the scenarist. "I know this is terribly difficult for you, but there are certain procedures that have to be followed in order to give the marshal's office the best chance possible to determine the circumstances."

Cicely winced. "It was an accident. Wasn't it?"

There was no good way to answer her. "We need to let them investigate to be sure."

"I think she has a point, Ceelee," Roslyn said. She urged Cicely toward the camp. "Come on. Let's get some coffee."

Cicely's shoulders slumped as she and Roslyn made their way toward the site. Poor woman. Charlotte didn't want to keep her from seeing her father, but it was for the best.

"Mr. Markham, can you stay here and make sure no one disturbs the scene?"

Markham glanced over his shoulder, into the crevasse. He shoved his hands deep into his coat pockets and met her eyes with a steady gaze. "I'll stay as long as I can."

"Thank you. I'll get someone to relieve you so you don't freeze." Charlotte started back to the camp, then turned. "I'm sure I don't have to ask you to not touch anything, Mr. Markham."

The cameraman gave her a wry look. "Not a problem."

Careful not to slip on freshly exposed ice or loose pieces, Charlotte returned to the mess tent. She could hear the buzz of conversation well before she reached the enclosure. It sounded like everyone was there. She pushed the door flap aside. Conversation stopped and all turned to her.

Taking a deep breath, Charlotte said, "I've asked Mr. Markham to keep an eye on the . . . the scene for now. Someone will need to spell him so he can warm up. When the train arrives, I suggest someone go back to town and tell the marshal's office as well as the coroner what's occurred."

"Why just one person? We all might as well pack and go."

Charlotte didn't know who had asked, not that it mattered. "Until the marshal or deputy can question everyone and investigate, we all need to stay here. Keeping everyone in one place will make it easier and faster for the inquiry."

Wallace Meade pushed to the front of the group. "Listen here, little lady—"

"I'm not your little lady, Mr. Meade." Indignation heating her cheeks, Charlotte held his gaze. He wasn't the first man to attempt to talk over her. "I realize I'm not in charge of your production or this site, but I have been involved in several investigations. The best thing we can do is stay put and wait for the deputy."

"What's there to investigate?" Meade asked. "Poor Stanley wandered onto the glacier and fell into the crevasse. Clearly this was a terrible accident."

From one of the tables, Charlotte heard a woman sob. Carmen or Cicely?

"It probably was an accident," Charlotte said, and noted Meade's self-satisfied grin. "But we don't know. If the coroner decides the death was questionable, it's best to start off with all the factual information possible."

She glanced around the tent to see if anyone else had objections. What was it James had said about having an attitude of implied authority? She had no authority whatsoever, of course, but this situation called for someone to take the lead. Standing toward the back, Caleb Burrows met her eye. He didn't seem to agree or disagree with her. Wouldn't a lawyer prefer to follow some sort of procedure?

"Fine," Meade said, acting as spokesman for the company. "Who'll go to town?"

Volunteers made offers, but Charlotte held up her hands, quelling the voices. "Under the circumstances, I think we need to send the most impartial person in camp. Someone we'd all trust."

"You?" Meade's single word wasn't quite filled with derision, but it was there. Perhaps he wasn't fond of being challenged.

"No," Charlotte responded. "My place is here. Rebecca Derenov should go."

"Me?" From her seat at a nearby table, Becca looked around at the roomful of adults. "But—"

"She's a child," Meade argued. "She can't carry this sort of responsibility."

"I assure you, she can," Charlotte said. She stood in front of Becca, ignoring Meade's sputtering protests. "Go straight to Deputy Eddington or Marshal Blaine. I'll write out something if you'd like, but I think it's best if you go. Don't say a word to anyone but them. We don't need a stampede of ghoulish looky-loos out here. Then I want you to stay in town with Esther or Mary. If either asks, you weren't feeling well."

Having had their conversation just the other day about keeping confidences, Charlotte was sure Becca understood the magnitude of the situation despite her tender age.

Becca nodded solemnly. "I can do that."

Charlotte smiled. "I know you can." She checked with the group again. "Is everyone agreed, we'll have Becca go?"

No one else opposed the girl being their messenger, giving Wallace Meade no support in his opposition.

Peter York cleared his throat. "What do the rest of us do in the meantime, Miss Brody?"

"The train should arrive shortly on its way down from Chitina," she said. "Becca will get back to town by early afternoon. The marshal or deputy and the coroner will come right out. We'll have to stay until tomorrow, at the latest, while they make their initial investigation. I'm sure we can keep ourselves occupied for twenty-four hours if it means learning the truth about Mr. Welsh."

There were murmurs of reluctant agreement, with one notable exception.

"I ain't stayin' here with a dead body," Paige Carmichael

protested. "No offense to Cicely and Mrs. Welsh, but that's too creepy."

"I *do* take offense," Cicely said, coming forward. Her eyes were red-rimmed and puffy behind her spectacles. Through the crowd, Charlotte saw Carmen seated at a table, her hands around a mug of coffee and a blanket over her shoulders, as if she couldn't get warm even in the close heated quarters of the tent. "My father may not have been the easiest man to get along with, but he deserves the respect of our finding out what happened." Paige shrank back a little at Cicely's words. The scenarist then faced Charlotte. "We'll do as you suggest, Miss Brody. It won't be easy for me or my mother, but if we can endure it so can the others."

No one dared to disregard Welsh's grieving daughter, not even Paige or Meade.

"All right. Thank you," Charlotte said to Cicely. "Becca, get packed. We'll need two or three volunteers to spell Mr. Markham watching over the scene to make sure nothing's disturbed. I'm sure once the deputy gets here, everything will be taken care of swiftly."

Except, she wasn't sure of that at all.

While they waited for the train to return from Cordova, Charlotte tried to gather as much information as she could from the company. A few had heard the same noises she had late last night, as well as the dog barking, but no one could swear what time it was.

"After eleven," Smitty said as he set up another two pots of coffee to brew. "We'd finished up here 'bout then and all was quiet. Even the party was down to nothing."

The music and laugher hadn't lasted as long as Charlotte thought it might. Perhaps Welsh was hard on anyone being late or complaining of a hangover.

Dave the dog handler barely recalled telling Byron to shush.

"He's usually quiet, but when something riles him, he's at it worse than a hound on a scent."

Tail wagging, Byron yipped then grumbled happily at the sound of his name.

Dave and Charlotte stood near the pen of dogs while he fixed the post. The dogs sat on their straw bedding, occasionally joining the conversation with a variety of canine sounds.

"Did you notice that this morning?" Charlotte asked, indicating the leaning support.

"Yeah." He used another couple of short bits of wood to brace the larger one. "But the dogs roughhouse all the time. Figured they knocked into it or something."

Later that afternoon, Charlotte was seated with Roslyn and Peter in the mess tent, getting an idea of how Stanley Welsh was regarded in the industry and as a personal friend. Both actors appreciated his enthusiasm, even if he came up with some mind-boggling ideas at times.

"He had a vision, that's for sure," Peter said with fondness. "I think he could have worked out the problems with the Natives eventually. Especially with Cicely writing the scenario. She had a way of making him see reason."

Father and daughter seemed to be at odds when Charlotte witnessed their interactions in the car and at the theater, but perhaps, given the chance, Cicely was able to prevail when they were alone.

"Poor Ceelee." Roslyn dabbed a handkerchief along the corners of her eyes. "She and Stanley were a formidable pair in this business."

"Do you think she'll give up writing?" Charlotte asked.

The actress considered it for no more than a few moments. "No. She'll grieve, of course, but she'll find the strength to continue. Cicely is a lot tougher than she appears." Roslyn smiled sadly. "She'll bounce back sooner or later, and I'd bet on sooner."

"You seem to know each other quite well," Charlotte said.

The other woman blushed and looked down at her mug of coffee. "We've worked together on several films and clicked. She and I have a lot in common." Roslyn raised her eyes. "We're . . . comfortable with each other. Cicely is my best friend."

"Practically inseparable, they are," Peter said, smiling. "Two peas in a pod."

Roslyn grinned at her costar. "We are, I guess. I should go check on her and Carmen. If you'll excuse me."

The actress rose and headed out into the frigid day.

Charlotte hoped the men standing over the crevasse were keeping warm. She made sure the cook sent out a full thermos of coffee and sandwiches for them, as they needed it.

In the distance, the CR&NW train whistle sounded. Several people in the tent gave low cheers or exclamations of relief.

Thank goodness. Charlotte rose along with Peter.

"Excellent." The actor donned his coat and gloves, as did Charlotte, and gestured for her to precede him. "Let's get this over with."

Others were already on their way to the platform. Charlotte asked Peter to stay on the camp side of the train to assure no one attempted to board. If there was a guilty party or someone simply wishing to avoid the inquiry, she wanted to know.

The train came into view as it crossed the bridge. It slowed and rumbled up to the platform with a bite of burning coal and a burst of steam in the air. The wooden planks beneath Charlotte's feet vibrated even as the engine throttled down. The conductor opened a single door, at the front of the passenger car, and Deputy James Eddington stepped out, squinting into the setting sun.

Charlotte's smile grew when their eyes met. James gave her a fleeting grin, but sobered quickly when Wallace Meade stepped up to him.

"Deputy, I hope we can clear this up soon. We want to give

Stanley and the family all due respect, of course, but I see no reason why this can't be wrapped up this afternoon."

James quirked an eyebrow at the other man. "Oh, you don't, do you? And why is that?"

Meade grasped his fur lapels, his chin up. "Obviously this was an unfortunate accident. Stanley went for a late-night walk and fell into the crevasse."

"Mr. Welsh didn't seem like a stupid man to me," James said, "and walking along a glacier in the dark is damn stupid."

"He may have been under the influence, if you know what I mean." Meade made a gesture of tipping a cup.

James clamped a hand on Meade's shoulder. "Tell you what. You do your job by organizing your people in one place so I can interview them. The doctor and I will do our jobs of figuring out how Mr. Welsh died. Sound fair?" He patted the producer's shoulder, then addressed the crowd. "Everyone head back to the mess tent and wait for me."

There was less grumbling than when Charlotte told them the same thing, but she supposed by now the crew was resigned to the fact that they'd be there a little longer. The doors to the cars remained closed, save for the one James had emerged from. The crew filed down the stairs off the platform, talking among themselves.

Wallace Meade didn't move. Once the others were out of earshot, he narrowed his eyes at the deputy. "I don't want these poor people to be delayed any longer than necessary. Stanley's body has been stuck in that crevasse all night and all day. He needs to be taken out of there as soon as possible. It's not right."

"Neither is a man dying, no matter the cause." James gestured toward the platform stairs. "If you'd join the others, please."

Meade cast a questioning look at Charlotte, who stayed put but said nothing as he crossed the platform and descended the stairs.

Charlotte and James stepped toward each other at the same time. He took her hands, then leaned down to touch his lips to her cheek. "You're shivering with cold," he said. "Let's get inside and get you warmed up."

She eased her hands from his and pressed her palms to his chest. Rising onto her toes, Charlotte kissed him full on the mouth. His hands fell to her hips and he pulled her closer, deepening the kiss. Electric pulses radiated through her from chest to belly to limbs, warming her nicely. His solidity, his steadiness, made her feel all would be well. Together, they would figure out what had happened.

Charlotte broke the kiss, smiling up at him as they both caught their breaths. "I missed you."

James pecked her on the lips, then released her. "It's only been a day."

"Imagine what would happen if I'd been gone a week." She laughed when he gave her an exaggerated waggled eyebrows lascivious look. "Did Becca get to Esther's? Where's Michael? Didn't he come with you?"

"Yeah, Becca's there for the night. She promised to keep her lips sealed about what's going on. As long as you give her the full story when we get back." James glanced over his shoulder at the open door. "Michael has a few things with him to conduct his initial investigation. I guess I should help."

They entered the passenger car where Michael was going through a bag that held several bottles and other paraphernalia of his duties as coroner. The conductor stood at the front of the car, checking his watch.

"We'll be back tomorrow morning, Deputy," the uniformed man said.

James tugged the brim of his hat. "Thank you, Mr. Briggs. I'll let the others know."

He and Charlotte moved down the aisle to Michael.

"People are going to start to wonder about you, Sis," he said.

"Me? What did I do?" Charlotte had been known to offer her opinion on topics such as women's voting rights and Prohibition, but nothing stronger than words had been bandied about. So far, anyway.

"I'm assuming nothing," he said, "but you do seem to be in the thick of things. Again."

Charlotte gave him a playful swat. "Right place, right time. Though poor Mr. Welsh . . ."

He certainly had been in the wrong place at the wrong time, however he ended up there.

Michael handed her a bag and another to James. "Yes, well, let's go see what happened. Though the sooner I can get him back to town and perform a thorough examination, the better."

James hoisted a small rucksack over his shoulder, adjusted his hold on the bag Michael gave him, then led the way back out of the car, down the platform stairs, and toward camp.

"The biggest one's the mess tent, yes?" he asked Charlotte.

She nodded, taking care of her footing on the frozen ground. "Everyone but the men I've asked to watch over the crevasse should be there. At least I hope so."

"Well done maintaining the scene, Miss Brody."

"I figured you and Michael might want to have it as close to unsullied as possible. Though I didn't think about any of the men watching being the perpetrator."

"What makes you think there was foul play?" Michael asked.

"I heard loud voices and some sort of ruckus last night," she said. "Late, after everyone else seemed to have gone to sleep. And the dogs became restless soon after."

"Could have been anything or anyone." James was always good at offering alternative explanations. Not to deny there was something suspicious, but to make sure he had as many avenues covered as possible. "We'll talk to these folks for a minute; then you can show us the path you believe Welsh took."

They had reached the mess tent. When they stepped through

the heavy flap, the conversation that was already buzzing became almost overwhelming.

"What's going to happen now, Deputy?"

"When can we leave?"

"I'm not staying here a minute longer. This film is cursed."

The comments grew louder, and the people closest to the door moved a step forward.

Unaffected by the pressing crowd, James set his bags down and pulled off his gloves. He touched his thumb and middle finger of his right hand together, put them in his mouth, and let off a piercing whistle.

Everyone froze and fell silent.

Brows furrowed in his "I'll take no guff from the likes of you" expression, James lowered his hand. "Listen up. I know you folks have been here longer than you wish under unpleasant circumstances, but until we get some answers about what happened, you'll stay where I tell you. I'll be asking some general questions and then talk to individuals. Dr. Brody and I will go to the scene to gather information. Now, get some coffee, find a place to sit down, and shut up." When no one moved, James's expression darkened. "Go."

Muttering and grumbling, they went to find refreshments and seats.

"I was almost compelled to go with them," Charlotte said quietly.

James snorted. "I know better than to expect such discipline from you."

They set Michael's bags off to the side, and Charlotte found an out-of-the-way seat nearby. Despite having her notebook in her pocket, she didn't retrieve it. People tended to talk more freely if they didn't think they were being recorded.

After everyone settled down and looked to James, he spread his feet and clasped his hands behind his back. "Good. Thank you. I know this is a difficult time," he said, his voice softer now, more sympathetic. "The doctor and I have been called out to determine the circumstances of Mr. Welsh's death, but we need your help. First, let's get a timeline of his activities. Who was the last to see him?"

Several people started talking at once. James held up his hands again.

"He had dinner here in the tent with the rest of us at seven," Peter York offered.

Roger Markham added, "Then we had a meeting about today's shoot and what we needed to change or keep, angles, time, that sort of thing, schedule for the scenes we wanted next. That lasted until nearly nine."

Caleb Burrows spoke from the back of the mess. "I met with Mr. Welsh about then to discuss the AEC concerns."

That was before Charlotte had seen the men by the bins near ten o'clock. Why meet again, outside and not in one of their tents? Were they afraid Miles Smith or Mrs. Welsh would interrupt?

"And it got right loud," someone said. "I could hear you going on from the film shed with the door shut."

Burrows's face darkened. "Mr. Welsh was having a difficult time understanding our concerns. Some of you just don't see what the problem is, portraying our people as primitive villains so you'll look good."

Several people began denying that *North to Fortune* was trying to do any such thing, their arguments getting louder, faces growing redder. Standing beside Burrows, Miles Smith clenched his hands into fists, his eyes darting among the crowd as if waiting for someone to come at him and the lawyer.

James's voice boomed out over them all. "Enough!" When they fell mostly silent again, he addressed Burrows. "When did you and Mr. Welsh part company?"

Burrows crossed his arms, chin lifted. For a moment, Charlotte wasn't sure if he was going to answer the deputy, but he did. "Nine-fifteen or so. We never really reached an agreement, but he was feeling ill, said he needed to go take some medicine. He left, I assume to go to his tent."

No mention of his later meeting with Welsh. That was odd.

James found Carmen Welsh where she sat with Cicely and Roslyn. The older woman was pale, her face drawn.

"Ma'am?" James said with a gentleness Charlotte knew he reserved for such moments.

Carmen gazed up at him, shaking her head. "I didn't hear him come in. I'd taken a sleeping draught earlier. I don't sleep well away from home."

"He stopped by to see me about the scenario," Cicely said. "We spoke for a few minutes." She glanced at Roslyn, who met her eye, then looked away. "Then he headed toward his and Mother's tent, I think. That was at nine forty-five, or thereabout."

The group fell silent after that, with everyone looking around to see if anyone else had anything to add. When no one spoke up, James shifted his gaze to Charlotte.

"You heard something."

Charlotte sat up straighter, surprised he called on her. "Yes. I don't know what time it was, but the lights were out. I heard some loud voices and what sounded like something falling."

She'd mention the conversation between Welsh and Burrows that Burrows hadn't revealed later, when she and James had a chance to speak alone.

"Anyone else hear that?" he asked.

Heads shook, no's were murmured. A couple of people corroborated, but they hadn't worried about what they'd heard or when.

"The dogs were bothered by something," Charlotte said. "One barked, and Dave told him to hush. He said he barely recalled that much."

"All right," James said. "Dr. Brody, Miss Brody, and I are

going out to examine the site. I want you all to stay here or go back to your tents. We'll need some help, I reckon, getting Mr. Welsh, so if someone has any ideas, I'd be obliged."

"We can use the rigging we had in mind for lowering Roslyn into the crevasse," a crewman offered. "Won't take long to set it up."

James gave the man a nod. "Come out when you get it ready." He turned to Charlotte and Michael. "Let's go."

"Why does she get to go?" Wallace Meade rose from his chair near the front of the tent. "Miss Brody has no more business in this investigation than any of us."

"Because," James said over his shoulder as he held the tent flap open, "I trust her."

Warmth from his support filled Charlotte as they made their way across the campsite. The sun was headed toward the horizon. It wouldn't be long before it was too dim to see much of anything.

"I think Stanley came this way," Charlotte said, leading them toward the dog pen. "Maybe from his own tent, maybe not." She pointed out which tent was occupied by whom. "That first one is Cicely and Roslyn's. Past theirs is the Welshes' tent. On the other side of that is Meade's. Becca and I are beside Cicely and Roslyn, then Paige and Elaine the costumer, and lastly Peter and Roger."

Other crew members, as well as Caleb Burrows and Miles Smith, occupied the remaining six tents.

"What about Burrows and Smith? Where are they staying?" James asked.

Charlotte pointed to a far corner of the four-by-three setup of tents. "There somewhere."

Charlotte led him and Michael between the first line of sleep tents and the mess tent, around the back of the mess tent, and past the row of sheds to Dave the dog handler's. Several of the dogs yipped and howled, excited to see people. Others stared silently, the ones with light eyes sending a shiver down Charlotte's spine. They were beautiful animals, but those ice-blue eyes seemed to look into your soul. One dog barked.

"I think that's Byron, the dog Dave hushed," she said, nodding toward the brawny mutt.

At the sound of his name, Byron wagged his tail.

"When we came by earlier," Charlotte said, "I noticed that some straw outside the fence line had been strewn farther up on the ice."

"Could have been the wind," Michael suggested.

"The wind has been coming down from the glacier," she pointed out. "Dave found this caught on the pen post that had been half pushed over." Charlotte took the bit of wool from her jacket pocket and handed it to James. "Mr. Welsh's slipper was being used as a chew toy. It's in my bag in my tent."

"From trousers or a blanket, maybe," he said, rubbing the rough fabric between his fingers. He looked up, squinting across the ice as he passed the fibers to Michael, who put them into an envelope then in his pocket. "I see the men standing guard."

"It's almost a direct path to the crevasse from here. If he was alone, Stanley was making a beeline in that direction for some reason." They started off again. Both James and Michael were searching the ground before them. "I didn't see much else."

"No, me neither. Doc?"

Michael shook his head. "How did you find him, Charlotte?"

"There were a number of us out here looking for Stanley this morning. We spread out a little, knowing the ice had some dangerous patches. As we got closer to the crevasse that Stanley was going to use to trap a character in the film, I just got a feeling." The queasy, stomach-flipped sensation made itself known again the closer they got to the men standing near the crevasse. "I was hoping it was just my active imagination at work."

"I'm Deputy Eddington," James said to the men. "Either of you have anything to tell me about this?"

They exchanged looks and shrugs; then one spoke up. "Not

really. Been taking turns just standing around, making sure no one messes with things." He gestured toward Charlotte. "Like the lady asked. What do you think happened?"

"We're gonna try to find out," James said. He and Michael stepped closer and looked over the edge. Charlotte joined them. James took a flashlight out of his coat pocket, turned it on, and pointed the light downward. "Not sure if there's something under him or if it's just a shadow. Not much room, but maybe the two of us can go down and examine the body, then rig him to be brought up."

Michael set his bags down. "Let me go down alone first."

Charlotte didn't bother to hide her shock. "Michael, it's awfully dangerous."

Her brother wasn't exactly athletic.

"I'll be on a rope all the while with someone up here holding the other end, right?" When everyone agreed that would be the standard procedure, Michael shrugged. "Can't think of anything that could go wrong then. And it'll allow me to perform a better in situ examination."

James directed the flashlight down into the crevasse again. "Fine by me, Doc. After you're done, I'll come down and we'll get him hoisted up to the surface." He addressed the men. "Go on back and get yourselves warmed up. We'll take it from here. And thanks."

The two guards shuffled back toward camp, passing the crewman who was in charge of the rope rigging and his assistant. They set up a series of anchors hammered into the ice, pulleys, and rope. Charlotte was impressed with the preparedness of the crew. Maybe Welsh had more forethought about the dangerous scene than the others had suspected.

The men had Michael step into a harness, secured a line to the metal ring near his waist, and then gave him some instruction on how to descend without swinging around. One of Michael's exam bags was tied to another rope so he would be able to use both hands.

When he was ready, Michael put his back to the crevasse and got onto his hands and knees. After running the line through the anchors and pulleys, the two crewmen stood one behind the other, feet planted and ice crampons on their boots digging in.

"Slow and easy, Doc," the lead man said.

With a reassuring smile at Charlotte, Michael lowered himself over the side. James helped him get into position. Charlotte's heart edged toward her throat, but she stepped closer to watch. *He'll be fine. He's on a strong rope. He'll be fine.*

The men made sure Michael's descent was as safe and steady as possible. Michael used his feet and hands to keep from banging against the ice walls. Some sharp protrusions stuck out, but he deftly skirted them. Finally, after what had to be no more than several minutes but felt like hours, his feet touched the surface ten feet down, beside Welsh.

"All right," he called up. "Send my bag, would you?" While he waited, Michael took a flashlight from his pocket and shined it down on the body. "Not a shadow under him, Eddington, a blanket caught beneath his head and shoulders."

"Where's the rest of it?" James lowered Michael's bag into the crevasse.

Michael squatted, trying to see beneath Welsh without touching him. "There's another crevasse under him. Not as wide, of course, but wide enough. Might have gotten wedged in there, if he'd fallen the right way."

Thank goodness for small favors.

"What else can you see?" James asked. "Any wounds? Blood?"

Michael pulled off his gloves and ran his bare hands over Welsh's body, gently probing his head, neck, shoulders, arms, ribs, hips, and legs. "Possibly a broken neck, but whether that was the cause of death is hard to say. No significant blood or wounds. A few minor abrasions on his head. Probably from the fall."

James gave Charlotte a pointed look, then asked Michael, "Do you think he fell in on his own or had some help?"

"No idea. He's partially frozen down here. I'll get a better sense after he warms up a bit."

James cast a glance back at the men still holding Michael's line. "We need to get Welsh harnessed. Any ideas?"

The lead man made sure his companion was prepared to take the line alone; then he joined James and Charlotte at the edge of the crevasse. After crossing himself, he scratched his chin, assessing the situation.

"Welsh isn't a big man," he said. "We can rig something. Need to go down there, but we'll manage."

Charlotte looked over the side. There was barely room for Michael, who was not a large man himself. Adding the slight-of-frame crewman would create difficulty in maneuvering, but there was no choice if they were to retrieve the body.

"Do what you have to," James said. "We need to get him out of there." He called down to Michael. "You okay, Doc?"

Michael scraped something off of Welsh's coat, which the director had worn over his striped pajamas, and put it in a small jar. "Just fine. I'll collect a few samples, then help get Welsh secured, since I'm already down here. But sooner would be better than later. It's damn cold down here."

"On my way, Doc," the crewman said, and hurried to the canvas bag he'd brought.

Charlotte watched Michael work. "He seems almost relaxed down there."

"Who," James asked, "your brother?"

She nudged his shoulder. "No, Mr. Welsh. Wouldn't you think that if he'd been walking along and fell over the edge he would have panicked and tried to catch himself? People flail about when they feel themselves falling."

"He might have," James said, but he didn't sound completely convinced. "Unless he was inebriated."

"The opening of the crevasse isn't all that wide," Charlotte pointed out. "Even inebriated, if he'd tried to catch the side, he would have hit the edges in his efforts, don't you think? There should be wounds on his hands, or maybe more bruises."

James frowned down at the body. "Damn it," he said quietly so the two crewmen wouldn't hear. "We might just have a murderer out here."

Charlotte had thought the same thing when she first saw Welsh's body, but had chalked it up to her journalist's mind and overactive imagination. Who would want to kill the director?

Plenty of folks, she realized. Welsh had a beef with half a dozen of the people sitting a few hundred yards away. And those were only the ones she knew of since the day before yesterday.

"Get him up here as soon as you can," James said to the lead man. "We'll get the dog sled over to transport him back to camp. Doc, you have something to cover him real good, right? No need to traumatize his wife and daughter."

"I do," Michael said, his voice echoing upward. "I'll do a proper autopsy back in town."

James took Charlotte's arm in a light grasp and walked her a few steps away from the men working the rope rigging. "I'll stay here to keep an eye on things. I need you to ask the handler to ready his dog team, under official request by the marshal's office."

Charlotte nodded. "I can do that. James, there's something else." He gave a questioning look that prompted her to continue. "Caleb Burrows is lying."

His blue eyes narrowed. "About what?"

"About when he last saw Stanley." Keeping her voice down so only James would hear, she told him what she'd seen and heard the previous night near the bins. "But Stanley walked away quite alive."

"Did Burrows follow him?"

She shook her head. "Not that I could tell. He seemed to go

around the back side of the sleep tents, toward his own, while Stanley went to his own."

James stared off into the distance, absently scratching at his bearded chin. "Doesn't mean he killed the man, doesn't mean he didn't."

"Then why not say they'd spoken a second time?"

"That, Miss Brody, is a very good question."

Chapter 7

There were a number of people in the mess tent when Charlotte returned. Some were playing cards or checkers, others were reading or chatting to pass the time while they waited on word from James. People often sought the comfort of others in trying times, and it was also the warmest place in camp, she wagered. Questioning faces turned to her after she closed the flap.

"Well, Miss Brody, have you and your deputy decided we can leave?" Wallace Meade asked. His tone made it perfectly clear how he felt about both of them.

"Not until tomorrow, when the train heads back this way," she said, ignoring his attitude. Everyone was in shock and acting off, she reminded herself. "But Deputy Eddington has more questions."

"What did he and the doctor find?" Cicely sat beside Roslyn, who covered her friend's hand in a comforting gesture.

There was no absolute proof of foul play, and to insinuate as much would do two things she knew James would want to avoid: upsetting folks further and letting the possible murderer know he was on to him or her. She especially didn't want to cause Cicely any more anguish. Having her father die was bad enough, but suggesting his death was intentional would be a whole new horror.

"He and Michael just want to clear up a few things before making an official determination." Hopefully that was truthful but vague enough to appease them. "They should be back soon."

Wallace Meade rose from his seat, shaking his head while a look of disgust showed on his face. He stalked out of the tent. The rest of the occupants went back to their games and conversation. On her way to pour herself a warming mug of coffee, Charlotte heard bits of conversation expressing relief that they would be able to head back to town soon, as well as a few once again claiming the film was cursed. What else had happened since *North to Fortune* had gone into production?

Charlotte wrapped her hands around her mug and headed to Paige, Cicely, and Roslyn's table. The scenarist and the lead actress looked up. Paige, who had her back to Charlotte, continued to play solitaire. The petite blonde's indifference certainly didn't mean she wasn't paying attention. Charlotte would have to word her questions carefully.

"May I join you?" Charlotte asked, indicating the open seat beside Paige.

Roslyn looked over at Cicely. The actress had read Charlotte's intention that she wasn't just being social. Roslyn would let her friend decide if she was ready for more questions.

Cicely gave her a solemn nod. She took a deep breath and released it slowly. "There's more, isn't there?" she asked quietly as Charlotte sat down.

"As I said, the deputy is trying to put together all the available facts. He asked if I'd help by talking to a few people." Charlotte placed her hand palm down and slid it across the table in a sympathetic gesture, but didn't touch the other woman. "I'm truly sorry for your loss, Cicely, and I don't want to make this any more difficult for you than it is."

Cicely's jaw muscles tightened and she blinked rapidly.

Charlotte inwardly cringed at causing the poor woman more pain. After a moment to collect herself, Cicely offered Charlotte a wan smile. "Thank you. If answering questions gets the situation settled faster, I'm for it."

Roslyn laid her hand on Cicely's forearm in support.

"I appreciate that," Charlotte said. "Your father had been ill for some time, is that right?"

"He started feeling poorly about a month ago, complaining of headaches and difficulty breathing. He told us the doctor said it was stress and a bout of bronchitis flaring up."

"Your mother mentioned medicine he was taking sometimes caused disorientation."

Cicely nodded. "Something his doctor made up for him. He only took it at night, unless he was having a bad time of it. Then Mother tried to get him to take some during the day. He'd been taking it more often of late."

"Do you know what's in it?" Charlotte asked. She had a vague suspicion of the main ingredient.

"Not offhand." Cicely smiled sadly. "Knowing Papa, it had a healthy dose of brandy. He carried it with him, most of the time."

Medicinal alcohol was allowed under Prohibition as long as it was prescribed by a doctor. Alcohol for religious uses was also permitted. Charlotte was sure more people would be finding religion and be ordained as a result of the ridiculous amendment.

"Not to say he was a big drinker," Cicely added hastily. "A glass of brandy or sherry in the evening was his habit. He didn't go to the party after the performance the other night either." Her cheeks flushed. "I probably shouldn't have said that."

It didn't surprise Charlotte in the least that the Californians had brought or acquired alcohol. Alaska had been a dry territory before Prohibition had been enacted, but people found plenty of ways to obtain their favorite beverages.

"It won't go further than us." Charlotte considered the circumstances of Stanley being out on the glacier. "From what the deputy learned, Mr. Welsh had been headed to bed at nine-forty-five or so, after talking to you. Was he prone to wandering or taking walks in the evening? Or would he have met with someone else that late?"

"Not that I know of. Papa was an early riser, and despite his tendency to push everyone, including himself, to the limit, he was a big believer in getting a good night's sleep before filming."

After he'd spoken to Cicely, Welsh had probably headed to bed. But what happened between that time and the hour Charlotte believed she'd heard the commotion? The camp had been quiet by eleven, according to Smitty. What time was the disturbance? And more importantly, what had caused the dogs to whine and bark? Stanley Welsh walking past their pen alone, or with someone, or had it been something else entirely?

"Do you think someone had spoken to him and hasn't said so?" Cicely asked.

Charlotte glanced around the mess. No one had come forward about seeing Welsh any later than Cicely. Which made sense if the last person to see him alive had been involved in his death.

"It's possible," Charlotte said, "but without admission or a witness, we may never know. Do you think your mother is up to talking to me or the deputy?"

"Mother took her sleeping draught earlier than usual last night. I doubt she recalls anything after that."

Charlotte didn't want to push the issue, but if Carmen Welsh could tell her anything more, it might help. "Deputy Eddington will want to speak to her, or perhaps she'd talk to me."

Cicely and Roslyn rose, Roslyn's hand still on her arm. "I'll let you know what she says."

After the two women left, Charlotte sipped her coffee, wondering how James and Michael were doing. Extracting a body from such a confined space couldn't be terribly easy.

"You think someone killed him," Paige said quietly, her attention on the cards laid out on the table.

Charlotte didn't bother hiding her surprise at the unexpected insight. She had to remember not to underestimate the blonde. "It's possible. Anything's possible when something like this happens."

"Even more possible when you consider how many people Stanley ticked off of late."

The fact the director had irritated people didn't surprise Charlotte in the least. She'd witnessed his exchanges with Burrows and the AEC, with Roger Markham. Even with Cicely. "You think someone was angry enough to hurt him?"

"Sure. Even me," Paige said with a short laugh. She met Charlotte's questioning gaze. "Not that I did, of course. Stanley was a decent enough guy, but he worked like everyone else in the business. Lots of promises and lots of excuses why they couldn't or wouldn't be met." The actress shrugged, but her indifference didn't ring completely true to Charlotte. "It's the way things work."

"You were getting frustrated at his lack of follow-through," Charlotte said.

"You bet I was." Color rose on Paige's cheeks. "For the past three pictures he cast me in, he'd promised bigger parts, more screen time. But somehow a different broad would always get picked for the juicy roles. You'd think sleeping with the guy would have given me an advantage."

Charlotte startled at her audacity. Paige readily admitted she was having an affair with Welsh and was angry about broken promises. Plenty of motivation there.

"But I didn't do anything to Stanley," Paige said, seeming to read Charlotte's thoughts. "He may have been leading me on some, and I was hoping for a break sooner rather than later, but it's just a matter of time before something comes my way."

There was self-satisfaction in her voice and expression.

"Why's that?"

"It always does. I have a knack, you see," the actress said. "Always land on my feet, like a cat." She gave Charlotte a wink and consulted her card game.

"Who knew about your . . . relationship with Stanley?"

Paige shrugged. "I didn't advertise it in *Variety* or anything like that. We kept it on the q.t., but there's probably a few who knew."

Who would have been most affected by the affair? "Carmen? Cicely?"

At least the young woman had the decency to look somewhat abashed. "Maybe. Probably. Not that they said anything. Not to me, at least." She quirked a slender eyebrow at Charlotte. "And Cicely knows better than to start playing 'Who Shouldn't Be Sleeping with Whom.' "

"Oh?"

Who would the scenarist be associated with? Peter? One of the crew? Charlotte had only seen her with her parents or . . . Roslyn? The women were quite friendly, affectionate toward each other even. *That* relationship would certainly get tongues wagging, and such a scandal would cause both women to lose out on opportunities. If Cicely knew about Paige, and Paige even suspected anything between Cicely and Roslyn, Charlotte was sure both sides would keep their mouths shut.

"I see. You said Stanley had been with others. Do you think Carmen would have gotten so fed up as to do anything about it?"

"Nah," Paige said. "Carmen liked the money and status that came with being Stanley's wife. He'd have to do something pretty drastic for her to get rid of him."

Apparently numerous affairs weren't drastic enough to these folks.

"And you weren't looking to be the next Mrs. Welsh?"

"God no." Paige laughed, drawing the attention of more than a few people. Lowering her voice, she said, "I wouldn't be able to deal with Stanley on a day-to-day basis. He was too temperamental. Better her than me, I say."

The actress seemed cavalier about her relationship with Welsh, but her earlier irritation at losing out on parts or not getting screen time didn't match her current offhandedness. Paige had been nearly furious in town, then irritated again on the train and during rehearsal just the day before. What had changed?

"I appreciate the information," Charlotte said as she rose. "If you can think of anything else that might help, let me or Deputy Eddington know."

Paige's eyes brightened. "That tall drink of water with the gorgeous dimples? You bet. I'll tell him everything I know, maybe even make up a bunch of stuff if that helps."

She laughed again before returning to her game.

Jealousy flared in Charlotte's chest. Her jaw clenched. Making a significant effort, she smiled stiffly. "Yes, he'll be happy to take your statement. If you'll excuse me."

Charlotte turned on her heel and strode toward the door flap. There was no cause to be jealous of Paige Carmichael. James was a good-looking man; more than a few women had said as much to Charlotte.

Back outside, a cold, cutting wind came down off the glacier. Charlotte took a deep breath, letting the chill clear her head. She wasn't usually the jealous type. What had gotten into her?

Maybe she was concerned that if she didn't allow their relationship to go further than heated kisses, James would seek out someone like Paige to satisfy him. While there was no promise of exclusivity on either of their parts, neither was seeing anyone else. But how long would he wait?

You're being ridiculous.

Charlotte took another slow, deep breath. Of course she was. She and James would figure out where they would take their relationship and how long it would be before they got there. He wasn't one to flit off to the next available girl.

"Charlotte," James called.

Her head jerked up. He strode toward her, low sunlight causing him to squint. Charlotte met him on the path. "Did you get Mr. Welsh out of there?"

"Yeah," he said, scratching his bearded cheek. "Funny thing."

"What's that?"

"He wasn't wearing gloves, though he'd had his other slipper on." James rubbed his hands together. "A man doesn't go off for a walk out here in slippers and without gloves."

"Not if he wants to feel his fingers and toes the rest of the night." Charlotte recalled the state of Stanley's body. "He may have used the blanket over his coat for added warmth, perhaps wrapping his hands in the wool kept them warm enough."

He gave her a skeptical look. "I don't know."

Charlotte shrugged. "If he was taking some sort of medicine that made him disoriented or not in his right mind, who's to say what he thought he was doing?"

James considered that. "I suppose. We'll keep that in mind. Michael will have more answers after his full autopsy, I hope."

"I'm sure he will. Is he on his way?"

"He and the others are securing Welsh in the storage shed for the night. We'll need to use the dogs again to get the body to the train in the morning." He nodded toward the mess tent. "Meade in there? Doc and I will need accommodations."

"He wasn't just now. I'm not sure what's left, as far as tents go. With Becca gone, there's an empty cot in mine." As the words left her mouth, Charlotte realized what she had said. Heat rushed to her face. "I mean . . ."

James cupped her cheek. Smiling, he leaned down and touched his lips to hers. "I know what you meant. I'll find a place. Michael can stay with you." He lowered his hand and looked up at the mess tent again. "Did you talk to any of the others?"

Grateful for the change in subject, Charlotte told him what Cicely had said about Welsh's illness and what Paige had said about their affair. Upon hearing that Paige didn't seem to care about becoming the next Mrs. Welsh, James looked skeptical.

"Not every woman is out to marry the man she's sleeping with," Charlotte said. She wasn't trying to defend Paige so much as keep any motivations for murder open.

"No," James agreed, "but the woman had been getting passed over enough that she may have felt it was her due to have some sort of break come her way. Maybe not getting it *again* pushed her past her limit."

"And she pushed Stanley into the crevasse?" Charlotte could see the fiery-tempered blonde doing that in the heat of the moment.

"We'll keep her in mind as your brother performs his exam."

Charlotte started toward the Welshes' tent. "I'm waiting for Cicely to see if her mother is up for an interview. Or would you rather speak with her alone?"

"I don't want to overwhelm the woman," James said. "Let me go see her."

Hiding her disappointment, but understanding this was, most likely, a murder investigation, Charlotte pointed out the correct tent. "I'll be in mine, over there," she said.

James tugged the brim of his hat. "I'll come for you later."

He walked to the Welshes' tent and called to the occupants. Cicely Welsh invited him in.

Though tempted to linger and listen, Charlotte decided it was too cold as the wind picked up. Besides, she trusted James to share information when he was ready to do so. Just as he trusted she wouldn't put anything into print that might jeopardize the case.

Theirs was a comfortable working relationship. Now if she could sort out their personal one, things would be much easier.

Back inside her tent, Charlotte turned up the kerosene heater. She straightened the blankets on Becca's cot in anticipation of Michael sharing the tent with her for the night.

Where was Michael? He should have seen to Welsh's body by now.

Bundling herself in her coat, scarf, and hat once again, Charlotte headed out to the storage shed where James said they'd keep Welsh until they left the next day. She passed several people along the way. Most nodded greeting. Others gave her sour looks, as if it had been her fault they were still there. Well, she supposed it was, but she wasn't about to feel bad for them when a man had died, or worse, been killed by one of them.

The door to the shed was ajar and she heard shuffling sounds from within. "Michael?"

"Come in," he called out.

She entered the hastily built, but sturdy shed and shut the door behind her. The wind whistled through the gaps between the planks. Cases of equipment had been stacked in the back corner. Under a single bare bulb over his head, Michael squatted beside the dog sled that had been pushed in as far as it would go. Stanley Welsh's body lay atop the sled, covered by blankets and strapped in. Michael examined the area around Welsh's throat.

"Find anything else?" Charlotte asked.

"I think there may be marks here," he said, pointing. "Once everything warms up it might be easier to tell. There's little to no blood. Internal injury due to the fall will show in the autopsy, but it wasn't that great a distance."

"What about his hands?"

Michael covered the head and shoulders with the blanket and stood, stretching his back. "Nothing significant. Why? Do you think he might have fought someone off?"

"Maybe," Charlotte said, "or if he slipped and fell, wouldn't he have tried to catch himself and scraped his hands on the ice?"

Her brother nodded thoughtfully. "Perhaps. And there's something else that doesn't sit right. No flashlight. Who walks along a dangerous ice field in the pitch-dark without a light?"

"No one thinking clearly, which may be the case. I think the medicine he was taking could have been partially responsible. But our suspicion that Mr. Welsh was murdered is gaining more traction."

Unfortunately, that meant there was a camp full of people who could have done it.

An expression of distaste lined Michael's features. "Eddington will have his work cut out for him." He dug into his coat pocket and withdrew a padlock. "George the rigging man gave me the key so we can lock the shed and not worry about anyone disturbing the body."

A shiver ran through Charlotte. "Good gracious, who would want to?"

Michael gestured for her to precede him to the door and he pulled the chain on the light dangling from the middle of the ceiling. "A famous person dies and you get all manner of odd ducks wanting to see. Or take photographs and sell them."

Charlotte exited the shed and waited for him to lock the door. "I suppose it's not an unusual thing. Disturbing, but not unusual."

He shoved the key into his trouser pocket. "Unfortunately. But Welsh should be undisturbed for the night."

She looped her arm through his. "Come on back to my tent and put your things away. You can sleep in the cot Becca had used."

"Where's Eddington staying?"

Charlotte waited for her brother to ask if the deputy would rather have the cot in her tent, but the comment never came. She let out a relieved breath.

"He'll talk to Wallace Meade or Smitty about a place to sleep."

Michael nodded but said nothing more on the subject. He had no illusions—or delusions—about her relationship history. He understood it had little to do with her sense of propriety and more to do with fear of repeating past mistakes.

They returned to the mess tent in time to hear James addressing the gathered crew. Wallace Meade stood with the deputy, facing the crowd. Charlotte and Michael slipped in and found places to stand along the side wall.

"It's only for another evening," the producer was saying. "I told Deputy Eddington we'd give him our full cooperation here and once we returned to town."

Well, that was a change of heart on Meade's part. Had he realized he was fighting a losing battle by opposing James and decided to cooperate? Meade was a successful businessman, one who probably knew when to cut his losses.

There were the expected grumbles, but no one outright protested. Not that protests would have changed James's mind on how the investigation would be run. He potentially had a murderer to catch.

"This is a terrible tragedy, of course," Meade continued, "and I'm sorry to say the production of *North to Fortune* will be shelved for the foreseeable future."

Everyone started talking at once, some questioning the decision, others agreeing wholeheartedly, citing "the curse." The death of a colleague was unfortunate and sad, but what else had them spooked?

"Why?" Cicely Welsh asked over the din. They turned to her, and she rose from her seat. "My father was passionate about this film. He had a vision of an epic experience that more than a few of us shared. It wasn't perfect, but we were working on it." She nodded to Caleb Burrows and Miles Smith where they sat at a table of several other Natives, mostly locals hired as background actors. "We already have half the necessary reels completed. With a few adjustments to the script, I think we can finish and create a film Papa would have been proud of."

No one spoke for a few moments.

Beside Cicely, Roslyn Sanford rose. "Count me in."

With Paige's revelation of the scope of their relationship in mind, Charlotte saw the adoration in the actress's eyes for the bespectacled scenarist.

"I'm in," someone called out.

"Me too. Let's get it done."

Others joined in to support the idea, but there were a few protestations. The strongest coming from Wallace Meade.

"Hold on there, everyone," the producer said, hands raised to get their attention. "I can appreciate your dedication to Stanley and the film, but there's a lot left to do. Who's gonna work that out?"

"Cicely can do it," Roslyn said. "I'll help. She and Stanley were working on the scenario together, and of course she knows the story better than anyone else." Roslyn smiled at the taller woman. "What do you say?"

A slow grin curved Cicely's mouth, but before she could respond, Meade cut in.

"Now wait a minute. Cicely is no director." He shook his head and waved his hands. "Impossible. She's a scenarist. This film is too big for a newcomer."

"I dare say, Meade." Peter York stepped forward. "Cicely is perhaps the smartest gal I know. She's been at her father's knee on plenty of films, so hardly a newcomer. She'd be aces. Right, everyone?"

For the most part the crew was behind the idea, agreeing with Peter and making Cicely blush.

Meade's face reddened. "I think we need to take a few days and consider the situation. Let's get back to town and we'll figure it out. Pack your personal items. We'll secure the site for now and decide who'll come out to break it down if it comes to that."

By the furrowing of her brow, the implication that the company might not return wasn't lost on Cicely Welsh.

"That seems fair," Cicely said tightly. "We can bring our things back easily enough when filming resumes. Thank you, everyone, for your support." She and Roslyn sat once more.

It was Meade's turn to give the scenarist a purse-lipped frown.

James called for their attention now. "We've arranged to have the train stop here at nine tomorrow morning. I want everyone on it. Once the doctor makes his assessment, I may have a few more questions to ask folks."

"When can we leave town?" a man asked.

"When I say so." James put enough of a growl in his voice to let them know he meant business. Then he addressed Cicely. "I know you want to get your father back to the States as soon as possible, miss, but I'm afraid this is still an open investigation."

"I understand, Deputy. We're all ready to cooperate fully."

Charlotte doubted that as she perused the faces of the men and women in the tent. Someone in here had been instrumental in Welsh's death.

Chapter 8

Michael was up and out of the tent early the next morning to supervise Welsh's body being transported to the train platform before anyone else headed over. He asked Charlotte if she'd be willing to keep Cicely and Carmen at the campsite while they loaded the sled onto the train. The women were going through enough trauma; seeing their loved one's body, even covered, might be too much.

Charlotte agreed to do what she could, and at breakfast suggested to Cicely they board last. Carmen was sitting with her daughter, looking pale and somewhat glassy-eyed. Had she taken a bit too much sleeping draught last night? Not that Charlotte blamed the poor woman.

When Charlotte managed to talk to James about his interview with the recent widow, he said she couldn't recall much of the night of Welsh's death, mostly due to the concoction she took. Both of the elder Welshes seemed to rely upon their doctors' prescriptions. Michael had found a half-empty bottle of Dr. Halpert's elixir in Welsh's coat pocket. According to the label, it contained several herbs, minerals, a touch of arsenic, and thirty percent alcohol.

Charlotte mentioned she'd seen the director drink from the bottle at least once during the rehearsed scene. Who knows how much he'd had before that evening?

"That might explain his disorientation," James had said.

Now, in the almost light of morning, Charlotte helped the crew pack up what they couldn't afford to leave unattended at the glacier. Under Smitty's watchful eye, everything else from bedding to lanterns to food would be accounted for and locked in the supply sheds.

"If we do decide to return," Cicely said as she checked the straps on a case, "we'll just bring it back out."

"Do you think Mr. Meade will agree to it?" Charlotte asked.

"He's put in a lot of money," Roslyn said. "If the picture doesn't get made, he and the investors will be in the red. Films aren't always profitable as it is, but Mr. Meade talked *Fortune* up to a lot of folks and has a number of big backers."

"If he canceled the film, would the investors demand to get paid back?"

Roslyn answered immediately. "Depends on the conditions of their agreement. Losing Stanley might be considered an unavoidable catastrophe that negates some, if not all, repayment. The studio could simply write it off as a loss, but I think there are plenty who would want their money back. At least with it finished and distributed it has a shot at making something for those investors."

Then why had Meade wanted to stop filming? Did he truly believe only Stanley Welsh had been capable of creating a money-making film? Was his admiration and respect for Welsh so high that he wouldn't consider anyone else? It was difficult to say. Perhaps it was time to ask the man himself.

The train rumbled up to the platform at nine, as expected. While freight and passengers were loaded, the conductor and engineer talked to Meade about the modified schedule. In the snatches of conversation Charlotte gleaned, the CR&NW had made two extra trips at the request of the marshal's office for the sake of the film crew. Who would be responsible for payment? Meade argued that the marshal requested the last trip, so that office should pay. James waved all the men off, telling the conductor to bring it up with Marshal Blaine.

"I'm just the deputy," James said as he hauled a crate marked UNDEVELOPED FILM to the freight car.

Charlotte stifled a laugh at the shared expressions on the other men's faces. James was as much the marshal in Cordova as Blaine, but if he was able to use his lower title to avoid tedious situations like who needed to pay a bill, he was happy to do so.

"You are terrible," she said to him as they passed on the platform.

He gave her a quizzical look, then grinned when she indicated the three men still arguing. "I am at that."

Once everyone was settled, the whistle blew and the conductor called "All aboard!" to the empty platform and campsite. James and Michael rode in the freight car with Dave, the dog team, and the sled with Stanley Welsh.

Charlotte watched as a gust of wind rippled the canvas roofs of the tents. A cloud of blowing snow tumbled through camp. If they decided to continue filming, the company could be back in a matter of days. If not, some of the crew and probably a few locals would return to break down the site. Meade had made previous arrangements for the materials to be sold to the Cordova Hardware and General Store, which would, in turn, sell the wood, fittings, tents, and anything else the Californians didn't want to haul south.

The train lurched once, then slowly began moving westward along the rails. The atmosphere in the passenger car was subdued, nothing like the more buoyant attitude on the way out.

Cicely and Carmen sat together, with Roslyn in the seat across the aisle. Carmen had said little over the last day or so. Cicely had asked for the location of the telegraph office in town, so she could inform the studio head of Welsh's passing.

She had also discussed the procedure for getting her father back to California with Michael, once he released the body. Would Carmen ever come out of her haze? Some didn't when a spouse died.

Peter and Paige sat behind Cicely and Carmen. The two spoke quietly. With their backs to Charlotte, she had a difficult time reading their body language. While they didn't seem overly chummy, they remained engaged more often than not as the train rumbled on.

Unlike Wallace Meade. He sat in silence several rows behind the two actors, arms crossed and brow furrowed. Was he trying to determine which would be worse, making or not making *North to Fortune*?

Behind Charlotte once again, Caleb Burrows and Miles Smith chatted quietly. Charlotte turned around. "Pardon the interruption, but can I ask you something, Mr. Burrows?"

The lawyer smiled at her. "Of course, Miss Brody. I won't guarantee an answer, but you can ask."

Charlotte shifted and turned, resting her leg on the seat and laying her arm across the back. "Given your druthers, would you rather see *North to Fortune* suspended or filmed and released?"

"Considering the direction Mr. Welsh had been going? It's better if it's never released. But you knew I'd answer that way."

"A lawyer once told me I should never ask a question that I didn't have an inkling of what the answer might be," she said.

Burrows nodded. "Makes courtroom proceedings much less strenuous."

"What if they decide to carry on with the film?" Charlotte suspected she knew the answer to that one as well.

"If they adjust the scenario so it isn't detrimental to the Native people, then I think the AEC would be happy to support it." Something changed in his dark eyes. "If they decide to carry on at all now."

"Miss Welsh seemed willing to work something out," Charlotte said. "She was rather upset that her father hadn't considered the Native point of view."

Burrows's gaze fell on the young woman at the front of the car.

Miles's did as well, but the younger man frowned and quickly brought his attention back to Charlotte. "I bet she talks a good game. I won't believe it until I see it."

"Hold on there, Miles. Miss Brody's right," Burrows said. "Miss Welsh was very supportive at the show the other night. She may be the path to correcting the film."

"And pardon my bluntness," Charlotte said, lowering her voice, "but with Stanley gone now, that path is much more open."

Burrows's features fell into an unreadable, neutral expression. "I hadn't considered that."

Hadn't he? Charlotte wasn't so sure.

Only a handful of passengers stood on the platform at the Cordova train station, waiting for the CR&NW to eventually head back toward Chitina and Kennecott. Several miners and a woman with two small children stared openly as the crew disembarked. Then the yipping dogs were brought out, already hooked up to the sled holding Stanley Welsh's body.

Hand tight on the lead dogs' line, Dave walked the six excited animals down a ramp and onto the street; then he called up to Michael, who had just emerged from the freight car. "See you over there, Doc."

Michael waved to him, then hefted two of his bags. James followed him out, yawning and scratching his bearded chin. They climbed the stairs up to the platform and made their way over to Charlotte.

"I'll drop my things off at my office, then head to the hospital," Michael said to James. "It'll take me a while since he needs to thaw some. I'll have a preliminary report in the morning. See you later."

He hurried off, bags thudding against his back and hip.

A gust of icy, wet wind blew in from the sea. Hands clamped to hats. Shoulders hunched.

"Looks like we're in for some weather." James checked the horizon and made a sour face. "Yeah, it ain't gonna be pretty the next day or so."

"What does that mean about our departure?" Wallace Meade asked, tugging at his leather gloves and gingerly flexing his hands. "We need to catch the southbound steamer."

"I thought you'd be discussing continuing with the film?" Charlotte asked. Meade obviously had his mind made up, but what about Cicely and the rest of the company?

"I don't see how that'll work out. It's best if we just get Stanley back home and buried."

James narrowed his gaze at the man. "None of you are going anywhere until the doctor determines cause of death. I may still have questions."

"You can't keep us here, Deputy." Meade straightened to his full height, chin up, putting him eye to eye with James. "You have no right."

What had happened to that spirit of cooperation Meade had advocated earlier?

James's blue eyes turned glacial, and his brows met over his crooked nose.

Uh-oh. Charlotte hadn't been witness to James's anger too often, but when it flared it was best to stay out of his way. Grateful he wasn't addressing her, she took a half step back.

"First of all, Mr. Meade," the deputy said, "as an agent of the law of the Territory of Alaska, I have every right to investigate a suspicious death, which this is now, as I see fit. Second, chances are your steamer isn't going to arrive, and if it does, it likely won't depart anytime soon because of the storm that's brewing. Third, I don't know about Miss and Mrs. Welsh, but I'd rather hear from *them* regarding the treatment of their loved one. Now get your ass back to your hotel and wait for me to tell you what'll happen next."

Meade gaped at him, perhaps unaccustomed to being spoken to in such a manner.

James turned his attention to the others on the platform who had stopped to listen to the deputy set the producer straight. "That goes for everyone. Gather your things and go back to the Windsor or wherever you're staying. You may be here awhile, so get comfortable and settle in. Cordova has some fine amenities to keep you entertained until decisions can be made."

And suspects fully questioned, Charlotte added silently.

The men responsible for the freight began hauling it to the side, waiting for a hired truck to help transport it to the hotel or wherever it was to be held. The unencumbered cast and crew hefted their personal items and filed down the steps from the platform to the street. Not a one grumbled about having to walk rather than take a car the few blocks to the hotel.

Wallace Meade waited for the platform to clear, then turned to James. Charlotte prepared herself for another run-in.

"My apologies, Deputy."

Charlotte and James exchanged surprised looks.

"I know you're doing your job," the producer continued. "It's just been so upsetting, this last day or so. We're all stunned by Stanley's death, and the possibility it was intentional? Unbelievable. So please, forgive my rudeness."

He stuck his right hand out in a peace offering.

James stared at the man's hand for a moment, then grasped it. Meade winced slightly.

The irritation hadn't completely left James's eyes as he nodded once in acceptance. "These things tend to get the best of us. I'll appreciate future cooperation, Mr. Meade, so we can get this matter settled and you and your people can be on your way."

Meade eased his hand from James's. "Absolutely, Deputy. You can count on it."

He tipped his hat to Charlotte, then retrieved his bag from the platform. Hefting the case in his left hand and cautiously using the right on the rail as he navigated the steps, he then strode down the street presumably toward the hotel with the rest of the company.

"That man certainly runs hot and cold," she said.

"Never a dull moment." James hoisted his bag to his shoulder, then reached for Charlotte's. "I'll walk you home."

Beating him to the handle, Charlotte picked up her bag. "I can manage," she said, smiling. "Besides, Becca will be in school for another few hours. I need to stop in at the paper and get something written up before I meet her at home."

"Can I at least walk you to the *Times* office?" He seemed disappointed that she'd taken her own bag, or that they wouldn't spend fifteen minutes walking together back to her house.

"I'd like that."

James preceded her down the slick stairs and prepared to take her hand should she slip. She didn't, and the two of them traversed the icy road to the newspaper office several blocks away. The train blew its whistle, warning of its imminent departure. Another gust of wet, freezing wind blew in, tinged with coal smoke.

"How bad a storm do you think it'll be?" Charlotte asked.

James squinted up at the sky. "We might not feel it too bad here, but out on the water, it'll be nasty. I'll get in touch with the navy station and see what they say. Storms like this have been known to cause ships to go down, so I'd reckon the steamers will be delayed. Make sure you have plenty of food and fuel, just in case they don't come in with supplies."

"You too." They had reached the office, and Charlotte turned to stand and face him. "Thank you for the escort. I'll make sure there's enough stew tonight if you're interested in a hot meal. Say seven o'clock?"

He leaned down and pecked her on the cheek. "I'll be there, thank you."

They bade each other good-bye, and Charlotte went in, not feeling cold in the least.

Andrew Toliver sat at his desk, shirt sleeves rolled up and papers strewn before him. The muffled hum and clatter of the Linotype came through the closed door on the right.

Anticipation lit Toliver's eyes. "Heard you all were coming back early. What happened? Did Burrows create some sort of ruckus?"

Charlotte quickly divested herself of her coat, hat, scarf, and gloves. Barely conscious of the fact she was wearing trousers, she hurried over to the chair on the opposite side of the desk and sat facing him. "Worse. Stanley Welsh was killed."

Toliver's eyes practically bugged out of his head. "What?"

Charlotte gave him the details of the events after leaving Cordova, from Welsh's arguments with Paige Carmichael, Roger Markham, Caleb Burrows, and Wallace Meade to the discovery of his body in the crevasse. "He wasn't an easy man to get along with," she said. "Even he and his daughter didn't see eye to eye."

"That's unfortunate," Toliver said, sad understanding in his eyes. "But were any of those arguments worth killing over? Angering, yes. Frustrating, yes. But to take a man's life? No, something deeper happened here, Charlotte."

"I agree that their arguments were somewhat superficial on the surface." Charlotte rose and started to pace, her preferred method when trying to follow threads of a story. "There's more. Perhaps not something deeper and darker, but more."

"Or," Toliver said, "whoever killed him didn't have much depth of reason but did have a terrible temper. Even a weak motive can be enough when anger and opportunity are present."

The nefarious twists and turns of a potential murder case flittered out of her head. Charlotte sat back down with a huff. "Well, that would be boring."

Toliver wagged a finger at her. "We aren't in the entertainment business, Miss Brody, we're in the information business. Though it's not impossible to do both. Write up something for tomorrow's paper and get it in to Henry quick as you can. There's still time for him to rearrange the layout before we go to print. Then I want you back with those people in the morning."

Charlotte snatched a pad of paper and a pen from his desk and got to work.

The second installment of her *Times* articles with the cast and crew took a decidedly sinister turn compared to the first, more glib piece. She wrote of the train trip out to Childs Glacier, of the rehearsal and blocking of character movement on the dangerous ice, of the anxiousness that pervaded the company. Not just the nerves associated with the making of a film, but fears that the production was cursed. Charlotte touched upon the dissatisfaction of the subject matter by some, then described how things seemed to be going well for the moment. The next paragraph began with the morning of Welsh's disappearance and subsequent discovery of his body.

She was careful not to call it murder, despite the suspicious circumstances, but did state that as a matter of procedure for an unattended, unnatural death, all avenues were being explored by the marshal's and coroner's offices.

When Charlotte had handed the sheets to Henry in the Linotype and printing room, the young man read through the pages quickly, his eyes growing wider with each line. Charlotte couldn't help but smile.

Who said information couldn't be entertaining?

"Wow," Henry marveled, looking up at her. "Is this for real? You found him?"

"I wouldn't have written it if it wasn't true," she said. "But not just me. Mr. Markham was there too, and a number of others. Even poor Cicely and Carmen Welsh." Charlotte felt a pang of sorrow for the Welsh women. A man was dead, and his family and friends would likely read this in the morning. Doubt crept into her conscience. "It's not too much, is it, Henry?"

"I don't think so," he said. "What did Mr. Toliver say?"

"He thought it was fine." But Toliver hadn't been there to see Cicely Welsh turn so pale she was almost as white as the ice, or watch Carmen faint into the arms of the man standing behind her.

You're getting soft, said a voice in her head. *A year ago, you wouldn't have thought twice about printing something just as detailed or more so.*

No, but a year ago she wasn't living and working in a small town where the subjects of the daily news were friends and neighbors. Since coming to Cordova, she'd learned to tread carefully when it came to certain events. Reporting on Lyle Fiske's death in November had been difficult for his widow, but Charlotte relayed the facts of that sordid case with little problem and without publicly embarrassing Caroline Fiske.

"Thanks." She started toward the door to the outer office, then turned back, guilt eating at her gut. "Strike the line about his sightless eyes staring up, all right? This is a news article, not a dime-store novel."

Henry pulled the pencil from behind his ear and scratched it across the page. "Anything else?"

"I think that's it. Good night, Henry."

"Good night, Miss Brody."

Charlotte shut the door behind her as she entered the office. Toliver was still at the desk, reading through a sheaf of papers while he absentmindedly rubbed the top of his shin where the cast ended.

"Henry's almost done," she told their boss.

"Good. Good." Toliver sat back and laced his fingers over his ample belly as he regarded her. "Go on home and get some rest. I have the feeling you'll be hopping like a rabbit here the next few days."

Usually, Charlotte would have offered to help Henry or start the printing press, but truth be told, all she could think about was a hot bath and a hot meal. Becca would be home from school soon, wanting to know every detail Charlotte could share about Stanley Welsh and what James and Michael turned up. They could talk about it over dinner preparations, and perhaps with James when he came over.

"I'll be at the hotel bright and early," Charlotte said as she donned her outerwear. "Good night."

Toliver bade her good evening and went back to his reading.

Charlotte hurried down the walk to the grocer's, the wind biting into her exposed cheeks. She pulled up her scarf and shot a glare at the darkening sky. Even she could tell the storm coming in would be a doozy. The bell over the door of McGruder's rang cheerfully, and the man behind the counter called out a greeting. Charlotte responded in kind, found the potatoes, carrots, and onions she wanted for her stew, and paid for them. Down the street at the meat market, a nicer cut of beef than she'd normally use for stew was wrapped in brown paper and tied with twine. She wouldn't have all day for the stew to actually stew, but the more tender meat should help move the cooking process along.

With all of her groceries in the bag she'd brought out to the glacier, Charlotte headed home. Ten minutes after she'd hung up her coat and winter things, Charlotte heard Becca bang into the parlor.

"Charlotte! Are you home?"

"In here," she called. Footfalls hurried toward the kitchen where she was cutting up potatoes and consulting her copy of *The Suffrage Cook Book*. "Take off your boots and hang up your coat."

The footfalls retreated to the entry and Charlotte smiled.

Becca padded back down the hall and practically flung herself into the room. "Well? What happened? How did Mr. Welsh die? Who did it? Where is he now?"

Charlotte held up her hands to stop the onslaught. "Nothing really happened. Michael isn't sure how he died yet. We don't know who did it. Michael is performing the autopsy at the hospital. Now wash your hands and help me. James will be over for dinner at seven."

Becca heaved an exaggerated sigh but did as she was asked. While the two of them prepared dinner, Charlotte gave her as much detail as she felt Becca should know. She reiterated that nothing was to go beyond the walls of the house or to be repeated to anyone.

"If you're serious about becoming a journalist," Charlotte told her, "you have to be able to withhold certain things until the entire story can be told."

"Even from friends and family?"

"Even then."

Charlotte thought about all the things she'd never told her parents or Michael. Or the bits and pieces she'd kept from James about the two murders she'd reported on here in Cordova. Oh, eventually she'd come clean to him, but at the time there were some things it was best he didn't know.

Chapter 9

After getting Becca off to school the following morning, Charlotte headed to Michael's office over the drugstore. He had moved from the tiny cabin farther down the street, which was now his residence. Separating home life from his practice had given her brother the opportunity to involve himself in the community on a more personal level. Michael seemed more at ease these days, more engaged with those around him. It pleased Charlotte to see her brother getting back to being the fun-loving person she'd grown up with.

The whitewashed door down from the drugstore entrance hadn't seen fresh paint in a few years, except for the sign MICHAEL C. BRODY, M.D. in black. Charlotte went in and climbed the stairs to his office. The advantage of being on the second story and having half of that level for his waiting area, office, and exam rooms was countered by the need for regular house calls to those who couldn't manage the steps. On the upper landing, the door to the office itself stood ajar. Before she went in, Charlotte could hear the *tip-tap* of a typewriter.

Seated behind the desk of the outer office, Mary Weaver transcribed Michael's handwritten patient notes. Her shiny black hair had been braided and coiled around the crown of her head. Charlotte couldn't see the skirt Mary wore, but her white blouse was pristine and freshly starched, as always.

Mary had taken over the receptionist and secretarial duties Charlotte had originally performed for her brother, who had been terrible at keeping up on the task. Charlotte hadn't been much better at it. Hiring Mary had probably been the smartest thing Michael had done for his practice. She was knowledgeable of basic office procedures, smart, and friendly. And she was known to a number of the local Natives, making them feel more comfortable about visiting a white doctor when necessary.

Mary glanced up from the report and smiled. "Good morning, Charlotte," she said. "The doctor isn't in yet."

Mary and Charlotte had quickly started calling each other by their first names, but Mary always called Michael by his title.

"Is it all right if I wait?" Charlotte asked. "I have a few things to talk to him about."

"Of course. Please." Mary indicated a couple of worn but comfortable secondhand upholstered chairs. "Can I get you anything?"

"No, I'm fine." Charlotte took one of the seats. "How are your mother and the children?"

She had met Mary's mother, four-year-old daughter, and six-year-old son at a small holiday gathering. The children stayed at home with Mary's mother during the day. Mary's husband had died a couple of years before, leaving her as the sole provider for the family. The assistance of the Eyak community had helped while Mary found work in town.

"They're doing well, thank you." Mary glanced down at the papers on her desk, then back up at Charlotte apologetically. "I should get these done before the doctor gets in."

"No, no, I'm sorry. Didn't mean to interrupt you." Charlotte smiled at the woman and picked up a month-old copy of *Harper's Bazaar*. There was also a *National Geographic* and a couple of days' worth of the *Cordova Daily Times*. Having reading material out for waiting patients was Mary's idea.

Mary went back to her typing and Charlotte read about the latest fashion trends. Well, the trends for the rest of the country, perhaps. Though she appreciated the occasional excuse to get gussied up, Charlotte was finding herself more and more accepting of the practical and casual approach to dress here in the territory. The wearing of trousers, as she had intended for the duration of her stay at the film site, didn't raise so much as an eyebrow.

Footfalls on the stairs warned that Michael was on the way up. Charlotte set the magazine aside and grinned when her brother came through the door.

"Good morning, Mary," he said, sweeping his hat off as he shrugged out of his coat. "Good morning, Charlotte. I figured you'd be here."

Mary rose and took his hat and coat from him, then hung it on a coat stand in the corner. "You have an appointment with Mr. Turner in fifteen minutes, Doctor."

"Right. Thank you. Charlotte and I won't be that long." Michael gestured for Charlotte to precede him into his office beside the exam room. There were more bookshelves and cabinets than he had been able to fit in his previous office. She sat in the hard-backed chair on the near side of the desk. He shut the door, then walked around the desk to his more comfortable upholstered chair. "Did you speak to Eddington last night?"

Charlotte narrowed her eyes. "What makes you think I saw James last night?"

Michael was well aware of her relationship with the deputy, but that didn't mean she had to tell him everything they did together.

"Your defensiveness, first of all," Michael said with a grin. "But he'd stopped by the morgue and mentioned he was on his way to your house for dinner."

"Oh." Charlotte released the tension in her shoulders and sat back. "Yes, he came over, but all he would tell me is that you hadn't finished and that it did look like Stanley was a victim of foul play."

"I'll conduct the internal exam later today." Michael opened the satchel he'd carried in and withdrew several sheets of paper. "There were no bleeding wounds on his body, other than minor scrapes. His neck, however, was broken, and there were lacerations and a skull fracture on the back of his head that were likely from high-impact contact with the side or bottom of the crevasse."

"Someone pushed him in?"

"After the fact, not to kill him," he said, turning one of the pages toward her. "I believe he was strangled."

Charlotte took the page and read. " 'External Examination: Bruising to throat consistent with obstruction of the airway and blood flow to the brain.' " Mental images of Stanley Welsh being throttled ran through her head. "It would take considerable strength to do that, wouldn't it?"

"He'd been ill for some time. That, or overmedication, could have reduced his ability to fight off an attacker. Or the person surprised him."

Charlotte considered the scenario. "So the killer—"

"Or killers," Michael interjected. "There's no evidence that it was one person or two. We should keep an open mind there. I'll still need to run tests on his stomach contents as standard procedure, and I'll check the medicine too, but that's the unofficial cause of death."

They heard Mary greet someone in the other office.

"There's Mr. Turner, early as usual, and likely to give poor

Mary grief if I don't see him before his appointment time."
Michael rose and exchanged his suit jacket for his white medical tunic. "I'll let you know if the tests come back with anything of note."

Charlotte rose as well. "Thank you. In the meantime, I'll see how James and Andrew want to handle the story."

Michael escorted her out of the office. "I'd imagine they won't have the same opinion."

"Probably not." She pecked him on the cheek. "See you later. So long, Mary."

"Bye, Charlotte. Tell Becca I look forward to seeing her tomorrow."

Tomorrow? What was Becca doing with Mary on a Saturday?

Charlotte's curiosity was piqued, but she didn't want to interrupt Mary's or Michael's morning by asking what she meant. Besides, if Becca wanted Charlotte to know, the girl would have told her. Charlotte nodded a greeting to Mr. Turner, then headed downstairs.

The wind was joined by wet, swirling snow, making the short walk to James's office seem like a miles-long trek across the tundra. By the time she reached the outer door of the building, which housed the marshal's office and jail on the ground floor and the post office upstairs, Charlotte was soaked and chilled.

Shivering, she went into the marshal's office. James crouched beside the stove, adding coal to the pan. He glanced over his shoulder and smiled.

"Good morning, Miss Brody."

Charlotte smiled back. "Good morning, Deputy. It seems your weather prediction has come true."

He finished with the stove, dusted his hands on his pants, and stood. "Unfortunately. I'm about ready for spring. But the weather will also keep the Californians in town, hopefully long enough to sort out what happened."

Charlotte joined him and held her hands out to the stove for warmth while he prepared a pot of coffee. "I was just at Michael's office. It's pretty much official now, isn't it? Stanley Welsh was murdered."

"That seems to be the case. Now we just have to figure out who did it."

"And why," she added. That was what fascinated Charlotte in murder cases: motive. What would it take for a person to kill someone? Where did anger turn into rage, so that physical harm to another person was the answer? "If we learn that, we can usually find out who."

James walked to his desk and sat, turning his chair toward her and leaning back in a relaxed manner. "I think we can rule out self-defense. There were no marks on Welsh that indicated he'd been the attacker. And no one else seemed worse for wear."

Cicely's bruised cheek came to mind, but she'd explained that as an accident while rehearsing with Roslyn. There didn't seem to be any other injuries on the scenarist. Nothing visible, at any rate.

Charlotte sat on the corner of his desk. "There are attacks and then there are attacks."

"What do you mean?"

The details of a story Charlotte reported several years before came rushing back. At the time, it had been a local sensation, but even in retrospect, a wave of sadness and anger swirled in her gut.

"A few years ago, the police were called to the home of a prominent family who lived not far from my parents. I usually avoided reporting on news involving neighbors or people my parents knew, but this one drew me in. Victor Chaffey, a local businessman, had been found stabbed to death at the foot of the stairs. His wife, Pauline, was holding a knife and covered in blood when the police arrived. She had called them herself."

"That made it easy for the cops," James said.

"Yes and no. Pauline admitted killing Victor, but she claimed he'd been abusing her for years." Charlotte watched James's face cloud over. He had a particular dislike for stories of abuse to women or children. "The trouble was, Pauline never had a mark on her. Not a bump, not a bruise, not a scratch. He had never raised a hand to her. Ever. She made that statement outright to the police."

Understanding dawned in James's eyes. "He did things like calling her names or making her feel worthless."

"That, among others. She claimed he took control of all her finances, chose her friends for her, and dictated what she'd wear and where she went. Some days, she said, he wouldn't allow her out of the bedroom, locking her in or threatening to kill her if she came out."

"She got fed up and killed him." James shook his head. "Why not just leave?"

Charlotte had asked herself the same question, and had put it to Pauline Chaffey in an exclusive jailhouse interview. "Because she had nowhere to go and no one to go to. Over the years, Victor had isolated her from her family to the point they hadn't had contact with her for nearly a decade. It wasn't just that she was fed up, James. She was terrified. The night she killed him, Pauline claimed he had threatened *her* with the knife because she hadn't had dinner ready on time. When he put it down and walked out of the room, something broke inside her. She grabbed the knife, followed him, and stabbed him in the back. Seventeen times, the coroner said."

James crossed his arms. "His back was to her? She outright murdered him."

Charlotte crossed hers as well. "Or was it, in a way, self-defense? Victor constantly threatened her, more and more over time. Was she supposed to wait for him to actually stab her first before she could rightfully defend herself?"

At her trial, Pauline's attorney had posed that very question, claiming mental duress after years of emotional abuse and terrified anticipation of Victor's promised attack. The prosecutor made a case for murder. In the end, Pauline Chaffey was convicted of second-degree murder, by reason of temporary insanity, and sent to a women's asylum. Charlotte hoped she was at peace in some way.

"You think the murder of Stanley Welsh was the result of his abusing someone? Who? Carmen?" James didn't sound convinced, but he was always very good at poking at her theories. It wasn't that he didn't agree, but it made them both think the case through from different angles.

"Possibly," Charlotte said. "Though they did appear quite attentive of each other. Not that a public face is always the most accurate."

Last November's murder of Lyle Fiske had proved that as well. Caroline Fiske, his widow, had been treated quite differently out of the public purview.

"No," James agreed. "Who else? Cicely? I doubt anyone but a family member would have had as much personal time with Welsh. And the two of them had their disagreements about the storyline in the film."

"Things could have finally come to a head over creative differences, or personal ones. Cicely and Roslyn claim her bruised cheek was from a boisterous rehearsal." Had that been the case, or had father and daughter fought? Charlotte rose and began to pace. "Paige Carmichael was having an affair with him. Maybe Stanley was running roughshod over her and she got tired of it and his failed promises."

Who else would have been angry enough to take his life in such a way as strangulation?

"Caleb Burrows had his reasons as well," James said, answering her silent query. "Though not due to years of abuse by Welsh. Perhaps years of dealing with men like him."

"Same with Miles Smith," Charlotte added. "Burrows had his second conversation with Welsh that evening that he isn't mentioning. According to Burrows, Welsh was still leaning toward a not-so-accurate portrayal of Natives, but was coming around. Was the later meeting I heard the follow-up to their argument that was finally smoothing things over?"

James quirked an eyebrow. "According to *Burrows* they were working it out. No reason for Burrows to hurt Welsh if they were, right? A beautiful friendship was forming."

Charlotte immediately realized what the deputy was doing. "You think Burrows could be lying, that Welsh actually had no intention of changing the story, and Burrows got angry and killed him over it."

"We don't know what they were specifically talking about that you heard," he said. "If you've killed a man, lying about any circumstances surrounding it can come quite naturally. Especially to someone who's trained to think on his feet and with no witnesses to naysay him."

She had to agree with James on that, but perhaps there was a witness.

"Burrows was bunking with Miles Smith. He might have seen or heard something."

James stood up and tended the coffeepot on the stove. "Or Smith did it himself, or was an accomplice."

Michael's suggestion that two people could have been involved in Welsh's death rang in her head.

"Or it was someone else entirely," Charlotte reminded him.

He handed her a cup of coffee. "Or that."

"Are you going to interview everyone again?" She sipped the hot brew. It was stronger than he usually made it, and no cream or sugar to be had.

"I'll have to, though whether I'll get much further is always questionable." James paused, eyes narrowed as he looked at her.

"What?"

"You'll be hanging around with them anyway, won't you? Getting your story for the paper. Asking questions, listening in on conversations."

Charlotte raised her chin in false indignation. "I do not 'listen in' on conversations, Deputy. I just happen to be in the right place at the right time." She grinned at him. "But yes, I will be doing just that. Are you asking me to provide you with information?"

"Every little bit helps," he said. "As long as you obtain it legally."

They had had more than a few discussions about that in the past, but both would have to admit to a certain amount of rule bending.

"I'm sure that can be arranged." Charlotte set down her half-empty cup and leaned forward to kiss his cheek. "I'll see you later."

James placed his free hand on the side of her neck and shifted so their lips would meet instead. Charlotte smiled as they kissed, tasting coffee on his mouth. She pressed her hand against his chest, the soft wool shirt a poor substitute for his skin underneath. Her fingers curled, grasping the material, and errant thoughts of being skin to skin with him made her breath hitch.

James deepened the kiss, his fingers sliding to the nape of her neck, tickling her hairline. She felt his other arm at her back, drawing her into him. Not forcing her, but suggesting, like a dance. It was a dance she missed terribly.

He broke the kiss and eased back half a step. His fingertips gently twirled the stray hairs at the base of her neck. "Sorry," he said, his voice low and rough. "I shouldn't push."

"Nothing to be sorry about, and you aren't pushing." Charlotte closed the space between them and took his lower lip between her teeth. She smiled when *his* breath hitched. "But one of these days, Deputy . . ."

His eyebrows rose. "Yes?"

She rolled her eyes and kissed him quickly before pulling out of his arms. "You'll just have to wait and see."

As she started to move away, he grabbed her hand, preventing her from getting far. Charlotte turned back, expecting another silly face or some remark. Instead, James's eyes had softened. He raised her hand and kissed the knuckles. His warm breath on her skin sent shivers up her arm and down her spine.

"I'll wait as long as you want me to, Charlotte."

James knew she needed time, and he'd certainly been more patient than other men she'd known. More patient than she herself had been with those men.

"I—" The words caught in her throat. "I appreciate that. And one of these days, I will tell you everything."

"Only what you want to," he said, smiling as he released her hand. "Now let me get back to work."

"I wasn't the one causing the delay, Deputy," Charlotte said as she sauntered to the door.

"Oh, but you were, Miss Brody." She glanced back to see him wink at her. "Indeed you were."

Laughing, Charlotte waved and left the office. She made sure her coat and scarf were in place before heading through the outer door, but goodness, she was practically baking. Lingering heat from being with James, she figured, and grinned all the way to the Windsor Hotel two blocks away.

The walkway in front of Cordova's fanciest hotel had been scraped nearly clear of ice and snow, but a new layer was forming quickly with the storm. Charlotte opened one of the double doors and was immediately hit with a warm wall of bacon- and coffee-laden air and excited conversation. The paneled lobby was humming with people, and it took Charlotte a moment or two to sort out who was there and what the hubbub was all about at nine-thirty in the morning.

At least half a dozen members of the film crew were gathered around some poor soul, all talking at once. A few others stood off to the sides, watching.

"Hold on! Hold on!" came a deep male voice from within the crowd. "I can't understand any of you if all of you are jibber-jabbering at once."

After a moment of relative quiet, they began again.

Charlotte skirted the edge of the group, attempting to see who was trapped at its center. She sidled up to a man she recognized from the *Fortune* crew but didn't seem involved in the situation. "What happened?"

The man glanced down at her. He was about ten years her senior, wearing a rough shirt and heavy trousers. One of Roger Markham's men, she thought. "Hey, Miss Brody. Kinda crazy this morning. A few of the rooms were ransacked while folks were at breakfast."

Instinctively, Charlotte retrieved her notebook and pencil from her coat pocket. "Ransacked? Was anything taken? Was anyone hurt?"

"No one hurt," he said, focusing again on his companions. "Not sure if anything was taken, but Mr. Meade there found a note."

He indicated where Cicely, Roslyn, and Wallace Meade were off to the side speaking with another policeman, Ned Keith. Ned was taking notes as Cicely spoke, and Meade mopped his reddened face with a well-used handkerchief. He seemed more upset than either of the women. No surprise, considering some sort of note—which was unlikely to be a good thing—had been left in his room. Ned paused in his writing to unfold a piece of paper he'd tucked inside his notebook.

"What did the note say?"

"Something like, 'Get out of our town or you'll be sorry.'"

Not the most original of threats, but it got the point across.

"I'm assuming it wasn't signed," Charlotte said.

The man laughed humorlessly. "Not hardly. I keep sayin' this film is cursed, but no one believes me."

After a death and a threatening note, Charlotte wondered what it would take for them to believe something—or rather someone—was keen to stop the film.

But why and who?

The two policemen finished gathering information. Charlotte loitered, taking her own notes, but no one had anything definitive. The occupants acknowledged they had left their rooms unlocked, thinking they would only be down at breakfast and gone for a short while. They also were quite sure nothing was stolen.

"Well," Ned, the senior officer, said, "all we can do for now is tell you to lock your doors. This ain't Los Angeles or Seattle, but we have an element here."

"What about the note?" Meade asked. "Going through our things was bad enough, but obviously someone wants us gone."

Ned held up the paper. "We'll hold on to it, but no telling who wrote it."

"The only ones who wanted us out of town was that Native group," one of the crewmen said. "Maybe you should start with them."

Charlotte couldn't help but respond. "You have no idea if that's true. You shouldn't jump to conclusions."

"I'm not," the man argued, "but who else had a beef with us?"

Ned held up his hands, stopping the exchange. "We'll ask everyone we can think of about it, but it's not like anyone's going to up and admit it. Go on about your business. If you do discover anything's missing, let us know. We'll be in touch."

He and the other officer left the Windsor. Some of the company headed up the wide staircase, back to their rooms. Charlotte overheard a few others talk about local clubs. The Mirage and the Tidewater would both open by noon for friendly gaming and socializing. There was mention of visiting a house or two later that evening.

Charlotte made a mental note to see Brigit and ask her if any of the crew stopped by her place. The madam wouldn't share specific details, but Charlotte was sure that if something significant happened or was said that affected the murder of Stanley Welsh, Brigit might bend her confidentiality rules a little.

Meade, Cicely, and Roslyn were the only members of the company remaining in the lobby.

"This town used to be safe," Meade said loudly. "I regret telling you and the others that we hardly ever lock our doors, and now look what's happened."

Cicely laid her hand on his shoulder. "It's not your fault. We thought nothing of leaving the room unlocked."

"The intruder just went through your things and just left the note?" Charlotte asked. "He didn't take anything?"

"Not as far as we know," Roslyn said, "though that's disturbing enough. Why, the thought of some stranger pawing our personal items . . ." She gave a shudder of revulsion.

"Thankfully, no one was in their rooms." Meade shook his head sadly. "I'd hate to imagine what could have happened if this . . . person . . . ran into one of us unexpectedly."

Considering someone had killed Welsh, Charlotte was surprised any of them had left their doors unlocked, even for such a short period.

"How does this affect your decision to continue filming?" Charlotte asked Cicely, but Meade answered.

"I think that's obvious," he said. "We're done."

Cicely frowned. "No, we can't be. I won't let something like this keep us from fulfilling Papa's vision."

"Don't be ridiculous." Meade sighed, then began speaking in a tone that had Charlotte envision a mother trying to convince a five-year-old to eat her vegetables, not as if Cicely was an intelligent, grown woman. "If someone is trying to send us a message, it would be foolish and irresponsible of us to ignore it. We've already lost Stanley to some nefarious person. This invasion and note are just a reminder that we aren't wanted here."

Cicely paled, the pain of the loss of her father too fresh.

Roslyn touched Cicely's arm, concern etched on her lovely face. She shot daggers at Meade. "You're upsetting her, Wallace."

The scenarist patted her friend's hand. Cicely lifted her chin, seeming to recover. "It's all right. Mr. Meade, I appreciate your concern, but I'll be damned if I let some coward who sneaks around rifling through rooms, leaving notes, and harming sick men scare me off. There are some who want to abandon *Fortune*. Fine, but I'm staying. I have enough support to finish the film, with my own money if I have to. I won't let my father down."

She turned on her heel and strode to the stairs, hands clenched.

Roslyn Sanford smiled as she watched Cicely depart. "Thatta girl." The actress glanced at Charlotte and Meade. "If you'll excuse me."

She followed Cicely up the stairs.

"Damn foolish girl," Meade muttered.

"I don't know," Charlotte mused aloud. "She wants to finish her father's work. I think it's a fine way to commemorate him."

"If someone else doesn't get hurt or killed in the meantime." Meade mopped his damp brow again, then stuffed his handkerchief in his pocket. "A film gets a reputation, Miss Brody, and no one wants to be associated with it. She'll have a devil of a time if too many walk away or can't participate because someone gets hurt."

Cicely Welsh reminded Charlotte of a number of women she knew, and quite a few she'd met here in Alaska: Strong. Resolute. Resourceful. "Maybe, but I wouldn't put it past her to try."

Meade stalked off, shaking his head and muttering about damn women. Charlotte should have found offense in his attitude, as she had in the past, but instead she found herself smiling. More and more men were learning that women weren't just going to collapse and let the male of the species take care of things. Women like Cicely Welsh, when given the opportunity, even under unfortunate circumstances, were bound and determined to fulfill their own destinies.

"Thatta girl." Charlotte tucked her notebook into her coat pocket and headed out to see Brigit.

Chapter 10

⬥

Charlotte hunched her shoulders practically to her ears and blew on her mittened hands as she passed Michael's cabin and turned down the road that led to Brigit's. There had been enough pedestrian and vehicle traffic to press the snow into a stretch of rough, compacted ice, yet slick in places that snatched your foot out from under you, if you weren't careful.

Safely on flat ground again, Charlotte was grateful someone had shoveled the walk leading to the front door of the unassuming house. She knocked, rubbing her hands together as she waited.

The door opened. Wearing a kimono-style blue robe with orange and silver accents, Brigit herself had answered, rather than her young son, Charlie, or one of the girls. Though she appeared tired, Brigit smiled and gestured for Charlotte to enter.

"You must be freezing out there. Come in and have some tea," she said.

The foyer, with its pretty wallpaper, could have been the entry to a modest house in any town. A door on the right marked PRIVATE led to Brigit's office. To the left, the parlor proved the house to be a little less modest. Faro tables and several small couches and loveseats adorned the room. A piano butted against the wall below the stairs leading to the girls' rooms. To the left of the stairs, a closed door led to the kitchen.

Charlotte removed her coat, hat, and mittens. Brigit hung them in the hall closet, then handed Charlotte a pair of soft slippers to wear instead of her boots. After changing her footwear, Charlotte and Brigit walked through the parlor.

A table and four chairs filled most of the floor space of the small but tidy kitchen. A narrow stove, a sink, and an icebox occupied space against the walls. A tea kettle burbled on the stove. Brigit reached up into an open cupboard for another cup and saucer.

"I meant to come by sooner," Charlotte said as she took a seat at the table.

"I know you've been busy. It's been all hustle and bustle here too." Brigit poured the water into a blue and white teapot, then covered it with a cozy. She set it on the table along with the two cups, saucers, and a plate of cookies.

Charlotte picked up a cookie. The buttery treat practically melted in her mouth. "Mmm. These are delicious."

Brigit sat in the chair to her left, smiling. "Thank you. I love the aroma of the cookies baking, but in all honesty I'm not fond of sweets."

"I'd be happy to take a few off your hands."

Her friend laughed. After a few minutes of catching up, Brigit poured them each some tea. The distinct aroma of bergamot wafted from the cup. Charlotte added a lump of sugar and a dollop of milk. Coffee she could take black if necessary, but for some reason her tea needed milk and sugar.

"Have any of the movie people been by?" Charlotte asked.

Brigit sipped her tea, nodding. "Several last night. Lots of chatter about the poor man who died. They couldn't seem to talk about anything else, when they were talking."

"We think he was murdered." Charlotte watched her friend's reaction. Brigit knew who Charlotte meant by "we," so she didn't bother explaining.

Brigit's slender eyebrows rose in curiosity. "Do you? Why?"

Charlotte relayed the basic details and theories of Stanley Welsh's death, certain Brigit would keep the information to herself. "We're still looking into a few things. Andrew wants me to cozy up to the crew, for obvious reasons, but they're all a bit nervous at this point."

"Can't say that I blame them." Brigit shook her head. "I swear, Charlotte, in all the years I've lived here I don't think there's been so many suspicious deaths in such a short amount of time. Three since August." She opened her eyes wide and covered her open mouth with her hand. "When *you* got here."

Charlotte knew her friend was teasing, and she put on an equally playful air of indignation. "Michael mentioned this as well. Are you saying I'm bad luck or a brilliant murderer who has pinned deaths on others?"

Brigit laughed and laid a hand on her arm. "Neither. Though either one would make a wonderful serial or dime-store novel."

"Maybe I should try my hand at fiction," Charlotte suggested.

"Maybe someday," Brigit said, "but I do enjoy your articles and editorials in the *Times*. What do you think of the film people? Which one could have killed the director?"

"At least three have reason, I think, as do Caleb Burrows and Miles Smith. All had opportunity as well. We just don't have anything about motive and opportunity. Not a lick of physical evidence."

"Burrows is an odd duck, isn't he?" Brigit said.

Charlotte didn't hide her surprise. "You know him?"

"In a manner of speaking," her friend said, lifting her tea to her lips. Her dark eyes danced. Brigit wasn't one to share names of her customers, so Charlotte wondered what she meant. Anticipating a request for clarification, Brigit continued. "He's repre-

sented friends of mine in the past. A very good lawyer, I understand."

"I'll give him a call if I ever get nabbed for those murders,"
Charlotte said wryly.

Brigit laughed again. "If I hear anything pertinent to Mr.
Welsh's death, I'll let you know. So far, the crew who's come in
here have been trying to impress us with their connection to the
film and all the movie people they know." She rolled her eyes.
"As if railroad magnates, politicians, and judges haven't passed
through this house."

Again, Charlotte itched to ask for names, just to satisfy her
own curiosity, but knew Brigit would say nothing more than
she already had.

Charlotte ate another two cookies and they both drank more
tea as they chatted about local happenings and mutual acquain-
tances. Brigit seemed to know most everyone in town, particularly the men, but was also a member of the Women's Business
Guild and sat in on nearly every city council meeting.

"Pen and Rowena are having a brunch next Saturday," Brigit
said. "You should come along with me."

Charlotte liked the two women who ran the ladies' finery
shop. She'd written about them in one of her articles for *The
Modern Woman Review*. The two had met in Nome years before, during the gold rush there, became friends, then moved to
Cordova and started their business. They even shared a home.

"Their partnership makes me think of Cicely Welsh and
Roslyn Sanford. They started out working together and became friends as well." Perhaps more than friends. The obvious
dawned in Charlotte's brain. "Are Pen and Rowena together? I
mean, together together?"

Brigit gave her a knowing smile. "I was wondering when
you'd figure it out. You're usually more astute than that."

"They don't make it all that obvious, not that I blame them.
Having such inclinations would be difficult here." Charlotte
imagined it was easier in a large town or city, rather than a place

like Cordova where everyone knew you and your personal habits. Friends back east, whom she knew to be involved in similar relationships, fiercely guarded their private lives.

Her friend's smile faltered. "Quite. Pen and Rowena have mastered their façade of being business partners and spinster friends. Some might suspect their true relationship, but as long as they maintain propriety in public, they'll be left alone."

Charlotte recalled how Cicely and Roslyn could easily be seen as just friends, their public affection limited to the occasional hug or touch of the arm or smile. But once she realized there was likely more to their relationship, it was obvious in the looks they exchanged that their feelings ran much deeper. Now, when Charlotte went into the ladies' shop she was sure she'd find herself scrutinizing Pen and Rowena for such exchanges.

"How long have you known?" Charlotte asked. She felt silly for not having realized it before. Wasn't it part of her job to be more observant of people and their behavior?

"Almost from the time I arrived here," Brigit said. She patted Charlotte's arm. "Don't doubt yourself. They're very good at keeping it quiet. It took me a few times of seeing them in more intimate settings before it became obvious. Those who know, and there aren't many, take care to maintain the ladies' privacy."

"I'll be sure to keep my head when I next see them," Charlotte said.

"I'm sure you will. So, will you attend the brunch with me? Pen and Rowena really admire your work. They want to bring you into the Women's Business Guild."

Charlotte shook her head, not in refusal of the invitation, but to confusion as to why they'd ask her into the Guild. "I don't own a business."

"No, but you're essentially a partner at the newspaper. Everyone knows you do the bulk of the writing these days. Andrew Toliver must be thanking his lucky stars you arrived here." Brigit quirked a slender eyebrow. "Though I know he's not the only one."

"Michael seems pleased as well—" Again, a lightbulb seemed to suddenly flicker to life and Charlotte grinned. "You mean James."

"Of course I mean James," Brigit said, shaking her head as if she couldn't believe Charlotte's denseness. "Why, that man hadn't smiled as often in all the years I've known him as he has in the last six months. You must be doing something right."

"Actually, we aren't doing much of anything except kissing." The taste and touch of James's lips filled her brain and heat infused Charlotte's cheeks. Surprise dropped Brigit's mouth open into an O. "I know, I know, but you can understand my reluctance, can't you?"

Charlotte had told Brigit all about Richard and her "delicate operation." In fact, Brigit, Michael, and Charlotte's childhood friend Kit, back in New York, were the only people who knew. That was plenty of people, as far as Charlotte was concerned.

Brigit's expression changed. She narrowed her gaze and studied Charlotte for a few moments. "But you want to be with him. You want there to be more than kisses."

"I do. Or I think I do." Charlotte stood and tried to pace the limited space of the kitchen. The movement helped her to sort out her thoughts as well as release some sudden pent-up physical itches she often experienced when James was near or his name came up. "I'm so confused, Brigit. I like him. A lot."

"And he likes you, a lot," Brigit added.

"I know. Every time we kiss, I want more. I want to touch him. I want him to touch me." That desire flooded her body on a constant basis. "But then something in my brain brings everything to a screeching halt. It's madness."

Charlotte realized her fists were clenched and her breathing had increased. She stopped pacing and took a deep breath.

"He feels the same, I'd reckon," Brigit said quietly.

Charlotte sank into her chair. Elbows on the table, she covered her face with her hands. "I know. And I feel awful about denying him. Denying *both* of us."

"You haven't told him yet, have you?"

She knew what Brigit meant without needing to ask. "No, I don't know how. I don't know what he'll say or do, and it scares me."

"So don't tell him." Charlotte looked up. Brigit continued. "You are under no obligation to tell him anything you don't wish to share."

"Isn't that a lie of omission?" Charlotte was sure it was something like that.

"He knows or suspects you've been with at least one man, yes?" Brigit shrugged. "Let him draw his own conclusions. You've told me he's not pushing you for details, so don't give him any you aren't ready to give."

"Even so," Charlotte said, "I don't know if I'm ready to risk it."

"Risk what? Having feelings for someone?" Brigit's laugh was tinged with sadness. "We all have to take chances there, dear."

"That, yes, but I was also thinking of a more . . . physical risk. I can't put myself in that situation again, Brigit. I just can't." Charlotte barely managed to keep the fear out of her voice, though her entire body trembled at the thought of getting pregnant. She still had no desire to be a mother, but her feelings for James were so very different from those she'd had for Richard. What would she do if the circumstances reoccurred? She had no idea, and honestly didn't want to find out.

"We can take care of that." Brigit rose and headed out of the kitchen before Charlotte had the chance to ask what she meant.

Her footsteps faded once she left the parlor. While Charlotte waited, she poured herself another cup of tea. The trembling in her hands abated by the time Brigit returned.

"These are the best on the market," Brigit said, holding three packets of folded paper. "I get them imported from Germany. Better than anything you can find in the States. Been using them for years myself, and none of my girls who use them regularly have gotten pregnant or fallen ill."

Condoms weren't infallible, even when used regularly, but if Charlotte took them, that would be one less barrier, so to speak, between her fears and desires.

Brigit set the packets on the table between them, then sat once again. She took Charlotte's hand and squeezed gently. "Pregnancy isn't your biggest worry, Charlotte, because you and I both know there are other ways to enjoy the company of a man without ever risking pregnancy or disease."

Charlotte nodded absently. If she couldn't be honest with James quite yet, at least she could start being honest with herself.

"You're a young woman with a healthy appetite who's been denying herself sustenance for too long." With her free hand, Brigit slid the packets closer to Charlotte. "You're due for a feast, my friend."

Later that afternoon, Charlotte walked up the steps to her house, shoulders aching from being hunched against the blowing snow. It didn't seem to matter how many layers one wore when the wind was so wet and biting. Spring was nowhere near as close as the calendar indicated.

When she opened the interior door, the warmth and aroma of baking cookies filled her senses. She smiled as she unwound the scarf from her neck and pulled off her mittens.

"I'm home," she called out.

"We're in here," Becca replied from the kitchen.

"We" meaning Esther was with her. Esther often came home

with Becca after school, more frequently on Fridays, like today. Charlotte enjoyed the banter and laughter that filled the house when the two girls were together. It reminded her of her own school days with Kit.

In the kitchen, Becca and Esther were seated at the table, eating cookies, drinking milk, and giggling over a magazine.

"Look at what Becca has, Miss Charlotte." Esther's bright smile lit her entire face. It had taken a little time for Esther to get used to her, but now the child was positively chatty when Charlotte was around. "Aren't they handsome?"

Charlotte peered down at the movie magazine. It was open to a page showing Peter York and another young actor from a film they'd starred in the previous year. "They are. And Mr. York is a very nice man on top of that, isn't he, Becca?"

"Oh, yes," Becca said around a mouthful of cookie. "He treats everyone like they're his friend."

"Did you know Angus Melin was from Nome?" Esther asked, pointing to the other actor's picture. "His father and my father went to school together."

"How exciting," Charlotte said. She sat down at the table and took a still-warm cookie from the plate. "What other films has he been in, do you know?"

The girl shook her head. "I just know about this one. That's why we were so excited to get the magazine. Mr. Carter at the drugstore let us go through a box of old issues."

Becca continued the story while Esther chewed. "Esther's father told us Angus Melin was in one of the issues from a few months ago but didn't know which one. Took us over an hour to find it."

"I salute your success," Charlotte said, raising her cookie. The girls giggled and went back to the pages. "Are you staying for dinner, Esther?"

That was another somewhat regular occurrence.

"Her mother said it would be all right for me to eat there, then spend the night," Becca said. She and Esther exchanged glances.

"There's a special get-together tomorrow starting early in the morning."

"Is there?" Had that been what Mary meant when she said she'd see Becca tomorrow?

"Is it okay?" Becca asked.

"Of course it is. Make sure you remember to bring your toothbrush with you this time." Becca seemed relieved that Charlotte had agreed. "Did you think I wouldn't let you go?"

Both girls' cheeks pinked.

"Well," Becca said, "with the way people are starting to talk about the AEC, like it's some sort of group of hooligans, I wasn't sure."

"I'm sure Esther and her family aren't about to be part of a group that would do bad things."

Esther shook her head. "Oh, no. Mama doesn't even spank us. Much."

"I know," Becca said, "but sometimes Mr. Burrows can get a little . . ."

She seemed at a loss for words.

"Passionate?" Charlotte suggested.

Becca smiled and Esther giggled. "Yes."

"That isn't a bad thing," Charlotte said. "It's good to be passionate about something you believe in, as long as you aren't condoning harm. I appreciate that Esther and her family are able to help you stay connected to your heritage."

The girls fell silent. Sensing their reluctance to continue in that vein, Charlotte took another cookie and rose. She hoped Becca understood that Charlotte was available to talk whenever she needed.

"Clean up the kitchen before you head over to Esther's," Charlotte said as she left the room. "And take the cookies with you. If they stay here I'll eat them all."

"That would be bad for your stomach," Esther said, giggling.

Several treats at Brigit's and now two at home? Charlotte had better have a healthy supper. "And my waistline."

Both girls giggled louder. Charlotte smiled as she climbed the stairs. They really did remind her of herself and Kit at that age.

Once in her room, she sorted through her closet, looking for something dressy but not formal. With Becca spending the night at Esther's, Charlotte thought perhaps a visit to one of the clubs might give her a more relaxed atmosphere in which to talk to the *Fortune* crew. Especially if any of them visited one of the "private" rooms in the back where Prohibition and Alaska's dry laws didn't seem to exist.

Once the girls were safely off to Esther's, Charlotte changed into a low-waisted, flowing-sleeved dress with a hem that fell to the middle of her shins. The deep plum color was a little darker than she would have picked for herself, but it looked fine against her pale skin. The neckline didn't plunge as far as some she'd seen; Mother would have balked at exposing too much skin. She'd given it to Charlotte for Christmas, explaining in the note it was the latest thing in New York and Paris.

"And now in Cordova," Charlotte said to her reflection as she applied a bit of rouge and some lipstick.

She donned her coat, hat, and boots and wished she had the protection of James's car as the wind nearly knocked her off the last slick step. For a moment, she considered going back inside. No, there would be a number of the film company out tonight, despite the weather, to help alleviate boredom. If she didn't go now, she might miss something.

One hand holding her hat on her head, Charlotte made her way down the slippery road to the Tidewater.

Jangling music leaked through the door of the club along with the hum of conversation and pungent cigar smoke. Charlotte reminded herself that the Tidewater was a social club for all Cordovans. Granted, it was mostly men and "working" girls who availed themselves of the games, music, and refreshments, but no one had indicated the club was restricted.

She took a breath and went in. The cacophony of sound hit her with full force. At least two dozen people—mostly men—were crowded into the main room. They sat at tables, stood at the bar, or dropped pennies into the assorted arcade games against the back wall. The player piano in the far corner plinked out a rendition of "Jazz Baby."

A large man with an elaborate mustache stood between the piano and a door marked PRIVATE, his arms crossed. Either the Tidewater took their music playing quite seriously or there was something going on beyond the door that the casual club visitor wasn't privy to.

Though her interest in what, exactly, occurred in such rooms was piqued, Charlotte wasn't there to investigate how citizens were skirting Prohibition and gambling laws. At least not this time. Even if she was interested, since she believed Prohibition was a bad idea, Charlotte wouldn't have exposed the perpetrators anyway.

No, she was here for a different reason.

Charlotte opened her coat and worked her way to the bar. She squeezed between people, smiling when they smiled and ignoring the "accidental" brush of hands across her bottom. She found a place at the bar and checked out the other patrons while she waited for the barkeep to notice her there. Several young women chatted with men, sipping colorful drinks and smiling indulgently. Charlotte didn't recognize anyone from Brigit's house, but she suspected two or three might be from the other houses in town.

"What can I get ya, sweetheart?" the barman asked when he stepped up to her.

She consulted the list of offered soft drinks adhered to the wall behind him.

"Lemon-lime soda, please."

Charlotte found a few coins in her pocket while the man poured syrup into a tall glass, then filled it with carbonated water. He gave the drink a quick stir with a long spoon and set it before her. She slid a dime and a nickel across the bar.

"Only ten cents," he said, dropping one coin in the till and slipping the other into his pants pocket.

She shrugged and smiled. It wasn't much of a tip, in the grand scheme of things, but a little generosity now might help her later.

Sipping her drink, Charlotte strolled behind the line of arcade games, stopping now and again to watch over shoulders as pennies or nickels were dropped into slots. Mechanized figures danced or played instruments or raced around a track. For a dime, patrons could peer into the brass viewer of a Mutoscope moving picture machine and be treated to the "Dancing Delights of Daring Darlings." Several men waited in line for that one, grinning and joking as they tried to sneak a peek past the current customer.

Standing at a baseball-themed game was one of the film crew Charlotte recognized by the shock of red hair beneath his cap. He'd performed at the theater as well. What was his name, Bobby? No, Billy. As one of the youngest members of Roger Markham's crew, she hoped Billy wasn't as guarded as the other men might be.

Charlotte stood quietly behind Billy's right shoulder, watching him play the game. He sipped his cola, then turned the lever that sent a metal ball from the pitcher's mound to where he activated a bat with another lever. The young man laughed as the ball flew past the infield, then between the left and center outfielders. The mechanized men on the field advanced with a whirr and a tinkling of music.

"Well done," Charlotte said.

Billy turned his head, pausing before releasing another ball. She smiled at him and his freckled cheeks reddened. "Thanks. You're Miss Brody, ain't ya?"

Charlotte was hoping he wouldn't remember her, but there was no helping it. "Yes, but please, it's Charlotte. Do you have a favorite team, Billy?"

He seemed pleased she recalled his name. "The Brooklyn Robins, of course, though they didn't do so good last year. We'll give 'em hell this season, for sure." Impossibly, the color on his face deepened. "Pardon my language, ma'am."

Ma'am? Ow. Charlotte wasn't *that* much older than him.

She kept the smile on her face. "That's all right. So what's a Brooklyn man doing working on a Hollywoodland film?"

His blue eyes brightened. "You know Brooklyn?"

Her visit to Brooklyn had been limited to the clinic Margaret Sanger opened a few years ago. Initially, Charlotte had gone to write an article about the birth control advocate and her colleagues. The hundred or so women who had attended the opening that October day all had the same thing to say: They were grateful. The following day, Charlotte had returned for more personal reasons. Unfortunately, several days after that, Miss Sanger and a colleague were arrested for providing birth control for that purpose, not for disease prevention as the law allowed, and the clinic shut down. Charlotte hadn't been back to the borough since.

"Not really," she admitted. "I grew up in the Yonkers area, but your accent kind of gives it away."

"Aw, I thought I'd'a lost that by now," he said. "I got the acting bug, but need to eat, so I work on sets and things. What's a Yonkers gal doing way the heck up here?"

"Trying to stay warm."

"Ain't that the truth," Billy said with an exaggerated shiver, and they both laughed.

"Looks like you can use another drink," Charlotte said, gesturing to his near-empty glass.

"Yeah, but I wish there was something a little stronger than a cola, know what I mean?" There was a significant gleam in his eye.

Charlotte glanced over her shoulder at the burly man standing before the door marked PRIVATE. The Tidewater was open to the public, but like a few other places, gaining access to private areas required membership. Membership to the Tidewater required being a Cordova resident, though guests were permitted. Most visitors found it easy to make friends with locals.

"I think I can help you there." She slipped her arm through his. "Come on."

Billy rubbed his hands together and all but strutted beside her as they made their way across the crowded room. As they approached, the doorman quirked a thick eyebrow at them. When they stopped in front of him, he scowled.

"Members only."

Charlotte smiled. "I'd like to join, if I may. I live here in Cordova. The name's Charlotte Brody."

"I know who you are. Still, need to have a man vouch for you."

Charlotte and Billy exchanged glances. The young man shrugged. He swallowed hard when he looked back to the larger man, his Adam's apple bobbing.

It was a silly notion, and Charlotte didn't feel like arguing the ideology of equality with the bouncer, but that didn't mean she wouldn't have some fun with him.

"Well, Mister . . ." She faltered and glanced at Billy.

"Ridgeway," he said.

"Mr. Ridgeway knows me. And by your own admission, you know me too." She found her coin purse in her coat pocket and opened it. "I believe membership is a dollar . . . and a half?"

The cost of membership was posted over the bar: one dollar. Greasing palms was not an unknown practice in her profession. It had procured a significant amount of information at times.

"Two," the man growled.

Charlotte managed to hide her shock. There went the nicer cut of meat she was hoping to purchase for Sunday dinner next week. She handed the man the two dollars. He slipped them in his pocket and withdrew a key.

"Don't I get a membership card or anything?" she asked.

"Take it up with Lou." He nodded toward the bar and unlocked the door. Inside, the conversation was louder, more boisterous than in the main room, and the cigar smoke was twice as thick. "Don't make a fuss, or you'll be out on your ear. No refunds."

"We promise to be good. Come on, Billy." Charlotte tugged on his arm.

Billy touched the brim of his cap, still looking nervous. The man grunted, then shut the door behind them.

Charlotte's eyes watered from the smoke. It was impossible to sort out the conversation at the half-dozen tables where several poker and faro games were in progress. There were only four women in the room, three hanging on men who played and one woman at a table of men with a decent pile of chips at her elbow.

"Bar's over there," Billy said.

Over at the polished oak bar, a few men were chatting and drinking what appeared to be whiskey. The bartender came over when Charlotte and Billy found a spot. She recognized him immediately.

"Good evening, Mr. McGruder. How are you today?"

The grocery man grinned at her. "Evening, Miss Brody. Never seen you in here before."

"My first time. This is my friend Billy," she said, "and he's a bit parched."

McGruder took in Billy's youthful face. For a moment, Charlotte thought he was going to ask if Billy was old enough to drink. Though he could refuse to serve Billy, it seemed rather silly to hold up the age law when selling alcohol was illegal in the territory to begin with. Though technically it wasn't being sold, was it?

"What'll you have, son?" McGruder asked.

Billy grinned. "Bourbon and soda."

He said it with a confidence that surprised Charlotte. She'd have to be careful not to underestimate the youthful-looking Californian.

"And for the lady?"

"Same," said Charlotte.

McGruder reached under the bar for a couple of tumblers. He loosened the stopper from a brown bottle, filled their glasses a third of the way, then spritzed a shot of soda from a blue siphon into each. He held the tumblers, giving Billy an expectant look.

"I think he's waiting for a 'tip,'" Charlotte said, opening her purse.

"Oh, yeah. Right. No, I got it." Billy reached deep into his pocket and took out some coins. "Um."

"Four bits'll about do 'er," McGruder said, grinning. Billy put fifty cents on the bar. The grocery man-cum-bartender set the tumblers down. "Let me know if I can get you anything else."

He scooped up the coins and dropped them into a box under the bar where they landed with a jangle against others.

Charlotte and Billy touched glasses and drank. It had been a few months since Charlotte last imbibed, so she was careful to sip her bourbon. Billy, on the other hand, tossed back half the glassful in one swallow. He winced and smacked his lips.

"Good stuff," he said hoarsely.

Was he serious or putting on a bit of a show for her?

"So tell me about working on a picture like *North to Fortune*." Charlotte leaned against the bar and gave him her best "I'm fascinated by your every word" gaze.

"It's the best," Billy said. "I'm meeting all sorts a people, getting to travel some. Mr. York and Miss Sanford are giving me pointers about acting. Having a grand time."

He finished his drink and dove into a description of a particularly raucous party the cast and crew attended early in the filming. While he spoke, Charlotte signaled McGruder to pour Billy another. She laid a quarter on the bar.

"Gee, thanks." Billy toasted her, then downed a good portion. He blinked a few times, grinning.

"It can't all be parties and big laughs," Charlotte said. "Everyone getting along all the time, everything going swimmingly."

His expression darkened some. "No, we had a few bad runs, even before poor Mr. Welsh died." Billy crossed himself. "While we was filming some interiors in California, a camera platform collapsed, nearly killed a guy. Mr. Markham was mad as a wet hen, I tell you what. Blamed us for slacking on the job, but I know Vinny and me, we tightened every nut and bolt and checked it twice. We know better'n to do a shoddy job." He drank most of what was left in his tumbler. "Mr. Markham, he don't fool around when it comes to makin' things right. 'Safety first and foremost,' he tells us all the time. All the time."

"Is that why he was so upset with Mr. Welsh over the stunts he wanted?"

Billy nodded vigorously. "Oh, yeah. He and Welsh tangled over that nearly every day. Markham's no fraidy cat—was in the war, yanno, that's where he got the limp—but he's got a thing about big shots putting their glory over the lives of the people beneath 'em. He told us some terrible stories."

There was a touch of horror in Billy's eyes. Charlotte knew the awful things that happened during the war from talking to veterans, refugees, and Michael, who had treated injured soldiers, though he hadn't been on the front line himself. If Markham had been injured because of someone's disregard for others, would he have been angry enough at Welsh for putting the film's cast and crew in danger?

She signaled McGruder for two more drinks. When they arrived, she played with the glass more than drank from it. Billy didn't gulp this one down, but the effects of the first two were making him sway a little.

"Any other problems?" she asked, barely wetting her lips as she pretended to sip.

He shrugged. "The usual gripes from Mr. Meade over spending too much money on this, that, or the other thing; but when the director wants a set built the size of a real house and snow scenes in the middle of a California heatwave, it costs, yanno?"

Recalling the way Welsh ran the show at the Empress and the rehearsal out on the glacier, Charlotte said, "Mr. Welsh was a stickler for details, was he?"

At least when it came to some things. If it was inconvenient to him or considered unimportant—like the depiction of the local people—then he seemed willing to fudge.

"And how. We painted and refurnished one interior set three times before he was happy with it." Billy grinned. "But no skin off my nose, right? It ain't me footin' the bill. I get paid for doin' what I'm told, even if I have to do it three or four times."

"That sort of thing must have made Mr. Meade unhappy, though." Charlotte could imagine the producer's ever-reddening face as Welsh called for constant reworking of a set.

"Even madder'n Mr. Markham. Mr. Meade is always goin' on about how expensive things were, even us. We had to threaten to strike a month back when he didn't okay weekend pay on something Mr. Welsh wanted."

"You absolutely deserve to get paid for work done," Charlotte said. "It's not your problem they can't afford it."

Billy lifted his glass. "Exactly what we said." He drained his third drink and set the tumbler down on the bar with a thud.

"Anything else?" Charlotte asked.

"Oh, family stuff that's better left at home but isn't, yanno?"

"Between Stanley and Cecily or Stanley and Carmen?"

"Cicely—I mean, Miss Welsh," Billy said. "They argued over the story some, but I heard one to-do about her wanting him to stay outta her personal life." He winked slowly, nodding. "If ya know what I mean."

Charlotte had a very good idea what he meant.

Before she could ask more questions, a light dawned in Billy's eyes. "Hey, are you tryin' to get me drunk or somethin'?"

Charlotte smiled. "Just talking."

"Yeah, but you're writin' about us and all. If I'm gonna be a what's it called, a stool pigeon, then I want somethin' out of it." He stepped closer to Charlotte and placed his hand on her waist. "Whaddaya say?"

Her smile froze on her face. She might have expected he'd want more than a few drinks as "payment," even if he hadn't realized beforehand that she was trying to pump him for information. But she'd only go so far for a story, and that limit had been reached.

"I say, I think it's time you went back to the hotel."

"Aw, come on, Charlotte." He gave her a boyish grin as his hand slid to her backside. "Fair is fair."

Her heart raced, but her cool expression didn't waver. It had been some time since she'd dealt with men who thought nothing of touching a woman uninvited. It still made her stomach clench. "It'll be fair if I don't break your hand. Please move it before I do."

A hurt look, like a puppy that had been kicked, came over him, but he did as he was told. "No need to get violent, yanno."

"Let me give you a piece of advice, Billy." Charlotte downed her drink. The burn felt good this time, and actually helped calm her. "Being a gentleman is never going to get you into trouble."

Hurt turned into a wince on his fair face. "Now you sound like my ma."

Charlotte laughed. "I'll take that as a compliment. Come on, let's get you back to your friends. And thank you for the chat. I promise not to reveal my source."

She took his arm and headed toward the exit. Before they reached the door it swung open. Deputy Marshal James Eddington stood there with two of Cordova's finest at his back. His eyes locked on hers.

Charlotte swallowed hard.

James closed his eyes and pinched the bridge of his nose, as if a headache was coming on. "Damnation."

Her thought exactly.

Chapter 11

After clearing out the "private" area and sorting out that it was, supposedly, the gambling more so than the drinking that had gotten the attention of the local law, James took Charlotte's arm. Escorting her to the doorway leading to the main room of the club, he pointed to a stool at the end of the emptying bar. "Sit tight. I'll be right back."

"You're not arresting me again, are you?" Charlotte was glad the question made him smile and not glare.

He turned back to the group of customers arguing about whose fault it was the police had been called. Charlotte watched the men and women leave the Tidewater. Somehow, no one had been arrested, and they went without further upset. A few quietly mentioned that the Mirage, another club off Main Street, was probably still open. Charlotte had to hand it to them for perseverance.

James gave a final warning to the last few customers, mostly the Californians, who had claimed they didn't realize the Tidewater was *that* sort of place.

Sure, Charlotte thought, *and they hadn't known Brigit's was a brothel either.*

The film crew guys filed out. Billy gave Charlotte a con-fused, halfhearted wave as he went by. Did he think she was a snitch? She waggled her fingers back at him. When he slowed his step and started to turn toward her, one of the other men grabbed his shoulder and shoved him out the door.

James and Ned, one of the police officers, spoke to Lou the bartender and the bouncer. Ned's partner was still in the back room talking to Mr. McGruder. Would there be charges? There was no evidence that money had changed hands for the drinks, but either James or Ned could probably come up with some sort of charges against the club for the faro or poker games. Unless all the participants had claimed they were merely friendly games being played with pretend money.

The Tidewater men nodded, then shook hands with James. James headed her way, but Charlotte watched the three he'd left. Another handshake between Ned and Lou. Did Lou just slip Ned some money? Had he done the same with James?

No, she didn't believe that. James would bend some rules, but bribery wasn't like him.

"Let's go," James said, slowing as he passed her to take her upper arm and help her off the stool.

Charlotte buttoned her coat as they walked and was grateful James had come over in his car. He settled her in the passenger seat, then cranked the engine to start. It took a few extra cranks for it to turn over, and the popping and growling sounded par-ticularly loud. He got into the driver's side and put the car into gear.

"Lou paid off Ned, you know," Charlotte said.

James spun the car around and headed up the hill toward her house. He peered out into the blowing snow and darkness. "I know."

"But not you."

"Nope." He glanced at her. "Surprised? Disappointed?"

"Neither," she said. "You aren't perfect, but you have your standards."

"Gee, thanks. I think."

She laughed. It was difficult to see his face in the dim interior of the car, but she was sure he was smiling.

James pulled up in front of her house. The car stalled. "Damn it. I need to have that looked at." He set the brake and faced her. "Did you get anything useful out of that boy you were with?"

Charlotte lightly slapped his arm. "Billy is almost twenty. I'm not *that* much older than he is, you know. And yes, I did."

"You are a lot more world-wise than he is. He had no idea you were out to get information out of him, did he?"

There was more pride filling Charlotte than there should have been. "No, not at first."

They sat in silence for a moment, then James said, "Well, what did you learn?"

Charlotte gave him the rundown of what Billy had shared. "Nothing surprising, really, but it certainly helped clarify some possible motives."

"Yeah, but motives alone don't dump a guy in a crevasse." James rubbed his hands over his face. "I need more and I need it soon. They're hightailing it out of here as soon as they can."

"You can order them to stay, can't you?"

"Easier said than done." He reached out and brushed the backs of his fingers down her cheek. "It's getting late."

It was, but Charlotte didn't want him to go.

"Walk me to my door," she said.

He didn't move for a few moments, then hurried out his side and around to hers. He opened the door and held her hand as she lit from the car. Still holding her hand, James led Charlotte up the stairs to the front door. She squeezed between him and the door, opened it, and drew him into the entry. James shut the outer door behind them. Charlotte turned the knob on the inner door. One hand around the cool metal, the other still warm in James's, she faced him and pulled him closer.

He swept his hat off his head, leaned down, and kissed her. Gentle at first, they touched lips, tugged with the lightest pressure of teeth. Flashes of heat traveled from Charlotte's lips to her chest and down to the pit of her stomach. She slid her tongue along the crease of his lips.

James's free arm rapped around her waist. He pulled her against his chest and deepened the kiss. Charlotte responded in kind. Their entwined hands tightened around each other. She turned the doorknob and pushed it in, then rested her hand on his shoulder.

Bodies against each other, Charlotte inched them into the house, as if they were dancing and she'd taken the lead.

James moaned and kissed her like never before, his tongue and hand caressing softly, then stroking with intensity. Every fiber of her being demanded one thing: him.

Suddenly, he broke the kiss and placed his forehead on her shoulder. Charlotte pressed her hand against the nape of his neck. Both of them breathed fast, almost gulping air.

"I should go," he said into the side of her neck. His breath heated her skin.

She grasped his hair and angled his head so she could kiss him. "You should take me upstairs."

"Charlotte—"

She kissed him again, harder, while drawing him inside the parlor. He shut the door behind them. They came up for air and stared at each other for a moment. Lips tingling, Charlotte smiled. Then without a word, holding his hand, she led him to her room.

The aroma of frying bacon and coffee wafted into the bedroom, urging Charlotte awake. Enticing, but the chill of her nose and the warmth of the blankets kept her in bed. She pressed her palm to the empty side of the mattress. Closing her eyes, she smiled as she recalled the glorious night. It had been everything she'd imagined it could be with James, and then some.

Her attempt to sink back into sleep was thwarted by more

basic needs. Charlotte got out of bed and quickly found her nightgown and robe. Checking the vanity mirror, the reflection showed a mass of wild blond hair surrounding a smiling face. Yes, she certainly had reason to smile. A piece of ribbon to tie her hair back, a visit to the bathroom, and she was down the stairs.

She stood in the kitchen doorway and watched James at the stove, his back to her. He checked the bacon for doneness while he whistled, a cup of coffee on the counter beside him. Dressed in his union suit and trousers, the straps of his suspenders dangled at his hips. His shirt, coat, and hat were on one of the chairs with his boots underneath.

"Good morning," Charlotte said.

He half-turned around, smiling. "Have a seat. Breakfast is almost ready."

She pulled out a chair and sat down. He poured her a cup of coffee, set it before her, and leaned down for a light kiss. She cupped his bearded cheek in her palm to keep him there a moment longer. He smelled of bacon and tasted of coffee.

"Good morning," James murmured against her lips. He straightened and went back to cooking. "I hope you like scrambled eggs. That's the only kind I can make."

"Love them," she said, laughing. "Though I said I'd make you breakfast this morning."

"You can do it next time."

Next time.

Yes, now that they'd slept together, she supposed there would probably be a next time, and perhaps a time after that, and a time after that, if they wished. There was only the matter of not making it public knowledge, for Becca's sake. And being careful not to risk pregnancy, but perhaps Brigit could continue helping in that area.

Don't get ahead of yourself, her inner voice warned her. *Last time—*

This wasn't like last time. James wasn't Richard. And she was smarter now. They'd taken things slowly over the last several months and had been careful last night; there was no reason to think that would change. If James didn't agree, then he wasn't the man she thought he was. But she was pretty damn sure he was.

"Here you go." He set a plate of bacon, eggs, and toast in front of her and a second at the spot across the table.

"Silverware and napkins are there," Charlotte said, pointing to the appropriate drawers.

He found what he needed, passed her a fork and napkin, and then sat. Both began digging in. Apparently last night's activities had stimulated their appetites this morning.

"What are you up to today?" he asked.

"More tailing the film crew. Andrew wants as much day-by-day bits on them as I can get." She shook her head as she cut a piece of bacon with the side of her fork. "Trouble is, with the murder and the room break-ins, they're not doing a whole lot more than arguing about continuing with the film or getting out of town."

"Maybe that's the angle to follow." James took a bite of egg and toast. He swallowed. "Who's arguing about the film being made?"

Charlotte wasn't quite sure where he was going with this, but she'd play along. "Cicely wants to continue, in honor of her father. Meade wants to shelve it. Some of the crew agree with one, some with the other."

"What about the AEC?"

She considered what Caleb Burrows had told her about his meeting with Stanley Welsh before he died, as well as his not mentioning their second meeting. "Burrows said Welsh was going to change the story, and if he did, then the AEC would be fine with the film."

"Do you believe him?" James watched her over the rim of his cup.

"Who? Burrows or Welsh?"

"Either."

Neither man had ever been accused of being completely honest. Welsh had been stringing along Paige Carmichael for some time, and kept story changes from Cicely and the actors of the film. Charlotte herself had witnessed his tendency to "yes" a person, then do things the way he wanted anyway. And Burrows, well, being a lawyer meant he was probably very good at twisting words in a way to make them seem how he wanted you to hear them.

"Neither," Charlotte said. "At least not completely."

"I'm not sure you can trust anyone completely." James dropped his gaze to his plate and scooped the last bit of egg onto his toast.

Unease flickered in Charlotte's chest. "Meaning?"

He raised his head to meet her eyes again. "Meaning, we all lie, at least a little bit now and again, to make things easier. I think most people do it for the sake of others, tell white lies to keep from hurting feelings. But there's no one I've ever met who's completely honest."

Was he including her in that assessment?

"Well, you are a lawman. Most of the people you've met are probably not in a position to be honest."

He laughed and raised his coffee cup. "Touché. Not that I think brutal honesty all the time is a good thing either. As long as no one gets hurt, where's the harm in a little fib now and again?"

What did he consider a little fib?

"Except in the Welsh case, someone did get hurt." She hoped that's what he was talking about, and not the two of them.

"Was a lie at the root of his murder or just part of the aftermath?"

Charlotte dabbed her mouth with the napkin. "I guess that's what we have to find out."

"Yes, we do." James rose, gathered their dirty dishes, and put them in the sink. "I'm headed into the office to write up the report from last night at the Tidewater. Do you want a ride?"

"No, thank you." She rose and started filling the sink to wash the dishes. "I need to clean up here and write a few things myself. I'll come by later, if that's okay?"

He smiled and kissed her. Not just a peck, but deeper. His hand slid from her hip to the small of her back. "Anytime."

James stepped away, leaving her breathless at the sink, and donned his shirt and jacket. He set his hat on his head, then slipped on his boots. "See you later."

This time, it was just a quick peck, and out the door he went. Within a minute, she heard the car engine balk once, twice, then finally catch.

The normal domesticity of the last few minutes with him struck her as pleasant but . . . odd. She shook off the feeling and got to work.

Charlotte washed the dishes, washed herself, and dressed in a simple blouse and skirt with a pair of long johns underneath. Last night's dress was fun and pretty, but her legs had near frozen on the way to the Tidewater. She twisted her hair into a bun at the nape of her neck and pinned the strands in place. Was it time to get it cut into the latest bob fashion? Several of the younger women in town had theirs done, as did Roslyn Sanford and Paige Carmichael. Charlotte was pretty sure the fashion and hairstyles of the visitors would ripple through Cordova.

Downstairs, she sat at the desk in the parlor and wrote up the events from last evening, leaving out her conversation with Billy, of course. No one had been arrested, so she didn't have to worry about embarrassing anyone. Mostly she hoped the few sentences of the paragraph would warn people to be careful when they went out for a good time.

"The Women's Temperance League will probably come after me for even that much."

Last November's run-in with Mrs. Hillman and her friends over Charlotte's criticism of the Volstead Act had come close to costing Andrew Toliver some advertising business. He had been behind her piece, of course, or he wouldn't have let her run it, though Mrs. Hillman's veiled threats had given him pause. Charlotte didn't want the *Times* to lose revenue because of her, but that didn't mean she'd lick the WTL ladies' boots either.

Charlotte tapped her pen against the edge of the desk. The conversation with Billy replayed in her head. Heated exchanges between Meade and Welsh. Arguments with Cicely over the story, and more personal topics. Financial straits and family problems.

Nerves were frayed even before they'd left California. Secret affairs were threatened with exposure. Careers and livelihoods were at stake. And Stanley Welsh had been smack in the middle of it.

Charlotte wrote Stanley's name in the center of a clean sheet of paper and circled it. She drew a line from the circle, wrote "Wallace Meade," and then circled that as well. She repeated the process with Cicely, Paige, and Roger Markham, who had been concerned about the stunts Stanley wanted to include and angry at being ignored.

In addition to the Californians here that Stanley had quarreled with, Charlotte included Caleb Burrows and Miles Smith. Then, a final line and circle around a big question mark, just in case she'd missed someone.

All had motive and opportunity. The men had the means to manually strangle Stanley without much difficulty, but Charlotte never put it past any woman to cause sufficient physical harm.

"Especially if she has help." She added Roslyn to Cicely's circle.

The two women had much to lose if Welsh exposed their relationship. Would he have done such a thing to his own daughter? Considering the view many took of sapphic relationships, how women Charlotte had known had to carefully conduct themselves for fear of being disowned by family or worse, it wouldn't have surprised her if Stanley Welsh felt the threats were justified.

As with Pen and Rowena, the shop owners here in town, perhaps Cicely and Roslyn could continue their relationship as long as their "open secret" wasn't so open. Should it become public, there was a real threat, personally as well as professionally.

What if Cicely had finally had enough? Enough of her father changing her stories without telling her? Enough of his harassment about her relationship? Enough of the crushing thumb of being Stanley Welsh's daughter?

Charlotte tapped the circle with Cicely and Roslyn's names. Together, the two women could have overtaken Stanley and killed him, then dragged him to the crevasse. The bruise on the scenarist's cheek could have come from a struggle. Cicely insisting to finish the film could be a ruse, or could have stemmed from guilt.

By the same token, Paige was probably not capable of dragging Stanley out across the ice alone, but perhaps she could have gone walking with him, strangled him, and then shoved him into the crevasse. It seemed an unlikely scenario, but not impossible.

Markham had the temper. If he flew off the handle, no one within his reach might have been safe.

Wallace Meade took on the air of a gentleman, but he'd had a rough-and-tumble childhood, working his way across the western states to Washington and eventually up to Alaska at a young age. He'd toiled and sweated with his back and hands before trading in his denims for a wool flannel suit.

What about Burrows and Smith? Either working together or

alone, they were capable of the physical aspect of Stanley's death. Burrows had been in the army and was trained in combat. Miles was as vocal in his anger as Markham, and he'd certainly been angry enough at the treatment of his people that, if Stanley had refused to budge, Miles may have reacted. The same went for Burrows. Though the lawyer might have a longer fuse, Charlotte got the suspicion it was attached to a powder keg.

Charlotte studied the array of suspects and their motives for a few moments. Sitting here wasn't going to get answers or proof. She capped her pen, folded the page with her article, and headed to the door. Her first stop would be the *Times* office to file her piece, such as it was. Then she'd head to the Windsor to see who was about. People were probably sick of talking to her by now, but that was too bad. Another chat with Burrows and maybe Miles Smith was in order as well.

Half a block from the house, she spotted Michael hurrying toward her. His breath puffed silver-gray in the morning air, and he held a canvas bag under one arm. Beneath his fur hat, his brow was lined, frowning in the depths of his blond beard.

"Is Eddington around?" he asked by way of greeting.

"First, good morning to you too," she said. "Second, what makes you think I know where he is?"

Though she did know, up until an hour or so ago. Charlotte continued toward the *Times* office with Michael falling into step beside her.

"Sorry. Good morning. And I assumed he was with you because he wasn't in the marshal's office."

"It's Saturday, Michael. The man's allowed a day off." Despite their being closer of late and sharing more of their lives, Charlotte wasn't about to tell her brother outright that she'd slept with James. He'd either assumed they already had or that it was inevitable.

"I'm aware of the day, thanks, but he wasn't home either. Someone at the café said they saw you leave the Tidewater together last night." He gave her a sidelong look. "What were you doing there?"

"Following leads." She tapped the bag he held. "What do you have here?"

"Another piece of the Welsh puzzle."

Charlotte couldn't keep the anticipation from her face. "Oh? What is it? Can I see?"

With his shoulder, Michael blocked her attempt to grab the bag. "You know as well as I do that if I show you before I show Eddington he'll flay both of us. You'll have to wait."

"He was headed to the office earlier, but probably stopped at home to feed the cat. He might be at work by now," she said.

"Aha!" Michael stopped dead in the middle of the street. "So he was with you. I knew it." His triumphant smile turned into a look of concern. "You were, um, careful, weren't you?"

The heat in Charlotte's cheeks countered the cold wind coming down the mountain behind them. She wasn't ashamed of having slept with James, but her sex life was not a topic of conversation she wished to have with Michael. "We were. Anything else you want to know?"

"God, no," he said, shaking his head vigorously. "Just making sure. Let me know if you need me for anything. I can prescribe prophylactics for medical purposes."

The advantage of being related to a doctor.

"Condoms from my brother would add a certain something to the romance, don't you think?" They both grimaced with discomfort. "We have it taken care of, but thank you." Lord, she hoped that would end the discussion.

Luckily, it did, and their conversation turned to members of the *Fortune* crew as suspects. Michael agreed that it would require a certain amount of strength to have strangled Welsh.

"He wasn't a small man," Michael said, "and even in a reduced state of awareness by medication or alcohol, it would take some muscle to do as much damage as he sustained."

"So you don't think it was a woman." There went half her suspects.

"I didn't say that. Women can be quite strong, or perhaps two could have killed him." He clutched the bag under his arm closer to his body. "There would be considerable strength necessary to drag him to the crevasse too."

"More strong man action or a pair of women?"

"Perhaps," he said.

Obviously Michael wasn't going to tell her what he'd discovered until they met with James.

"Let's go by the Windsor on our way," Charlotte said. "I want to see if anyone's about."

"Haven't you gotten all you can from questioning them?"

"The main suspects, yes, but you'd be surprised what the others on the crew know that they don't realize they know."

Charlotte told Michael what Billy had said last night at the Tidewater. She left out the part where James and the Cordova police raided the club, but he probably knew that bit already. News traveled faster at the cafés and barber shops than in the *Cordova Daily Times*.

By the time she finished, they reached the front of the Windsor Hotel just as Dave drove up with his team of dogs, the Brite-White Laundry company logo stenciled on several sacks in the sled. The six canines dutifully slowed and halted at his shout of "Whoa!" They panted happily while Dave set the ice hook and headed inside.

"I've been thinking about learning to drive a team," Michael said. "It would give me a way to reach my patients who live outside of town."

"And where would you keep the dogs between appointments?" Charlotte wondered. "In your cabin or upstairs in your office?"

"Hmm, good point. Maybe I could borrow Dave's."

Charlotte knew her brother had become happily settled in Cordova and enjoyed life in Alaska, so it didn't surprise her if one day he did learn to drive a sled and team.

"Come on, let's see who's at breakfast." She started to urge him into the hotel when Wallace Meade and Roger Markham came through the door. "Good morning, Mr. Meade. Mr. Markham. You're up early."

The two men greeted her and Michael cordially.

Dave's dog Byron, at his "wheel" position closest to the sled along with Shelley, started barking.

Markham shot a glare at the dog. Byron barked louder.

Meade tugged on his gloves, taking extra care with the right. "A brisk walk in the bracing chill of an Alaska winter does wonders for a man's physical and mental well-being. Being down south for so long, I'd nearly forgotten how invigorating it is up here."

"It is that." Charlotte raised her voice over the noisy canine. "Tell me, have you made a decision about continuing the film?"

Meade answered her in an equally raised volume. "I made my decision first thing, but Cicely has managed to convince a significant number of the crew to go back out." Meade and Markham exchanged looks that said the two of them had likely gone toe to toe on the matter. "Far be it from me to deny the young woman the opportunity to honor her father."

His change in attitude puzzled Charlotte. Cicely must have presented a strong argument, or managed to tap into the man's sympathies, to keep the producer on the project.

"What about Mrs. Welsh? Will she be staying in town?"

"Carmen has decided to return to the site with Cicely," Markham said. "Understandably, she doesn't want to be away from her daughter just now."

Meade asked Michael, "I assume you'll be releasing the body soon?"

"Not quite yet."

"What's the holdup, Doctor? Cicely and Carmen would like to have him tended to as soon as possible. We—they don't need to draw this out. The longer it takes for you to release his body, the more likely some sort of media vulture will land on the story and blow things out of proportion."

Michael put on his "sympathetic but determined" face. Charlotte knew it well. "I understand completely, Mr. Meade, but until I'm satisfied that the cause of death is accurate, I'll need to keep Mr. Welsh at the morgue. I promise to let Mrs. and Miss Welsh know when they can have their loved one released to the undertaker."

Meade's mouth pressed into a grim line of annoyance, his gaze darting between her and Michael. Charlotte suppressed a grin. Obviously Wallace Meade wasn't too keen on the Brodys, but she hoped her next question wouldn't be met with rejection.

"When is the crew headed back to the glacier?" Charlotte asked. "I'd like to continue my coverage for the *Times*. I could get some positive news out there about the production before any of the vultures even start circling."

Though Charlotte didn't consider herself one of those, nothing piqued interest and sold copies like sensational events involving famous people. But this wasn't about generating revenue. She was more interested in solving the crime.

For a moment, Meade seemed uncertain about her resuming; then he nodded thoughtfully. "That would be helpful, I suppose. Cicely wishes to return in a couple of days at the latest."

Dave the laundry man exited the Windsor carrying two stuffed canvas sacks of what was likely bed and kitchen linens. When the team of dogs saw him, they all started whining and yipping in excitement; their master's return meant they'd soon be off. Charlotte had never seen animals so enthused with their tasks as sled dogs seemed to be.

Dave yanked the anchor and urged them on with no more than a "Hike" that was mostly drowned out by the yips. The dogs dug in. Lines strained. The sled moved forward, swooshing down the road to another customer.

Quiet returned to the street once again.

Wallace Meade gave Charlotte and Michael a slight smile as he tipped his hat. "If you'll excuse me, I have a few errands to run." He addressed Markham. "Meet me at the train station in half an hour."

Markham puffed on his cigarette, eyes narrowed. "I told you I'd be there." He tugged the brim of his cap, turned on his heel, and walked away, his limp barely noticeable.

The producer grunted as he watched the cameraman depart, then turned to Charlotte again. "We'll send around a note as to when we'll be departing, Miss Brody."

"Thank you, Mr. Meade. Good day."

"Good day." He ambled across the road, toward the heart of town.

"I know he's trying to make the situation easier on the Welshes," Michael said, "but I hope he realizes I'm taking care so I can be accurate. I'm not trying to drum up any sort of unnecessary excitement."

"I know you aren't." Charlotte looped her arm through his. "I'm sure he and the Welshes understand that too. It's a terrible time for them all."

"Do you still want to go inside to see if there are some more movie people to talk to?" he asked.

Charlotte watched Meade as he stopped to chat with another gentleman, then lost sight of him when he continued on past the tobacco shop and down to Main Street. "No, I think I'll stop by later, though. Come on. Let's go see if James is at the office."

*   *   *

Michael held open the door to the federal building to allow Charlotte to precede him. She, in turn, opened the interior door that led to the marshal's office for him. The stairs up to the post office were lit by a couple of small hanging lamps. Charlotte made a mental note to check the *Times*'s post box before leaving.

Inside the marshal's office, James sat at his desk, smoking a pipe and typing on a shiny black Royal typewriter. The rhythmic *clickety-clack* of the type bars on the paper-covered platen were quite familiar to Charlotte. He glanced between his hands and the page, his fingers sure and quick over the black enamel keys.

"Impressive," Charlotte said as she and Michael entered. "Your typing skills are improving. I should hire you as my secretary."

James lifted his head, fingers stilled, and grinned at them. "I'll send you my rates. Good morning, Doc. What do you have there?"

Michael opened the bag as he walked toward James's desk. "The blanket used to drag Welsh onto the ice. It has bits of straw and other debris embedded in it. There's also a tear on the side toward the middle of the long edge where it caught on the dog pen."

If Welsh had the blanket around his shoulders, and wandered out on the ice on his own accord, the tear wouldn't be in the middle like that. "Not the bottom or corner?" Charlotte asked.

"No, and it was a long, irregular snag," Michael held the beige tuft up to the torn edge. "Using a microscope, I noted the fibers are consistent. It's very high quality wool, smooth, and with good color. Much nicer than the blankets on the cots in your tent, Charlotte." He turned the blanket over. "There's also a stain here and on his jacket, consistent with the medicine Welsh took. There was little left in the bottle to compare, but the aromas are similar. I'll run tests when I get the chemicals I need. They should be on the next steamer, whenever it gets here."

"Perhaps, if his hand was unsteady, he spilled it on himself," she suggested.

"Or spilled it elsewhere and tried to clean it up. Difficult to say."

"The snag on the side." James gestured to have Michael return to that portion of the blanket. "That suggests either one very strong person, or a pair, dragged him over and dumped him into the crevasse after killing him somewhere in camp."

Michael nodded. "That would be my theory, yes."

"Not Paige Carmichael then," Charlotte said. "At least not acting alone."

Her brother gave her quizzical a look. "Was she ever a serious suspect?"

"Perhaps not a leading contender, but until she can be completely ruled out, she had motive. Stanley continuously gave her the impression that his next film would be hers. He never delivered."

"A woman scorned," James said, shaking his head.

His tone hit Charlotte in the middle of her chest. "A woman promised and misled, is more like it. From what I've heard, much of the industry is knowing the right people. Paige was doing what she thought would work best to get the jobs she wanted."

"She was sleeping with the man so she could get ahead in her career." James crossed his arms over his chest. "She assumed he'd favor her and was wrong. It's not fair, but she's not exactly leading the parade on ethics either."

"Nor was he by cheating on his wife," Charlotte countered. "I'm not saying Paige is faultless. She was using Welsh—or trying to—and he was using her, but he got what he wanted while keeping her dangling on the line like a fish. A person can only take so much of that."

"Exactly my point," he said. "He wasn't living up to his end of the bargain. She could have become angry enough to kill him."

"It wouldn't surprise me in the least."

Charlotte and James held each other's gazes for a long moment. She was sure her own expression mirrored his tightly pressed lips and furrowed brow.

Michael glanced back and forth between them. "So . . . is she a suspect or not?"

She took a breath and mindfully relaxed the tension in her jaw. "Deputy?"

James pinched the bridge of his nose, eyes closed. After a moment, he looked at Charlotte again and said, "She isn't the primary suspect, but I'm not going to rule her out either."

Michael sat on the edge of the desk. "I'm glad that's cleared up."

Charlotte couldn't help but smile at his rare sarcasm. "As it stands, I think focusing on someone more physically capable of the act of strangling and dragging a man would be best."

James nodded slowly. "Agreed. So that leaves, what, a dozen or so suspects? The majority of the company is men who do a lot of physical labor."

"But only a few had motive," Charlotte reminded James. "What about the method of death?" she asked Michael. "You concluded strangulation. That would require considerable brute strength."

"The killer may have used something to render him unconscious," Michael said, "or taken advantage of his diminished condition. I took a closer look this morning, and the bruising on Welsh's neck was more defined. After opening him up, I saw the hyoid was fractured inward. Whoever killed Welsh used their bare hands."

He stood in front of Charlotte and placed his hands on her throat one at a time. He didn't squeeze, of course, but the sensation of hands at her throat was disconcerting. She had felt it before, not so long ago, and the memory sent a chill down her spine. She refused to let it get the better of her.

Michael continued describing his findings. "Left hand first. Right over top of it and slightly higher. There was a thumbprint-like bruise on the left side of his neck, as well as finger impressions on the right, and another thumbprint higher up on the right side."

"The killer led with his left. A southpaw?" James asked.

Michael lowered his hands. "Possibly. Charlotte, who in the crew is left-handed? Surely there are one or two."

Shaking off her experience, Charlotte quirked an eyebrow at him. "Do I look like Sherlock Holmes? That's not something I've paid attention to. When I go back to the glacier with them, I'll make note. Though being left-handed isn't going to prove anything."

James rose and crossed the office to the coal stove, where the coffeepot was kept warm. "No, but it may be something to help whittle down suspects. Coffee?"

Charlotte and Michael accepted the offer.

"What about Caleb Burrows and Miles Smith? Burrows was one of the last to see Stanley alive," Charlotte said as they took their seats once again. "Other than the killer."

"Unless, of course, Burrows *is* the killer," James added.

"He certainly had motive, opportunity, and ability." Charlotte considered the lawyer and his assistant. "Young Miles could very well have helped. He has a temper."

Michael stiffened. "Are you accusing those men because they're Natives?"

Charlotte blinked in surprise. "What? No, of course not. I'm *suspecting* them because they were there and had a very passionate stand against what Welsh was trying to do with the film. Please, Michael, you know me better than that."

He laid a hand on her arm. "Sorry. You're right, I do know you better. It's just that tensions between the Eyaks and the whites can get out of hand from time to time." He gestured toward James. "You've seen it, Eddington."

James nodded. "I have. It's been fairly quiet for a while, but the brouhaha over the film has stirred things up. Ned at the police station was telling me about recent fights he's broken up.

New difficulties bringing up old troubles. Hell, continuing troubles."

Charlotte had written up more than a few of those in the last six months.

"Those are just a symptom of a larger problem," Michael said. "Mary tells me terrible stories of how her people have been treated. Cheating in trade or business dealings, outright violence. But also subtle things like being ignored at the grocer's or remarks made when someone thought she couldn't hear or understand." He shook his head. "I know she doesn't tell me half of what has happened to her or people she knows."

"Then Welsh and Meade come here thinking their depiction of Natives as villains will be embraced," Charlotte said. "I don't blame the AEC for being upset."

James rubbed his eyes. "Upset enough to kill is what I'm concerned with. Which is why Burrows and Smith are still on the list. And why I've cleared it with Blaine to accompany the next trip out to the glacier while he stays here and works with the local cops."

It made sense to have the deputy marshal on-site to prevent further trouble and continue the investigation, but Charlotte had a sudden, unreasonable feeling he was going out to keep an eye on her.

Nonsense. He has a job to do.

"Maybe it's time to get their perspective." Charlotte drained the last of her coffee and brought the cup over to the sideboard. James would rinse it out later, as was his habit. "Do you happen to know where the AEC is meeting today?"

"I think they usually meet at the Smiths' house," Michael said, "but I'm not sure if that's a good idea, Charlotte."

"Why not? All I'm going to do is ask." She buttoned her coat and tugged on her mittens. "And if they don't want to talk to me, that's fine."

Michael and James both stood. Michael shoved the blanket

back in the bag and handed it to James. "That's never 'fine' with you," her brother said. "If I know you, you'll find a way to get them talking."

James came around the desk and stood beside her, looking wary. "And possibly cause them to close ranks."

"Whatever they decide, it'll be fine." Charlotte rose on her toes to peck him on the cheek. "Now, where do the Smiths live?"

Chapter 12

Charlotte filed another tidbit at the *Times* office, then helped Andrew set the Sunday paper, as Henry had been unable to work that afternoon. At nearly four, she glanced up at the clock and made a hurried departure. Luckily, the paper was ready to go to print and Andrew assured her he could manage without her.

She had just enough time to run to the bakery before it closed and pick up the last frosted yellow cake. Climbing the slick road as she made her way to the Smiths' home, Charlotte hoped the cake box survived the bursts of wind and snow and wouldn't become a sodden mess. Her mother had always told her that baked goods made visits more amenable, particularly if one dropped in unannounced. Would it work in this case? The Smiths and the AEC had no reason to invite her in, cake or no cake.

She approached the tall, narrow house with trepidation fluttering in her gut. Charlotte had never had difficulties with anyone within, but she was unsure how the group actually felt about her. Being a reporter made her someone to be wary of, and her role as Becca's guardian might be seen as interference.

Straightening her hat and clothes as best she could while balancing the cake in one hand, Charlotte took a settling breath, then knocked. Mrs. Smith opened the door, her dark eyes full of curiosity. She wore a white blouse and long blue plaid skirt, her gray-streaked black hair tied back in a long ponytail.

"Yes?"

Charlotte smiled. "Good afternoon, Mrs. Smith. I know you're having a gathering, and I hope I'm not intruding."

Why did people say that when they certainly did mean to intrude?

"We're almost finished, Miss Brody," the older woman said, her words soft and accented. "Are you here to collect Becca?"

"If she's ready." Charlotte heard voices coming from the parlor or dining room and she made a polite show of looking in that direction. "As I said, I don't want to interrupt."

Mrs. Smith smiled slightly, but kindly, and Charlotte knew the woman was on to her. "No interruption at all. Please, come in."

She held the door open to allow Charlotte to enter.

Inside, the voices coming from the parlor, behind a partially closed pocket door, conversed in the Eyak language punctuated with the occasional English word, like *film*, that perhaps didn't translate. Was Becca fluent in her father's tongue? She had never spoken it at home.

When Mrs. Smith closed the door, Charlotte held the cake out to her. "A token of appreciation for helping Becca, as well as an apology for coming unannounced."

The other woman smiled again, inclining her head. "Thank you, Miss Brody. If you'd be so kind as to wait in the foyer, I'll let Becca know you're here."

Charlotte thanked her, angling her head to see into the room as Mrs. Smith entered it. She caught no more than a glimpse of men and women sitting in a group. The door muffled the voices, but the silence that soon followed Mrs. Smith's entrance was telling. Charlotte could imagine the surprise on their faces at her presence in the house. Was Becca in there, just as shocked? Embarrassed?

She'll understand. I hope.

Mrs. Smith returned after a couple of minutes. She smiled at Charlotte again. Surely that was a good sign. "Becca went up to gather her things. Please, come in, won't you? My husband and the others would like to speak to you."

Charlotte slipped off her boots and opened her coat, but didn't remove it. Not tracking muck into the house was one thing, but Mrs. Smith hadn't offered to take her coat, meaning Charlotte wouldn't be staying long. She'd have to make the best of the time she had.

She followed Mrs. Smith into the parlor. All of the AEC members present watched her with a combination of wariness and curiosity. None appeared to be openly hostile toward her. Charlotte did her best to smile politely while making brief eye contact with each of them.

Jonas Smith rose from his seat at the far end of the group and offered his hand. "Miss Brody. I would say that your visit is a surprise, but we had the feeling you'd be here sooner or later."

Caleb Burrows rose from the chair beside Smith's, a tea cup and saucer in his right hand. As usual, the lawyer had an amused, knowing half grin on his face as he lifted the cup in his left hand and sipped.

The three other gentlemen rose as well. The ladies—an older woman, Michael's assistant Mary Weaver, and AEC Vice President Violet Langler—remained seated. Smith introduced everyone, and the men returned to their places, leaving Charlotte standing before them as if on trial.

"I appreciate you asking me in, Mr. Smith." Charlotte inclined her head, acknowledging the generosity of the group leader. He could have made her wait in the foyer. He could have demanded she leave his home. By inviting her in when she had shown up unannounced, Charlotte felt she'd been given a fortunate opportunity. Perhaps the AEC was willing to share their side of the story.

"Becca told us you've been asking her more questions about her association with us," Burrows said.

"In an effort to learn more about her heritage and how she's getting along, yes," Charlotte replied. "You're important to her, so you're important to me."

Gertrude Trask, a thin, gray-haired woman in a long dress and thick leggings, shook her head. Her dark eyes bore into Charlotte. "She's half white," she said in reference to Becca, her accent more pronounced than the Smiths'. "How would she or you know what's important?"

"Isn't Becca's being here an indication of that?" Charlotte asked. "I have no intention of denying her knowledge of who she is and where she came from."

The implication that not allowing Becca to learn these things would be worse wasn't lost in the eyes of most of the others, especially Caleb Burrows. Several nodded. Miles Smith, arms crossed, leaning against the wall in a corner, said nothing.

Charlotte addressed the elder Mr. Smith. "I have questions, of course, and they don't all pertain to Becca. This is your home, your meeting. Please, tell me what you wish to speak about."

Any information they could provide, whether about Becca's involvement with the AEC or the Council's feelings about the film and Welsh's death, would be advantageous both personally and professionally.

Smith glanced at the other members. He spoke softly to a young man in a straight-backed chair. The man rose and moved to the side, near Miles. Smith offered the chair to Charlotte. She sat on the edge, knees together and ankles crossed, hands folded in her lap.

"Mr. Toliver has been willing and able to keep our concerns about the film out of the newspaper," Smith began, "but many in town know how we feel. The time has come to make our views public. Too much has happened, and with the death of Mr. Welsh, there will be rumors and speculation about the involvement of the AEC."

There was already speculation, at least on the part of herself and James.

Mr. Smith continued. "It's critical that the people of Cordova know that no member of the AEC was involved in any of the terrible things that have happened. Not in regard to Mr. Welsh nor with the incident at the hotel."

Charlotte avoided looking at Burrows or Miles Smith. "While I understand this, Mr. Smith, two of your members were at the site the night Mr. Welsh died. Until the culprit can be determined, I'm afraid everyone who was out there at the time is being considered."

"Even you?" Gertrude Trask asked.

"The marshal's office chiefly looks at motive and opportunity. I had no reason to harm Mr. Welsh," Charlotte said, "so no, not me. Though no one is completely above suspicion."

"Our displeasure is considered sufficient motive for murder," Burrows said, his words matter-of-fact yet filled with cynicism.

"I'm afraid so." There was no sense trying to hide the fact. They all knew who was out at the glacier, and that heated words had passed between the men on more than one occasion. "The deputy marshal and the coroner have been sorting through the evidence they've gathered."

No need to disclose that there was little enough of that at this point either.

Karl Karlov, who ran one of the barbershops, glared at her through narrowed eyes. "You're associated with both men, Miss Brody, feeding them information."

"I'm involved because I was there and it's my job, yes, which means I'm seeking the truth as much as they are." She shifted on her seat and glanced at each of them. "No one is trying to persecute anyone unjustly. We want to know what happened to Mr. Welsh. His family deserves to know. Justice is as important to us as it is to you."

Gertrude Trask snorted. "Justice. What do you people know of justice?"

Charlotte's instinct was to defend herself and the majority of people she knew, but that wasn't what the woman wanted to hear. "I know there have been terrible things done to your people. I make no excuse for that. But I would hope you'd believe me when I say I want justice for anyone who has been harmed."

"She helped find the murderer of that girl last fall," Mary said, offering Charlotte a nod of support. Charlotte nodded in return, grateful.

"A white girl," the older woman retorted with derision. "Would she have done the same for one of ours?"

Mary and Charlotte held each other's gazes. Mary knew more of Charlotte's involvement with the later case that resulted in Becca's situation. Was she taking that into account? Charlotte felt the weight of her judgment as well as that of the others as they looked at her. Finally, Mary gave her a small smile. "Yes, I believe she would have."

There were a few nods of agreement, and Charlotte felt the weight lift some. Not all would trust her, but not all whites did either.

"You have the faith of the AEC," Caleb Burrows said. "We'd like your newspaper to follow through on its commitment to fair treatment."

"I'm glad to do it," Charlotte said, "and I'm sure Andrew Toliver will be happy to publish anything you wish."

"We have something prepared and ask that you and Toliver contribute support in your own words as well." Burrows set his cup and saucer on the table, then rose. With his thumbs in his vest pockets, he paced the room as he spoke, as if addressing the court. "We will have *our* voices heard, and you can help.

Together, we'll explain why the depiction of Natives in the current incarnation of the film is detrimental."

"It would be an honor to do what I can for you," Charlotte said. "Though this film is the tip of a very large iceberg."

"Large and ages old," Jonas Smith said, shaking his head.

Burrows stopped pacing and faced her, fire in his eyes. "What do you know of the history of whites in Alaska, Miss Brody?"

"Very little, I'm afraid." She was embarrassed to admit that other than the basic lessons in the purchase of the land from Russia, "Seward's Folly" as it was known, she couldn't relay much in the way of significant fact about the interactions between peoples.

"Whites came in here and did their damnedest to take over natural resources like fur, timber, gold," the lawyer said. "Some would like you to believe it was all done with the Natives smiling as an equal partner, but that's not the whole of the truth. There was no declared war or big battles, as with the Natives down south, but there were troubles and bloodshed. Yes, on both sides. Eventually, a settlement of sorts was reached. Not necessarily in our favor, but we were outgunned and just wanted to live in peace."

Smith added, "We're encouraged to want the things white culture offers, but denied opportunities in employment and education to achieve those things. Our children are being reeducated away from our culture—literally taken from homes—an act as abhorrent to us as it would be to you. Yet we're still treated as inferior when we do attempt to conform. Then someone like Mr. Meade or Mr. Welsh comes along and wishes to perpetuate falsehoods about us. You can see why we get upset."

Charlotte sat for a minute absorbing all they'd said. There was more to it than that, of course; they had merely given her a quick lesson in what had gone on before, what was still occurring, and why they'd had enough. She sympathized with them, and wanted to help the AEC, but there was something else to consider: Had anger and frustration manifested into murder?

She lifted her head to say as much to Mr. Smith, then noticed Becca and Esther on the stairs. Becca's face was drawn and pale. Was she embarrassed and angry to have Charlotte show up unannounced?

Suddenly feeling as if she had invaded her young friend's privacy, Charlotte rose. "I appreciate your time and willingness to talk to me. I want to assure you that Mr. Toliver and I will do all we can to present fair and balanced information regarding the treatment of the Eyak people. Not just for now, while *North to Fortune* is being filmed, but on any issue."

Burrows frowned and several of the others muttered among themselves. "They plan on finishing the film?"

"It looks that way," Charlotte said. She watched Becca and Esther slowly walk down the stairs. "I think Cicely Welsh will be more receptive to your request for parity."

"Let's hope so," Burrows said. "Allow me to walk you out, Miss Brody."

Charlotte bade farewell to the AEC members and preceded him to the foyer. Becca and Esther followed, Becca silently donning her coat while Esther whispered to her. Charlotte had the feeling it would be a cold, quiet walk home.

"Will you be returning to the site with the film crew?" Burrows asked.

"That's my plan." Charlotte pulled on her boots. "Will you?"

The lawyer pressed his lips together. "I'm not sure. We'll discuss it."

"Cicely wants to head back out in a day or so, so you may want to discuss it quickly."

Burrows smiled as he took her hand. His fingers closed around hers, warm and strong. Strong enough to strangle a man? "I appreciate the information. Have a good evening, Miss Brody."

"Good evening, Mr. Burrows." Charlotte turned to Becca. "Do you have everything?"

The girl nodded, unwilling to speak to her. Charlotte's heart sank. What had she done to their relationship?

Charlotte endured Becca's silence all the way home, then through supper. She didn't bother asking any questions other than, "Could you pass the salt?" or "Do you want dessert?" These required only action or the nod of a head.

Her own parents would never have allowed Charlotte to get away with such behavior, but she wasn't Becca's mother. She was Becca's friend. Perhaps that wasn't the correct way to run their relationship, but now was not the time to become parental.

But what did Becca need more, a parent or a friend? Charlotte wasn't sure she was ready for the former, and she may have made a mess of the latter.

At nine o'clock, while the two of them sat in the parlor reading, Becca finally broke her silence.

"You could have warned me you'd be coming," she said, not looking up from her book.

Charlotte set aside her P. G. Wodehouse novel. "It was somewhat of a spur-of-the-moment decision. I wanted to talk to Mr. Burrows. It didn't have anything to do with you."

Becca lifted her head, her dark eyes pained and intense. "Didn't it? If I hadn't been there, giving you an excuse to barge in, would you have gone then or some other time?"

She had a point but wasn't completely in the right.

"I don't know," Charlotte said with honesty. "Yes, you were a good reason to show up unannounced, but in no way was I trying to embarrass you or spy on your meeting. I needed to know what the AEC wanted to do about the situation."

"And you weren't going to ask me," Becca said.

"No, we talked about this. You want to keep your own counsel regarding your association with the AEC, only coming to me if you learned of anything dangerous or illegal. I didn't go to the Smiths' to check up on you, or imply you told me anything that prompted my visit."

Becca rose from the sofa, knuckles white as she clutched her book. "But they *will* think that. Don't you see, Charlotte? They're just getting to accept me, to trust me, and then you show up. Some of them will think I told you things I shouldn't have."

Standing slowly, Charlotte clenched her jaw as anger rose. Not at Becca, but toward those who would think such a thing. She supposed it was unavoidable, but try telling that to a thirteen-year-old who only wanted to be accepted. "I'm sorry, Becca. I should have considered the possibility. With Mr. Burrows and Miles having been out on the site, you must have figured out I'd need to speak to the AEC at some point."

The fight seemed to go out of the girl as her shoulders sagged and her chin dropped. "I know. I was just hoping it wouldn't happen while I was around, is all."

Charlotte took a couple of tentative steps toward her. Becca looked up. Tears welled in her eyes. Charlotte held her arms out. Becca stepped forward and Charlotte embraced her.

"Oh, honey." She closed her eyes, her cheek against Becca's bowed head. "I'm sorry. I didn't mean to make things difficult for you, but I have a job to do."

"I know," came the muffled reply. "Esther and the other kids are all right. They like you well enough."

Charlotte smiled. She supposed that's the best any adult could hope for from a group of adolescents. "That's nice to know."

Becca eased out of her arms. Her eyes were only a little puffy and red. "The grown-ups aren't so sure about you, though."

That made Charlotte chuckle. "I'm not surprised. I think most journalists face that problem." But maybe that wasn't what Becca meant. "Or is it because I'm white?"

"A bit of both, I think," she said, wincing. "Some, like Miss

Gert, tell terrible stories about what happened to their families. She went to a boarding school where they beat her for trying to speak Eyak."

The horror in Becca's eyes made Charlotte's stomach clench. Things like that were still happening, but she bet it wouldn't be in *North to Fortune*.

"I understand their mistrust," she said. "I want to mend what little I can by helping."

"I know you do." Becca sat on the sofa. Charlotte sat beside her. "Is there a way we can do it together?"

Charlotte smiled and took her hand. "I think so, but I won't get you involved with the investigation." Becca started to protest. Her indignation of being left out of the excitement was a relief to Charlotte. *That* she could deal with. "No, I have to put my foot down. It may get dangerous. In fact, I'll be heading back out to the glacier site in the next couple of days. I'd like to ask Esther's family or Mary if you can stay with them until I get back."

Becca's disappointment was clear, but she nodded understanding. "We have book reports due this week, so I guess it's for the best. I just wish I could have been in the film."

Charlotte kissed her on the temple. "I know, and I'm sorry about that part, but your safety will always come first."

"What about yours?" Fear and concern marred her young face. Becca had lost her parents, her brother. She was acutely aware of how quickly things could turn.

"Deputy Eddington said he'll be there," Charlotte assured her. "I'll be safe as a bug in a rug."

Becca smiled with relief. "Good. I know he won't let anything happen to you." She rose again and gathered her book. "I'm going to read in bed for a while. Good night."

"Good night."

At the foot of the stairs, Becca turned to face Charlotte, a sly gleam in her eye. "Though with Deputy Eddington there, I wonder how much work either of you will get done."

"Oh, you." Charlotte laughed and reached for a pillow on the sofa. Becca gave a laughing yelp as Charlotte threw it. The pillow hit the bannister, and Becca ran up the stairs.

Listening to the girl laugh made Charlotte's heart happy, but a dark sense of reality set in when she reflected on Becca's words. What if something did happen to Charlotte someday? What would that mean for Becca?

Chapter 13

The second departure from the train station two days later wasn't nearly as high-spirited as the first with Welsh's death looming over them, subduing conversation and emotion. Even Paige Carmichael hadn't uttered a single word of complaint when they'd been reminded the snow squalls could very well be worse out on the glacier.

From the number of people on the platform in town, it looked like most of the crew had opted to join Cicely in finishing her father's dream. The few who had decided to stay behind would keep an eye on the others' belongings until the location shoot was over.

The train was due to arrive shortly, Charlotte noticed on the schedule board. It was currently at the ocean dock unloading copper ore and loading up on freight before picking up passengers headed to the glacier, Chitina, McCarthy, and Kennecott.

Cast and crew members were trickling in by foot or hired car, but two notable members were missing. Where were Roslyn Sanford and Peter York?

"How long do you anticipate being on-site this time?" Charlotte asked Cicely. They waited under an overhang outside the station-proper rather than inside. Carmen Welsh and a number of the others were packed inside the little building. It was cold and blustery outside, but you didn't feel like a sardine either.

"No more than the originally planned week," the scenarist said. She spoke to Charlotte, and Caleb Burrows, who stood with them, but glanced around the platform and down the snowy street. Looking for her stars, no doubt. "Probably less. I do want the authentic scenes in there, but we'll make changes."

"Such as?" Burrows asked.

"I've rewritten the rescue scene," she said. "Instead of putting her on an iceberg, I have Dorothy being kidnapped by a rival gold miner. The local Natives will help Lawrence rescue her. Then Lawrence and Dorothy will be so grateful they'll share the profits from the gold mine with their new friends, saying they should have done as much to begin with."

"That sounds like a fine change in the scenario," Charlotte said. "What do you think, Mr. Burrows?"

Burrows, scarf over his nose and mouth and his hat pulled low on his head, nodded. "Much better. Though the AEC is still interested in scenes you've done so far."

"I know." Cicely held her mittened hands to her face and blew, momentarily fogging her spectacles. "I think it would behoove you or one of the AEC members to return to California with us to look at the film we've shot already. We can either reshoot or retitle scenes as necessary."

Wallace Meade, who had just come up onto the platform headed to the station house, stopped abruptly. "Hold on there, Cicely. I never approved of such a thing. How much are we talking here? And what about the integrity of the film? We don't want *North to Fortune* to be full of inconsistencies. That will kill us in reviews."

Behind the round glass of her spectacles, Cicely got a steely look in her eye that Charlotte had seen more often since her father passed away. She realized just how much Cicely resembled the late director.

"I won't go back on my word of correcting the film, Mr. Meade. I promised Mr. Burrows and the AEC we'd do what we could to make it right. That's all there is to it."

She even sounded like Welsh.

Meade's face turned bright red, and not from the cold. "You listen to me, young lady. I'm willing to go along with the continued shoot in honor of Stanley, but you are not in charge by any stretch of the imagination. Get that through your pretty little head right now."

He stomped off to the other side of the platform and barked at several of the men hauling equipment up from a truck. Dave and his team of dogs came around the corner of the building, panting and yapping. They passed below Meade, who stepped farther onto the platform as if to avoid the team despite being nowhere near them. Dave called the dogs to a halt and prepared to load them in a car behind the passenger cars when the train arrived.

Meade yanked open the door to the station house. As he entered, one of Smitty's assistant cooks started to exit. The two men exchanged a few curt words, then Meade continued inside and the cook wandered to the end of the platform to smoke a cigarette.

"I'm sure you won't need one of us to travel to California," Burrows said, drawing Charlotte's attention back to the conversation. For an aggressive lawyer, he seemed to have the ability to soothe a situation just as easily as he riled up folks. "There are a couple of Alaskans down in your neck of the woods already. Angus Melin has worked with Mr. York. He could take a look at the scenes."

Cicely's eyes brightened. "Oh yes! He was supposed to be in *Fortune* as well but was contracted to play a Polynesian in a different film and couldn't get away."

Charlotte shook her head at the peculiarity of Hollywoodland. A Native Alaskan couldn't return to his homeland to play one of his own because he was required to play a native of a different country? And several of the actors with minor roles who had come along with the Californians weren't Alaskan or any sort of Native as far as Charlotte knew. At least Welsh had hired some locals to fill in.

Burrows's smile tightened. Was he thinking the same thing about Melin and the "Alaskans" who were to be in the film? "I'll have the AEC send a letter of request to him, with a copy going to you and Mr. Meade."

"That sounds fine. Thank you." Cicely grinned, then excused herself and hurried away when one of the crewmen called to her.

Charlotte stepped closer to Burrows. "That's how the AEC learned of the film's content, isn't it? Angus Melin was shown the scenario. He knows people here."

She should have made the connection earlier, when she came upon Esther and Becca reading the movie magazine; the actor was a friend of Esther's father.

The lawyer rocked back on his heels. Though his lower face was covered by a scarf, there was no mistaking the amusement in his eyes as the corners crinkled. "Very good, Miss Brody. Though it wasn't a secret, Angus preferred not to have it widely known. I fear it did, however, please Welsh and Meade not to have him included in *North to Fortune*."

"Why?"

Burrows shrugged. "I believe they were trying to avoid having a troublemaker along. To be honest, I think Angus would have been the least of their problems." Something caught the lawyer's eye behind Charlotte. He tipped his hat and bowed slightly. "If you'll excuse me, I want to take care of something before the train arrives."

He turned on his heel and walked to the doors of the station building.

Charlotte looked in the same direction to see what had initiated Burrows's rapid departure. James climbed the stairs to the platform, a rucksack over his shoulder and a slight frown on his face. Was Burrows avoiding him?

"The train should be here soon," Charlotte said as he came up to her. She rose onto her toes to kiss his cheek, but his frown remained. "What's wrong?"

"You shouldn't go back out there."

She stepped away, puzzled. "Why not?"

James took gentle hold of her upper arm and guided her to a quiet corner on the platform. He glanced around to make sure no one was paying attention to them. Eyebrows drawn down, he said, "Just got word from the local coppers that Peter York was attacked last night."

Charlotte's breath caught. "Peter? When? Where? Is he all right?"

"Bruised, but moving about."

She instinctively looked around the train station. Cast and crew were either standing in small groups chatting or readying freight to return to the site.

"Do Cicely and Meade know?" she asked.

"I don't think Meade knows, but Cicely does." James nodded in the scenarist-cum-director's direction. "Roslyn was with him this morning, helping him pack."

No wonder Cicely didn't seem overly concerned that her star players weren't at the station yet.

"Has he seen a doctor? Maybe we should get Michael."

Charlotte started to move toward the stairs, but James stopped her. "He'll be fine. I just left them. They should be here soon."

That made her feel somewhat better, but James's initial demand she stay in town rushed back.

"What does the attack have to do with me?" Then she saw it in his eyes, the intensity that came with overprotectiveness. "You think it was related to all the other things going on. Welsh, the rooms being ransacked, the note."

His eyes turned glacial. "York heard one of the men say, 'That should do it. Earned our tenner.' I don't think it had anything to do with his wallet, though they robbed him too."

"But you don't know for sure."

There was certainly an element in Cordova who would happily relieve anyone of their money, particularly if they thought the victim was well-to-do. But she had a similar feeling the attack on Peter may not have been random.

He jostled her arm slightly. "I don't need hard evidence to see what might be going on here, Charlotte. I think someone put those men on to York. Someone who wants to scare people off the film. They won't leave you out of it because you're a woman or because you're a local."

Charlotte crossed her arms, her back stiff. "Are you forbidding me from going, Deputy?"

"I—" He cut himself off, pressing his lips together, and released her arm. After taking a deep breath, his eyes went from angry and intense to concerned and intense. "I know that would only prompt you to go anyway. I'm strongly suggesting you stay here. Strongly."

Did he think that their being intimate gave him say in how she lived her life or did her job? Hardly.

"I appreciate your concern and understand your reasoning, but you're right, I'd only defy your wishes. I'm going."

"Even if I ask you as someone who cares about what happens to you?"

Her resistance and stubbornness softened some, and Charlotte laid her palm on his cheek. "You have a job to do. So do I. It'll be fine. We'll help each other find out who did this."

"I can't convince you otherwise, can I?" He seemed more disturbed by that fact than usual. As progressive as James could be, some of his Southern gentleman charms like protecting women remained, but Charlotte wasn't about to hide behind his sense of chivalry.

She kissed him. "No."

When they parted, James removed his hat and ran his hand through his hair. "I figured as much."

"I'm glad you're learning so quickly."

The slamming of car doors drew their attention. Roslyn and Peter had emerged from one of Clive's taxis. Cicely hurried over to them. Peter grinned and nodded at whatever she'd said. Was his left eye swollen? It was difficult to tell. The trio made their way toward the platform, Peter moving gingerly. In the distance, the train whistle blew.

James hefted his pack higher onto his shoulder. "Do me a favor while we're out there, Charlotte?"

She almost said "Anything" but didn't want to make promises. "What?"

He picked up her bag, a gesture she knew would make him feel a little better. "Don't get into too much trouble."

Charlotte laughed. "I'll see what I can do about that."

Snow swirled away from the wheels of the train as it crossed the icy river flats. Luckily, there hadn't been much in the way of drifts to slow the train's progress, but the continued suppressed mood aboard made Charlotte wonder if the company would manage to pull together and finish the film. Everyone headed to the glacier had said they were for it, but once Peter York's assault became public knowledge, would Cicely have the force of will and leadership skills to maintain her influence over them?

Charlotte watched Peter as she chatted with Roslyn, Cicely, and Paige. He smiled often, as usual, but winced and held his side when the train rocked a little too hard.

How was he going to perform such a physical role for the film?

"Which of them would have sent a couple of thugs after Peter?" Charlotte asked James quietly.

James had his hat tilted over his eyes and his chin at his chest, appearing to be asleep, a copy of Burroughs's *Tarzan of the Apes* in his lap. He lifted the brim of his hat and looked at the group through slitted eyes. "They all can afford to hire toughs for the job, but actually go that route? The only one I wouldn't suspect is York himself, but men have done stranger things."

"That would be rather drastic, to hire men to beat you just to throw the crew into a dither. Besides, Peter really isn't a suspect, is he?" Charlotte thought about the suspect array she'd drawn up at home. Who else would have had the wherewithal to have Peter attacked? "Burrows and Smith know a number of people in town."

"True. Though it wouldn't take much of anything for a visitor to figure out where to find someone and hire them for the job." James tilted the brim down again and closed his eyes. "Don't worry about who hired whom so much as why."

Charlotte said the first thing that came to mind. "To scare the crew. More violence happening could make them rethink their decision and leave Cicely without means to finish filming. Or if Peter can't perform, they may have to quit altogether."

"Agreed. Anything else?"

She considered another angle. "If Peter was specifically targeted, however, it might mean he knows something and was being warned."

James grunted. "Hadn't considered that."

Charlotte smiled and nudged his shoulder. "Good thing I'm here."

He opened his eyes halfway and gave her a sidelong look. "Uh-huh."

With no intention of revisiting that argument, she said, "That seems to be what we keep circling back to, isn't it? Stopping the film from being made."

"Unless that isn't the reason for Welsh's death." James settled in again, eyes closed. "Time to figure that out."

There was much of the same activity and clamor as the first arrival when the train reached the platform at Childs Glacier.

There were fewer people to offload freight, but less freight as well. The dogs, as usual, seemed to be as excited as ever, and when they finished their duty of delivering larger crates to the necessary locations, Dave directed the team out across the frozen flats for a run. Never had Charlotte seen or heard six happier dogs.

To conserve fuel in the kerosene heaters, Charlotte bunked with Paige and Elaine the costumer. Three cots in the tent made for a tight fit, but it would be warmer and more efficient. Smitty the supply master was a stickler for efficiency of labor and material usage. The arrangement also gave Charlotte a chance to chat with Paige while Elaine was overseeing the preparation of costumes in the shed.

"I appreciate you letting me stay with you," Charlotte said. "I promise not to be a burden."

Paige glanced up from where she was fitting sheets over the mattress of her cot and smiled. "Not a problem. Though I'm sure you'd rather be with that deputy. I would, if I were you."

Charlotte's cheeks heated. She and James certainly hadn't tried to hide their relationship, but she didn't think they'd been overly demonstrative. "I imagine there would be all manner of trouble if we tried to share a tent."

The actress rolled her eyes. "Tell me about it. Heck, there are some directors who won't let married people share dressing rooms and the like. It's ridiculous."

Charlotte had to agree that it did seem more prudish than necessary. "Maybe the directors feel that too much intimacy and closeness creates tension."

Paige shrugged, then flicked over the bed one of the two wool blankets they'd been issued. "All I know is that keeping people apart can be just as tense. Sex is good for relaxation, know what I mean?"

Indeed, she did, but it could also add a source of upheaval to any relationship.

"Can I ask you something about your relationship with Stanley?" Charlotte kept busy with making her own bed in an attempt to appear as casual as possible. There were two blankets to each bed, both of lesser quality than the one found with Welsh, from what Charlotte could tell.

"Sure, but I think you have the gist of it." From her tone, Paige was just as willing to be nonchalant.

"I do, but there's something I don't quite understand." Charlotte sat on her cot facing the other woman. "Why, Paige? I saw you in rehearsals and on the stage. You're quite good. Why did you feel the need to sleep with Welsh?"

Paige paused in her domestic chore, her head dropping for just a moment before she lifted her chin and turned to Charlotte. There was a hardness in her blue eyes, but a hint of sadness as well. "Because I'm no beauty like Roslyn Sanford. I'm not funny like Mabel Normand, or sweet and innocent like Mary Pickford. Am I keen on the idea that sleeping with the director *might* get me a break? No, but I'm not the first and I won't be the last to do it, I tell you what." A small smile curved her bow of a mouth. "And in all honesty? I like men."

Charlotte couldn't fault her that at all. "But I'd imagine it was frustrating too."

She had seen and heard Paige's reaction to Welsh pushing her aside.

"It was, but I'm nothing if not persistent." Paige sat on her bed. "You think I might have killed him."

"I think you had motive, yes, but so did several people." Charlotte hoped she hadn't tipped her hand. "You never said where you were that night."

Paige shook her head and gave a humorless laugh. "You know what's funny? I *did* try to seduce Stanley that evening. Caught him on his way back from the latrine. But Stanley got distracted, then hurried off. Thought I saw someone by the corner of his tent, but I'm not sure."

Is that when he and Burrows met near the rubbish bins?

Charlotte sat up straight. "Why didn't you say this before?"

"In front of his wife and Cicely?" The actress rolled her eyes. "I'm not that crass. Besides, I didn't see who it was. If I were you," Paige continued, "I'd be asking Carmen a few more questions."

"Carmen?" Charlotte let her surprise show. Not that she'd ever crossed the wife off the list of suspects, but Carmen certainly wasn't at the top. "She was asleep."

"Was she?" Paige clearly thought the women had probably lied about that. Charlotte had to admit it was possible. They only had Carmen's word, though Cecily had corroborated that her mother regularly took a sleeping draught.

"How would she have gotten Stanley out there alone? She doesn't seem particularly strong to me." Carmen could have strangled him, if he was influenced by his medicine, but as with Paige herself, Charlotte didn't think Mrs. Welsh could have dragged her husband that far.

"True," Paige said, "but Carmen was very tra-la-la for a woman who knew her husband slept around, if you know what I mean. We didn't flaunt it, of course, but she knew about me and Stanley. And Stanley and other girls, truth be told."

"Maybe they had an agreement."

Paige stood and shrugged. "Maybe, though she was awful militant when it came to where he went and what he did. Stanley and I rarely saw each other outside of the studio. Everything not related to a film went through Carmen. She made all their social arrangements and even picked out his clothes. She fixed all their meals too, even though they could afford a cook on staff, because Stanley needed food prepared a certain way."

Charlotte tilted her head. "Had a doctor prescribed a particular diet?"

"Not that I know of. Stanley's family was from Prague, and I heard his mother made sure Carmen learned how to make six kinds of dumplings and cabbage strudel before they married. Since then, Carmen always made his food when they ate at home." Paige donned her coat and hat. "Listen, I don't want you to think I have anything against Carmen, because I don't. She's got her ways about her, sure, but never did anything to me. I'm gonna grab some coffee. I'll see you later."

Paige sauntered out of the tent, leaving Charlotte to wonder about Carmen Welsh. The new widow may have looked the other way when it came to her husband's affairs, but that didn't mean she didn't have feelings about them.

Charlotte stood outside of Carmen's tent. "Mrs. Welsh? Are you in there? It's Charlotte Brody. I was wondering if we could chat for a few minutes."

Other members of the cast and crew hurried about camp as wind and snow blew down the mountains, across the glacier, and right into their midst. The idea of filming before the sun set was quickly fading from possibility. Not far away, Cicely Welsh spoke to Roger Markham, arm waving out toward the ice field. Markham nodded and pointed as well, obviously more agreeable with what Cicely had in mind than what Welsh had proposed.

A blustery gust rippled the tent wall, revealing a smudge on the otherwise pristine canvas under the protective cover. What was that?

"Come in, Miss Brody," Carmen called.

Grateful to get out of the cold, Charlotte quickly opened the tent flap and just as quickly secured it behind her. Unlike the other accommodations, the Welshes' tent had been left untouched when the cast and crew had returned to Cordova, save for personal items. The cots, linens, and makeshift clothing racks and shelves all remained as James had described them the morning they'd discovered Welsh's body.

Carmen stood in the center of the tent, her coat open as the kerosene heater warmed up. She wore a dark blue wool suit, likely the most somber clothing she had with her, as one didn't travel expecting to don widow's weeds. Her suitcase was open on her neatly made cot. Some items had been hung up, others placed on the shelves.

"Please excuse the mess, Miss Brody. What can I do for you?"

Charlotte noticed the second cot—Welsh's—was still made up. No one had bothered to strip it before they returned to Cordova, and it seemed that Carmen was in no rush to carry out that chore yet. Perhaps it was more comforting to have the cot made up as if Stanley would be returning, rather than a bare mattress.

The two thick blankets were neatly tucked around the mattress, but something struck Charlotte. The blankets on the director's bed were solid brown and fluffier than the beige with blue stripes wool blankets on Carmen's. Though Carmen's blankets appeared to be of softer, finer quality than the wool blankets on Charlotte's own cot, more like the one Welsh had with him when he died.

"I was curious about something," Charlotte said, her gaze darting to the covers. "Mr. Welsh kept his medicine at hand, in case he needed it."

"That's right."

"Would he have taken the bottle when he was just going to the lavatory tent or to retrieve another blanket?"

Carmen shook her head slightly, her brow wrinkled. "At home, he kept it on the table by his bed, like the one there. He must have simply forgotten it in his coat pocket that night. Maybe that's what he was looking for in the dark, then decided while he was up he'd use the lavatory."

Charlotte's heart hitched. "You were awake?"

Paige had suggested Carmen might not have been as out of it as she'd claimed.

Carmen blinked at her, confused for a moment before something dawned in her dark eyes. "Oh, I thought I'd slept through his leaving the tent, but yes, I think I remember him fumbling with his coat over there on the rack." Her brow furrowed. "At least I believe he did. Could I have been imagining it?"

Charlotte considered the widow. Was she truly confused or trying to put one over on Charlotte? "I suppose it's possible you were awake for a brief time, especially if Mr. Welsh was fumbling about."

Between the darkness and his own state, Welsh could have been making enough noise to wake his wife. There had been the sound of something falling, Charlotte recalled.

"I found his shaving kit on the floor that morning. He must have knocked it from the shelf there." Carmen lowered herself down onto the edge of her cot. "You know, Stanley wouldn't have been looking for another blanket from the supply shed. He was terribly allergic to wool, and that's all they had there when we asked Smitty about extras." She gestured toward his bed. "Those are heavy cotton and silk blends that we bought especially for this trip. We brought them up ourselves."

The blanket found under Welsh was similar to the ones currently on Mrs. Welsh's cot, Charlotte assumed. And definitely wool from what Michael had said. Unless Welsh was severely affected by his medicine, or more concerned with staying warm than itching all night, Charlotte was pretty sure he wouldn't have taken a spare blanket from the supply shed.

If the director wouldn't have been out looking for warmer covers, whose blanket had gone into the crevasse with him?

"Mrs. Welsh, can I ask you about Mr. Welsh's relationship with Paige Carmichael?"

Carmen stiffened, her chin rising slightly. A small, tense smile curved her red lips. "You mean about their affair? She wasn't the first, Miss Brody, and likely wouldn't have been the last."

"You knew of them?" What sort of marriage had they had?

Carmen lowered her gaze to where her hand smoothed the

blanket beneath her. "At first, I was devastated. I'd done so much to attract him, to please him, but it wasn't enough." She looked up at Charlotte again, her eyes filling. "But Stanley explained it to me. He was a passionate man in all his endeavors. One woman couldn't withstand all that. So he saw other women, but always came home to me."

Tears fell and she lowered her gaze.

Oh, brother. Carmen didn't seem like the type to fall for the "I'm too much for one woman" line, but who really knew what anyone thought behind their public face?

"I'm sorry, Mrs. Welsh. I didn't mean to upset you." Though how Charlotte thought a discussion about her dead husband's infidelity wouldn't upset Carmen crossed her mind a little too late. *Nicely done*, the sarcastic voice in her head whispered.

"Do you think—" Carmen brought her fist to her mouth as if to stifle a sob. "Do you think Paige had something to do with Stanley's death?"

"She's not a strong suspect," was all Charlotte would say. She honestly didn't believe the petite blonde was physically capable of strangling Welsh and then dragging his body two hundred yards. Unless she had an accomplice they didn't know about.

Carmen nodded, her head still lowered.

"Again, my apologies." Charlotte retreated from the tent, securing the flap behind her.

While she felt bad about dredging up Welsh and Paige, Charlotte couldn't help but be intrigued by the information she'd learned. The snagged wool and drag marks beside the dog pen, and Welsh's allergy, gave credence to the theory that he hadn't wandered off onto the glacier on his own after getting another blanket. Had he gone out to meet Paige after Carmen was asleep? Who had distracted him from her wiles?

Shoulders hunched against the wind and blowing snow once again, Charlotte mulled over the new bits of information as she made her way to the main tent. A few of the cast and crew were seated inside, chatting or playing cards. The others may have still been settling in or helping with equipment for the next day. Smitty and his two assistants were busy at the cook stoves behind the tables that would soon be laden with food.

Steam and delicious aromas wafted over as the three men toiled in shirtsleeves and aprons, mixing, peeling, or stirring. Smitty, thick arms bared to the elbow and tattooed lady dancing on his forearm as he worked, joked and chatted around an unlit cigar in the corner of his mouth.

He glanced up as Charlotte approached. "Uh-oh, boys. Looks like fun time's over."

The two other men made playful sounds of disappointment, grinning as they continued with their tasks.

"Far be it from me to impede on your amusements, gentlemen," Charlotte said, laughing. "Though I'd appreciate a word or two, Mr. Smitty."

His bushy eyebrows rose. One of the men gave a soft wolf whistle.

"Quiet, you," Smitty said as he set his bowl down on the table. "Let me grab us a couple cups of coffee."

Charlotte nodded thanks and made her way to the farthest table from any others. The few folks in the tent watched curiously as Smitty joined her and set down the mugs.

"What can I do for you, ma'am?"

Charlotte wrapped her hands around the warm ceramic. "You play a critical role here on location. So much to coordinate. I was wondering about your inventory and how you keep track of everything."

"It's as accurate as it can be under the circumstances," he said, shaking his head. "These folks ain't regular army, yanno, so I have to watch things like a hawk. If I can't account for supplies, Mr. Meade gets boilin' mad."

That didn't surprise Charlotte in the least. "He's careful about money."

Smitty shrugged. "Yes and no. I mean, he has me practically counting the number of beans we serve, but then insists on steak for dinner."

"That does seem unusual." Charlotte checked to make sure the others in the tent had deemed her conversation with Smitty too boring to follow. To be on the safe side, she lowered her voice. "What about the blankets? I noticed there are different, shall we say, qualities and materials."

"Yeah, most of us get a couple of decent wool blankets. The muckety-mucks were given a higher-quality wool. Gotta keep them toastier than the rest of us." He was grinning when he spoke, giving Charlotte the impression that he was used to the "muckety-mucks" in any operation, be it army or film, getting better quality items or food than the enlisted men.

"Has anyone been complaining of the cold?"

"Of course," Smitty said. "We're not used to this sort of weather. I told Mr. Meade folks would be barking about the cold and we'd need more blankets or more kerosene, but he said we'd all make due for the short time." The former soldier shook his head. "An army or a film crew depends on even its lowest-ranking member being as well-supplied as possible. Can't have folks freezing or getting sick and expect them to get the job done."

"Good point." Charlotte sipped her still piping-hot coffee. "So no one's been trying to sneak more covers or fuel or anything?"

"Nah, they're a good group and know they only have to ask for anything they need. Besides," he said, patting his hip, "I keep the supply shed locked. These guys are great, but I don't need stuff disappearing."

"You have the only key?" Charlotte mentally crossed her fingers, hoping he'd say no.

"Yep."

Damnation.

"Except when someone borrows it, but I have them bring it right back."

Charlotte's hopes rose. "Anyone borrow it lately? Say, on the day Mr. Welsh was found?"

"Nah, too much going on elsewhere." A thoughtful expression furrowed his brow. "Though the following day, when we were packing up to leave, the door was unlocked for most of the morning while the boys and I put things away. We didn't want too much left in the tents, not knowing when we'd get back out and all."

"And you took inventory as you stored things?"

"Sure. Didn't want stuff walking off. Mr. Meade says we'll be selling a lot of the supplies back to the merchants or to whomever wants 'em."

"Isn't it just as easy to take inventory when all of this is over?"

"Easier, yes, but that ain't how I run things, ma'am." He was smiling again. "When I'm in charge of keeping track of supplies, they are kept track of. Everything's accounted for, down to the last bag of beans."

"And the number of blankets?" Perhaps she was showing a bit too much of her hand, but Charlotte wanted to know how Welsh had gotten his extra, allergy-inducing wool blanket if the shed was locked. Or when his killer had been able to replace their own?

"Yep, 'cept for the one the doctor took with Mr. Welsh, all were locked in the shed before the train left." Smitty scratched at his chin. "Course, people were bringing stuff in and marking their names off a list. The boys and I double-checked the count before locking up and it was all jake."

So the killer could have slipped into the shed with their items, marked off the return of two blankets when only one was brought back, and no one would have known the difference in the end. Double damnation. If only she and James had considered the blanket situation before the following morning. They could have gone to each tent to see who was short a blanket.

"What about the accoutrements in the Welshes' tent? Were those part of your inventory?"

No one else had much in the way of furnishings, as far as Charlotte knew.

Smitty shook his head. "Only the cots, linens, and Mrs. W's blankets. She asked that we not disturb things, even though we didn't know if or when we'd be back out. Said she'd get someone to pack their personal items later, if need be. I'm not one to argue with a widow."

"Understandable. Thank you very much for your time, Mr. Smitty." Charlotte smiled at the quartermaster and rose. "You've helped a great deal."

Smitty stood as well. "Happy to oblige. Mr. Welsh wasn't always easy to get along with, but he was a decent sort. Hell, I even tried to make one of his favorite dishes. Was grateful and all, but said it was too garlicky. Thought he liked garlic."

"Why's that?"

The crewmen gathered their coffee mugs. "Smelled it on him all the time. Figured he enjoyed it. Anything else, Miss Brody? I gotta get those rolls made."

"Not that I can think of." Charlotte buttoned her coat and set her hat on her head. "Thank you again. See you at dinner."

Smitty nodded, then turned to the cooking area, issuing orders to his assistants as he walked toward them.

Warmed from the coffee and the heat from the cook tent, Charlotte went in search of James. The whistle of an incoming train sounded and Charlotte instinctively looked in that direction. A puff of black smoke rose from behind a low hill. Within seconds, she felt the rumble of the engine and saw it as it came into view, slowing at the nearby platform in order to make an unscheduled stop on its way to Cordova.

There wouldn't be tourists out this time of year. The film company had requested the railroad curtail unnecessary stops while they worked, to keep folks out of the way. Several of the film crew peered over at the tracks as a boy of thirteen or so jumped down off the train and ran toward the camp, one hand clamped down on his hat. He spoke to one of the men on the outskirts of the site. The man turned and pointed up the ice slope, toward Charlotte. The boy nodded, then ran to her.

Charlotte's heart seemed to still and cramp. What was wrong? Was Becca hurt? Michael?

"You Miss Brody?" the boy called, out of breath as he approached. In his other hand he held a sheet of cream-colored paper. "I got a message for Deputy Eddington."

Relief washed through Charlotte, but if someone had telegraphed or telephoned up to Chitina and sent this boy down with a message for the deputy, it wasn't good.

"He's in the middle of an investigation," she said, turning toward the glacier. "Out there, I believe."

The boy stared out across the ice as he caught his breath. "Marshal Blaine needs him back in town right quick. Or rather, Mrs. Blaine does. She's the one who called."

"Oh no," Charlotte said with real concern. While she didn't know Marshal Blaine very well, he almost always had a smile and a kind word for her when they met. "Is it serious?"

"It's his heart, I guess." The boy shook his head. "Don't know what shape he's in, but he ain't good."

"When does the train pass back through?" she asked.

"Not till tomorrow." Anything could happen between now and then. "I heard Mrs. Blaine talking to my pa over the telephone. He's the telegraph man in Chitina. She sounded pretty dang upset."

Charlotte knew Mrs. Blaine to be a fairly even-tempered woman who had seen it all. If she was loud enough over the telephone that the boy heard her end of the conversation, things weren't good for Marshal Blaine.

The boy rubbed his arms, shivering. "What do you want me to tell the conductor?"

Charlotte glanced at the train waiting at the platform, then up toward the glacier where she could just see James's tall figure approaching. "Tell the conductor to wait. Deputy Eddington will be there as soon as he can to head back to Cordova."

Chapter 14

Charlotte met James, who had been retracing the path the killer or killers likely took to dispose of Stanley Welsh. He was taking the route in reverse to help see things from a different angle when Charlotte stopped him. She relayed the verbal message about Marshal Blaine, as well as handing him the paper that had been delivered. He read it over, his brow creases deepening.

"I told the boy to have the conductor wait for you," Charlotte said.

He stopped reading and met her eyes. "You should come back with me."

She shook her head. "I have a story to finish."

"And I have a murderer to catch. A murderer who is likely out here with you." There was concern as well as anger in his voice.

Charlotte drew a slow breath, tamping down her own worry and agitation. "James, the Blaines need you there. Mrs. Blaine asked for you specifically."

The hardness in his eyes softened some. He had worked for

the marshal for several years and knew the Blaines weren't the type of folks to get upset over nothing.

"I don't want to do this."

Charlotte wasn't quite sure if he meant leaving her there or having to deal with Marshal Blaine's illness. She wrapped her arms around him, pressing her cheek against the front of his mackinaw. His arms encircled her shoulders.

"I know," she said softly. "Come on."

Without so much as a word of agreement or discussion, they continued along James's original path back to camp, exchanging thoughts on the case. It wasn't a direct line to the tent where he would need to collect his gear, and the conductor was probably getting antsy waiting, but neither James nor Charlotte were too concerned about another few minutes.

As they approached the dog pen, the six canines gave them a hopeful look of escape but soon went back to snoozing in their hay piles when neither James nor Charlotte made any effort to engage them. Even Byron, Dave's brutish-looking but friendly wheel dog, did little more than thump his tail.

"I spoke to Mrs. Welsh and Smitty." She told James about Welsh's allergy and the locked supply shed. "Unfortunately, the killer managed to cover up the fact their second wool blanket had been dropped in the crevasse."

"That pretty much confirms that Welsh didn't go out on the ice alone," James said, "but doesn't give us anything in the way of a direction to follow toward who did it."

They walked between the supply sheds and the main tent, both alternately scanning the snow-packed path and the temporary buildings.

"Whoever did it," Charlotte said, "likely dragged him behind the meal tent, past the supply sheds, then past the dogs before heading onto the ice. That way the big tent would hide them if anyone was out and about."

"Chances of anyone being out are small in the middle of a frigid night."

"True, but would you want to risk being seen by some brave soul with a small bladder?"

James laughed. "No, I suppose not." His amusement didn't last long. "I can't see anyone being capable of dragging a body far before they're winded, somewhat slick surface or no."

Charlotte considered the tents nearest the ice. "Mine and Becca's. Cicely and Roslyn's is beside us, closer to the mess. Behind us were Paige and Elaine, and the Welshes behind Cicely's. Past those, Peter and Roger, and Meade's."

"Burrows and Smith and the rest of the company were farther away," James said, pointing to the right. "Over there?"

"Yes, that's right."

"If Cicely or Roslyn had killed him in their tent, do you think they would have dragged him all the way to the backside of the mess, past two other tents?" James asked.

Charlotte shook her head. "That does seem rather silly. If I had just killed a man and wanted to get rid of the body, I'd do it as quickly as possible."

"Exactly." He set his hands on his hips. "Why were the tents assigned as they were?"

"Mrs. Welsh wanted to be away from the front of the main tent so she wouldn't have to hear the company coming and going," Charlotte said. "But Stanley was experiencing a stomach ailment, so he wanted to be somewhat closer to the latrine."

"Not the most pleasant location, but with everything freezing the smell wouldn't be bad."

Charlotte wrinkled her nose. "I hadn't thought of that."

"You haven't lived with an outhouse in the summer," he said. "Winter isn't so bad, though."

"Thank goodness for indoor plumbing."

James started forward and Charlotte kept in step with him. He walked the trodden path between the mess tent and the line of three others.

"Are these still assigned to the same folks?" he asked.

"The one Becca and I was in is currently empty, but I think so."

Cicely and Roslyn's was first. James quietly circled the tent, looking at the canvas, the ground. He lifted his head and looked out toward the ice field.

"Not ideal to drag a body directly from here," Charlotte said. "But scared, desperate people do odd things."

"That is true," James said, bringing his gaze back to her. "The straw scattered in front of the dogs' pen, and the fact there's some imbedded in the blanket that went into the crevasse with Welsh tells me the body was dragged closer to there, not directly from here."

"Around the back of the main tent?" Charlotte imagined Cicely and Roslyn taking Welsh all the way behind the mess tent, then along the path between the supply sheds and in front of the dog pen. Would they have considered the longer, more strenuous route less of a risk than directly going out on the ice? Between the two of them, they could have. "I think they're still suspects."

James nodded slowly, a thoughtful expression on his face. "All circumstantial theorizing, though. Not a shred of physical evidence to connect them to the body."

"Except for Cicely's bruise." Charlotte didn't quite believe that the scenarist had been injured while she and Roslyn were rehearsing, but no one could prove otherwise.

"Still not evidence," he reminded her, "unless someone can corroborate its origin, and no one can." Seeing nothing more, he moved on to the next tent. "The Welshes?"

"Yes, though Carmen was probably in a drugged sleep while Stanley was being killed, she thinks she woke up for a moment and saw him fumbling at his things."

"So she says." James's voice held more than a hint of disbelief, as his job required.

"Paige didn't believe it either, but I don't trust *her* to tell the complete truth."

"You think Carmen could have killed Stanley and dragged him to the crevasse alone?" Now he sounded incredulous, and Charlotte couldn't blame him.

"Who said alone?" She gestured to the camp. "There are able-bodied men all over the place. A few kind words, promises, and a payoff could get a woman some muscle."

"Like the men who beat the hell out of York," James said.

Charlotte hadn't considered Carmen as a suspect in the assault on the actor, but it wouldn't be unheard of for a woman to hire someone to take care of physical jobs for her. Especially one who didn't seem to like to get her hands dirty. "Possibly, but again, no evidence against her for either crime."

"She was very cooperative regarding her husband's personal belongings, letting me look through their tent. What sort of killer allows that?" he asked.

"A very shrewd one," Charlotte said.

"Maybe. That's Meade's tent at the end." James led the way to the producer's tent. "Convenient to the back of the mess and the path in front of the dog pen."

"He's strong enough," Charlotte said. "When we were unloading the freight that first day, Meade pitched in and handled some very heavy boxes on his own."

"Motive is good too, if what your fresh-faced boy Billy said about Meade and Welsh fighting over money is true." James frowned at something on the tent wall. "What's this?"

Charlotte stepped closer. A dark brownish smear marred the canvas. "Is it blood?"

He scraped at the edge of the mark with a fingernail. "Looks like it. But no way to know whose."

Stanley Welsh didn't have much in the way of visible injuries, Charlotte recalled. The worst injury was on the side of his head. "Unless Stanley rubbed his head on Meade's tent after he was dead, I wouldn't think it was his."

James wiped his hands on his trousers. "It may—"

"Is there something I can help you with?" Wallace Meade asked loudly from behind them.

Both Charlotte and James turned. Meade strode down the path between the mess tent and the three sleeping quarters.

"What's this on your tent?" James asked, gesturing toward the mark.

Meade came closer and squinted at the smudge. "Blood," he said matter-of-factly.

He held up his right hand and gingerly removed the glove. A bloodstained bandage was wrapped around his hand. He showed James and Charlotte the palm and its dime-sized red blotch. As he shoved his hands into his pockets, Charlotte glimpsed a similarly sized mark on the back of his hand.

"I was going through some correspondence and my letter opener slipped. Nasty jab, it was." Meade eyed them both. "Anything else you'd like to know?"

Plenty, thought Charlotte, but when she caught James's eye she noted the slight shake of his head. She held her tongue. James straightened to his full six-foot-plus height, his blue eyes hard.

"I'm doing what the territory and federal governments have charged me to do, sir," he said to Meade. "The fact a man died on your site as the result of foul play should concern you."

The producer stiffened, his eyes narrowing, but then he seemed to realize who he was, in fact, speaking to. His shoulders dropped slightly. "My apologies, Deputy. If there's anything more I can help you with, just let me know."

James tugged the brim of his hat. "I'll do that. Good day."

He and Charlotte stepped aside to allow Meade to enter his tent. His gloved hand grasped the canvas right over the bloodstain. At least they knew it was Meade's blood and how it got there. But something about the wound niggled at Charlotte.

Charlotte took James's arm and drew him back to the Welshes' tent. She lifted the cover over the opening. A smear, similar to the one on Meade's tent, but smaller.

"What do you think?" he asked.

"I think it's odd that the two tents have the same sorts of stains. And that Meade must use one helluva letter opener," Charlotte said. "How did he get blood on both sides of his hand? Fighting with Stanley?"

James shook his head. "Probably not. When people fight, both parties tend to end up with some sort of wound. Scrapes or bruises. Welsh didn't have anything on his hands, and the bruising your brother found was concentrated around his neck, not on his face or body." He grinned at her raised eyebrow. "Yes, I have noted such things in my personal experience, both as attacker and defender."

"So however Meade sustained the injury, it wasn't in a fight or with a letter opener. And why is there blood on the Welshes' tent?" Charlotte heard voices coming from the front of the mess tent. It sounded like the company was taking a break from the morning's film schedule. "Still, not much to go on."

"Other than that Meade is lying," James said.

"But why?"

"That's a very good question."

He turned her so they faced each other. Staring into her eyes, he caressed her from shoulders to elbow. "Come back to town with me. I'll feel a lot better knowing you're safe."

It was tempting to say yes, but he wasn't the only one with a job to do. "It's only a few days. I'll be fine."

"A lot can happen in a few days, in a few hours," he said, his brow furrowed. "At least promise to just watch and listen."

"I'll be careful." She rose up on her toes and kissed him, not quite agreeing to what he'd asked for. "Come on, the conductor's waiting."

After saying good-bye to James, Charlotte joined the company when they returned to the glacier for filming. Cicely's revision of the scenario dispensed with Roslyn's character Dorothy falling into the crevasse. Understandable, considering the circumstances. Now, there was a rogue working for the evil mining company who kidnaps Dorothy. He was currently holding her at gunpoint while the cameras cranked and she waited to be rescued by Peter's character Lawrence and his Native friend Lewis.

Peter moved normally, as far as Charlotte could tell, but he was definitely uncomfortable. His periodic winces added to Lawrence's concern over Dorothy.

"What do you think?" Charlotte asked Caleb Burrows, who stood with her.

Arms crossed, Burrows watched the action play out on the ice. "Better. The partnership between the men is preferable to when they had Lewis being a ridiculous caricature."

Cicely called for a stop in the action via the megaphone, then spoke to the players and crew without the cone. A very different approach than her father.

"Do you think that would have been so if Stanley hadn't died?" Charlotte asked. She watched the lawyer's face, but he didn't react other than pressing his lips together in thought.

"Doubtful," he finally said, eyes still on the crew. "Welsh was a good one to make vague promises, then conveniently forget what he'd said. Unless we got it in writing, signed in blood, I doubt Stanley Welsh would have followed through."

Paige Carmichael had said essentially the same thing about Welsh's promises to her. He always found excuses to go back on his word. That pattern had certainly made Paige angry.

"Let's do it again," Cicely called out. "Ted, you have Roslyn at gunpoint after chasing her onto the ice. Good. Now, Peter and Lewis, come on scene. Ted, you turn and see them. Peter, go after the gun. You're fighting over it and boom! It goes off."

All of the players froze, eyes wide.

Only Roger Markham and his other cameraman moved at all, peering through their viewfinders and cranking. The second man, engrossed in the scene, suddenly tripped and slid. As he fell, he curled his body in an effort to cradle the expensive camera. Taking the brunt of the fall on his back, however, he hit his head. The camera bounced against his shoulder and landed on the ice with a crack of wood and glass. The door to the housing popped open and a reel of film rolled out.

Gasps and expletives sounded. Everyone rushed over to the fallen man as carefully as they could cross the ice to avoid the same fate. He sat up slowly, dazed, and rubbing at what was sure to be a heck of a goose egg.

"Are you all right, Andy?" Roslyn asked.

Andy seemed to be none the worse for wear, but the film they'd shot was lost.

"Okay, everyone," Cicely said, obviously disappointed as she rubbed the side of her hand across her forehead. "Let's break for lunch. We'll do another take later, if the light and weather cooperate."

Roger Markham picked up Andy's camera. Andy collected the spoiled film, shaking his head as he and the others started to walk carefully down off the glacier. Despite the interruption of the day's filming, the mood of the company seemed light and friendly from what Charlotte could tell as they passed her and Burrows.

Roslyn stopped beside Cicely, the two had their heads bowed toward each other, speaking quietly. Roslyn laid her hand on Cicely's arm, then hugged the newly minted director. Cicely closed her eyes, smiling.

Their affection for each other was obvious. If her father had threatened them, threatened to expose their relationship, would one or both of them have killed the man? Strangulation was often a crime of immediacy, opportunity, and passion, not typically how one planned to kill another person.

"Shall we head back, Miss Brody?" Burrows offered his arm.

Charlotte looped her arm through his and together they fol-

lowed the crew to the camp. "What would you have done if Mr.
Welsh hadn't died and refused to change the story?"

"As I said, we would have filed a libel complaint."

"Which would have probably been ignored or dismissed."

Burrows nodded. "Probably, but it would have brought attention to the discriminations. Would we have won anything?
Not likely. Would it have caused Meade and Welsh some problems? One would hope."

"Talking to either of them was getting you nowhere; there
would have been no other course of action," Charlotte said as
they drew closer to the main tent and the group of film people
ahead of them.

"There's always something that can be done, Miss Brody.
Not necessarily pretty, but something to accomplish the job."

The question was, what would that "something" be for a man
like Burrows?

As lunch finished and the wind continued to blow snow, Cicely Welsh and some members of the company lingered at a
table, dirty dishes set aside and pages of the scenario spread before them. Cicely's quiet manner was quite different from her
father, Charlotte observed. Perhaps that's why some, like Wallace Meade, didn't think the scenarist would be capable of making the transition to director. They were used to a director who
dictated. Cicely was more inclined to listen to her players and
crew, taking in their expertise before making a decision.

Charlotte refilled her coffee cup, then sat beside Meade, who
watched the group across the tent with his arms folded and his
brow furrowed. Every now and again, his gaze darted to the
cooking area where Smitty and his men worked. The three ban-
tered as they cleaned up and prepared the evening meal, paying
little attention to those around them.

"Cicely seems to be doing a fine job, don't you think, Mr.
Meade?" Knowing the man's opposition to continuing the film

with young Miss Welsh at the helm, Charlotte was sure the question would receive a significant response. She was not disappointed.

"Directors direct, they don't go about asking everyone down to the set painters what they think." His scowl deepened.

"I think she's well aware of her inexperience," Charlotte said, "and is seeking the advice of people who have been doing this for a while. Like Roger Markham. I heard him explaining what he could and couldn't do with his cameras."

Meade gave Charlotte a sidelong glance. "Yes, I'm sure Markham is relieved to have Cicely to deal with rather than Stanley. She's much more likely to give in to his recommendations."

Was Meade insinuating that the cameraman had something to do with Welsh's death? Markham had been protesting practically from the day they arrived in Alaska that the director was asking too much, putting cast and crew in too much danger. Had his concern for the safety of the company led him to a rash action?

"On the bright side," Meade continued, "it saves me from footing the bill for a boat that Stanley wanted for that iceberg scene."

Ah, yes, the focus of a producer's concerns: money.

"Is *North to Fortune* over budget?" Charlotte had heard an original budget of thirty thousand dollars, a mind-boggling amount to begin with. Where was the money coming from? Meade mentioned studio budgets and private investors, but would never go into any more detail than that.

The tight smile in his face told Charlotte much more than his words. "Incidentals and unexpected expenses happen on all projects, especially ones of this magnitude."

In her conversation with Billy, Charlotte had learned about a few of those added expenses. "You mean like Stanley Welsh ordering a set repainted or rebuilt numerous times."

Meade's eyes hardened. "That's what I'm here for, to remind these folks that their art costs money."

"Do you think Cicely will listen better than Stanley?"

The producer looked at the table where the others worked over the scenario. Cicely and Roslyn, sitting side by side, were smiling, and Roger Markham actually laughed. "She sure as hell can't be much worse."

A blast of icy wind rippled through the mess as one of the crew came in. Heads turned and shoulders hunched against the sudden cold. The pages on the table fluttered about.

"Maybe we should hold off on that scene," Markham said. "I'm all for realistic, but no cause to risk our necks."

Cicely's lips pressed together. Clearly she wanted to continue, but cold and blowing snow would make it difficult. "Agreed, but go out and see if you can get some storm footage, Roger. We can edit it in as needed or save it for stock."

Roger headed out to do his director's bidding.

"In the meantime," Cicely said, "why don't we rehearse the fight scene here? The more comfortable you all are with the action, the easier and faster it will go when it comes time to film out on the ice."

Tables and chairs on one end of the mess tent were set aside. Cicely sat facing the "set" and placed the actors where she wanted them. Anyone not in the climactic scene stayed behind Cicely.

It was similar to watching a stage production. There were lines of dialogue spoken with as much emotion and realism as in any play, despite the fact it would never be heard by the audience. The actors, Charlotte realized, were just as earnest as if they were in front of an audience. The words Cicely had written contributed to their characters, to the action. Even if the audience didn't hear it, even with limited text on the title cards, the story would come through.

Roslyn Sanford's Dorothy was a delicate balance of innocence, bravery, and fear. Peter's heroic determination to save his lady love came out in the flash of his dark eyes and the expressions on his face. Charlotte could see why the woman at the boat dock and many others found him attractive.

After several run-throughs, at least three of which were stopped when someone started laughing, the scene played out smoothly. Ted held Roslyn at gunpoint, or rather finger point, then Peter and Lewis wrestled him for the weapon. A "Bang!" from Cicely and Ted was "dead."

"Well done," Cicely said, standing. The broad smile on her face was reflected in the others. "We'll do it for real tomorrow."

Ted held up his hand, forefinger out and thumb up. "And I'll have a real gun, right? Bang!"

Everyone laughed.

"Of course," Cicely said. "The prop and costume folks will have everyone taken care of."

Paige edged closer. "Can we go over my bit some more, Cicely? I want to make sure I'm as ready as the others."

Was Paige trying to play up to Cicely as she had Stanley?

The somewhat amused expression on Cicely's face said she may have been thinking the same thing, but she gave the actress a friendly smile and said, "That sounds great. Let's go over here."

Beside Charlotte, Meade drained the last of his coffee from his cup and rose. "If you'll excuse me, Miss Brody, I have some correspondence to attend to."

"Be careful," Charlotte said. When he gave her a questioning look, she gestured toward his bandaged hand.

Grumbling something she couldn't catch, Meade strode to the dish deposit cart. The stout, dark-haired man on Smitty's crew met him at the cart and took the cup. The man said something, smiling at Meade and showing a lot of teeth. Was he asking the producer about a part in the film? Though unable to see Meade's face, Charlotte noted he shook his head and quickly exited the tent.

Cicely, Paige, and Roslyn went off by themselves to a side

table while the others put the mess tent back in order. Charlotte stood, ready to return to her tent, then spotted Caleb Burrows sitting quietly in a corner. She took a step toward him to ask how he felt about the revisions, but the lawyer rose and left the mess as if he had an appointment to keep. He hadn't appeared agitated. What had triggered his abrupt departure?

Chapter 15

✧

Well after dinner, most of the company had remained in the mess tent to rehearse and visit over pie and coffee. A few, including Roger Markham and Elaine the costumer, had left right after eating, Markham citing the need to prepare for the following day's shoot.

Some joined the actors while others played cards, chess, or checkers. All were chatty and lighthearted, discussing the changes in the story and the new fight scene. Peter and Ted were particularly animated as they went over a few finer points of the choreography. They gestured and "fought" while still seated, knocking into cherry-smeared plates and empty cups, which led to a great amount of laugher.

Charlotte laughed along with them. It was difficult to achieve the full impact of a deadly scene when your lower half was trapped beneath a table and china went skittering.

Whoever had brought the Victrola out to the site had moved it into the mess tent, and the latest Irving Berlin tune filled the air.

While the cast and crew appeared to enjoy the camaraderie she had seen when they first arrived, Charlotte noticed Wallace Meade was sitting alone, papers strewn in front of him, coffee cup at his elbow. He frowned down at whatever he was reading. He absentmindedly fiddled with his silver letter opener, tapping it on the table or stabbing it into the wood.

With his left hand.

A thrill of realization shimmered through Charlotte.

Now wait a minute. His right hand is injured, so he's favoring it. Avoiding the use of the wounded hand makes sense.

Yes, but how had his right hand become injured? Meade claimed it was from that same letter opener. Which meant he'd been holding it in his left hand—his dominant hand—when it slipped and jabbed his right.

Michael and James had suggested the killer was left-handed, but that wasn't proof. And recalling her visit to the Smiths' home, Charlotte remembered Caleb Burrows was a leftie as well.

Charlotte noted the bloodstained bandage around Meade's right hand. Even if his letter opener story were true, how had he been wounded on *both* sides of his hand?

The assistant cook approached Meade while Charlotte tried not to make her observation of the producer too blatant. He filled the producer's cup, bending low enough to say something in the older man's ear. Meade stilled, his hand tightening around the pen he held. He didn't make eye contact with the cook, and his lips barely moved as he spoke, but Charlotte would hazard a guess that whatever he said was not appreciation for refreshing his drink.

The cook poked Meade in the shoulder. The music on the Victrola wound down as the surrounding conversation hit a lull, allowing Charlotte to hear a snippet of the man's words to Meade. ". . . later, or there'll be trouble."

He then turned away, whistling as he sauntered back to the kitchen area as if nothing had happened.

Meade's gaze darted around the tent and fell on Charlotte. When their eyes met, he quickly gathered his papers and left.

What was going on there?

What kind of trouble was a cook's assistant making for Meade?

Meade had looked worried, but was he scared of something?

Charlotte brought her cup and dessert plate to the dish cart. The assistant cook smiled at her and asked if she enjoyed the pie. He was just one of Smitty's men, wasn't he? The sinister look about him was purely her imagination.

You're being silly.

Maybe. But maybe not.

Charlotte relayed her thanks for a fine meal, gathered her coat, hat, and scarf, and followed Wallace Meade outside. Head bowed against the wind and blowing snow, she started toward Meade's tent, but a flicker of light from the right caught her eye. She looked in that direction to the row of sheds on the opposite sides of the mess tent.

The prop man, Elaine the costumer, and even the players themselves were in and out of the sheds all the time. There was nothing terribly unusual about a light being on in one, even at this hour. Except this time there was, as most everyone else in the company was in the mess enjoying the evening of music and laughter. The thin bar of light leaking between the gaps in the shed wall might have been missed or ignored by most passersby who wanted to make it from tent to tent without a face full of snow.

Charlotte carefully made her way over. She put her ear to the crack between the frame and the door. The wind coming off the glacier chilled her exposed skin and made it difficult to hear what was going on within.

Probably just the property master or Elaine. Or perhaps Markham. Though with the afternoon's filming having been canceled, they probably took advantage of the unexpected free time in order to have a relaxing evening.

Only one way to find out.

Slowly, Charlotte eased the door open, peering in as she did so in preparation of closing it again if need be.

At first, all she saw was stacks of boxes and a rack of hanging furs and costumes with a narrow aisle between them. She opened the door just enough to slip in and closed it gently behind her, watching and listening for any indication she'd been heard. When no one came into view or called out, she crept up the aisle, careful not to jostle the costumes or crates, and peeked around the rack of furs.

Standing in profile to her, Wallace Meade fumbled with something in front of him on a waist-high crate. A lantern on a taller crate illuminated the area. Haphazardly stacked boxes partially obscured what he was up to, but Charlotte heard the *tink* of small bits of metal on metal. Meade wore a grim expression of concentration.

Charlotte stood on her tiptoes to try to see what he was doing. Before she could discern what he had in hand, Meade turned his head. Her heart jumped as their eyes met. She started backward, bumping into the stack of crates. He raised his left hand.

"Stop," Meade commanded.

The gun he pointed at her seemed to fill her vision. It looked a lot like the gun Ted was to use to hold Roslyn captive, the gun that would go off during his struggle with Peter and Lewis. If the trigger was accidentally pulled in the course of the faux fight, someone could be hurt or killed. Even if the bullets were discovered in the chamber before anything terrible occurred, word of yet another potential "accident" could see the company abandoning the production.

"Killing Stanley wasn't enough? You want the film to be shelved so badly that you're willing to hurt or kill someone else?"

"Reasoning didn't work, Miss Brody, nor did begging." Meade drew back the hammer with his thumb. "If it takes another body for them to finally walk away, so be it."

He didn't care if that body was Ted's or Peter's or Lewis's. Charlotte swallowed hard. Or hers. Her heart pounded in her ears, almost drowning out the howl of the wind and the rattle of the shed roof. Would anyone hear a shot fired over the wind and the music and the laughter? If she could keep him talking, perhaps she could manage to get away.

"What did Stanley do that was so terrible, Mr. Meade?"

"Tried to ruin me, is all." His face darkened with anger.

"He spent money like it grew on trees," she added, guessing that was reason enough to anger the entrepreneur, hoping to get him to elaborate.

"I expected to go over budget some," Meade said. "I was caught up in the excitement of *Fortune* as much as Stanley. Maybe more so. I sold off some stock. A lot of stock. Stanley kept spending, promising we'd make it back. Because he knew the film business, knew that this was something people were hungry for. When I ran out of things to sell, I borrowed from some very impatient men."

"You had to stop Stanley from spending so much."

Meade shook the gun at her and Charlotte jumped. "He was bleeding me like a stuck pig. If I didn't stop him, sooner or later I'd be found in a river or an alley somewhere. They put one of their goons on me so I wouldn't bolt."

Goon? The assistant cook? He was the only support staff employee Meade seemed to ever pay any sort of attention to, and not happily.

"You went to Stanley that night, to tell him to stop being so damn irresponsible." Sounding like she sympathized with him might get the story out of him. And perhaps buy her a few more minutes.

"No, he came to me, to tell me that he'd taken another five thousand dollars from the account. Insurance, he called it. Five grand! I couldn't believe it. We had just talked about keeping costs down. I had the damn cook water the soup and coffee. Where did Stanley think that money came from?"

"So pigheaded," Charlotte said, but Meade kept talking, as if he needed to get the incident off his chest. The more he spoke, however, the less likely he was to let her go. Yet she didn't dare interrupt.

"I just got so damn mad and before I knew it, my hands were around his throat and he was on the floor. Dead." Meade shook his head slowly. He looked more perturbed than remorseful, as if Stanley dying on him had been just one more way the director had managed to make his life difficult. "I hadn't meant it, but he was just so . . . There was no way anyone would see that as an accident. I had to get rid of him, make it look like he'd fallen in."

"You put him on your blanket and dragged him to the crevasse."

"His damn slipper fell off near the dogs' pen. That mutt grabbed it before I could and another one bit me." He held up his bandaged hand. That explained why there were injuries on the palm and on the back of his hand. "Then that one started barking his fool head off."

Byron. What was the saying about not trusting anyone your dog doesn't like?

"Killing Stanley didn't do what you thought it would." Charlotte tried to moisten her lips, but her tongue and mouth were equally dry. "Neither did ransacking the hotel rooms or having Peter York attacked."

"I told those thugs to break a rib or two, not just mess up his pretty face. Incompetent boobs." Meade's brow furrowed. "But I didn't ransack the rooms."

"I did." Caleb Burrows spoke softly from behind Charlotte.

Her heart felt like it stopped, and Meade's gun jumped in his hand, though he kept it pointed in her direction. Between the pounding of her own heart and the sound of the storm, she hadn't heard the lawyer come in. Neither had Meade.

"You?" Charlotte was tempted to face him but didn't want to take her eyes off Meade. "Why? What were you looking for?"

"Something Welsh had that I needed," Burrows said. "I waited in the lobby for everyone to go down for breakfast then snuck upstairs."

"You went through the other rooms and left the note to cover your tracks," she said. If Burrows also had a gun, she was in deep trouble.

"I didn't write any note," Burrows said.

"I did that," Meade admitted. "Figured I'd try to get what I could out of the situation."

The reason dawned on Charlotte. "You wanted to scare the company off."

"Nothing worked. What would it take to get them to quit?" Meade glared at Burrows, the sneer on his face revealing just how he felt about the lawyer. "Decided you wanted the money after all, eh?"

"Money?" Charlotte turned her head enough to catch Burrows's eye, but quickly returned her attention to Meade. "The five thousand dollars?"

"The insurance Stanley talked about," the producer said. His gaze darted between her and Burrows. "Our upstanding guardian of the law here was supposed to convince the AEC to quit harassing us. I told Stanley he was a fool to trust him."

"No," the lawyer protested. "I gave the money back. Left it in his tent the night he died. I wanted the letter he'd written to the AEC telling them all I'd done to betray them. That was *his* insurance against me. I couldn't let that get out."

Was that whom Carmen had seen in her tent that night, Caleb Burrows? Had she mistaken him for her husband?

"That wouldn't look good at all, would it?" Meade's mocking tone irritated Charlotte. She could imagine how Burrows felt. "Bad enough for a lawyer trusted by those naïve folks to take a payoff, but any chance of you getting onto the territorial legislature would be blown to bits."

A white man pursuing a political position might be allowed to sweep a minor bribe under the rug. A Native man, however, would have to have an irreproachable reputation. Would Caleb

Burrows have misrepresented himself to the AEC for money? Charlotte had no delusions of the lawyers' behavior; any man could be tempted by the right price. Seeing how passionate he was regarding the treatment of Natives, she was surprised he'd nearly succumbed to temptation.

"It was wrong to take Welsh's money in the first place, I know that," Burrows said. "It's something I'll have to reconcile with myself for a long time. The Native voice shouldn't be hushed at any price. But as I said, I returned the money. Left it in Welsh's tent. I just wanted the letter, which I found. That is less of a crime than murder."

"Where's the money now?" Charlotte asked. Carmen would have found it as she went through Welsh's things, wouldn't she?

"Safe. I'll hand it to my guy personally, once we're back in California," Meade said.

"You went into his tent," Charlotte said. Maybe Carmen had seen Meade searching for the money after learning about it from Welsh, not Burrows bringing it to him. That would explain the blood smear on the Welshes' tent. "You needed the money to appease the mob. If you convinced the studio to declare the film canceled, legitimate investors could write off their loss. You'd have fewer people to repay."

"Film's a risky business, Miss Brody, but it shouldn't ruin a man or his reputation. Stanley told me Burrows had returned the money, but he'd planned to offer more to get the AEC off our backs for good." The producer's hand tightened on the pistol grip, turning his knuckles white. "I couldn't believe it. We had just gone over how in the red *Fortune* was. He never listened to a damn thing I ever said."

"So you killed him," Burrows said.

Meade's mouth curled into a cruel smile. "Bribery may be a lesser crime than murder, Mr. Burrows, though it depends on who does the bribing and who kills whom. You had as much reason to kill Stanley as I did. If I kill *you* while you're trying to silence the unfortunately and fatally wounded Miss Brody, I doubt anyone would get too upset. Hell, I might be considered a hero for solving Stanley's murder."

Charlotte's brain registered that something about Meade's stance or arm position had changed.

Move!

Before she could react, strong hands grabbed her shoulders and swung her around. All at once, Caleb Burrows was between her and Meade, and a gunshot rang out in the small space.

Burrows's weight fell against her back, shoving her down the narrow aisle toward the door. "Go."

Charlotte stumbled forward, taking half a moment to look back. Burrows lay on his stomach blocking the aisle between the rack of furs and the stack of boxes. He held one hand to his back, his face contorted with pain.

"Run!"

Charlotte ran. She yanked the door open. Wind ripped it out of her hand and banged it against the shed wall. She held up her arm to keep the door from bouncing back and hitting her.

"Help! Help me!" she cried out as loud as she could as she ran toward the mess tent, the wind snatching her words away. Would they hear her over the wind? Over the music?

The dogs began to howl.

The lights on the pole swung frantically. Light and shadow danced across the paths and tent walls. A bulb banged against the pole and flashed brightly before going out.

"Help! He has a gun!"

Snow and ice kicked up by her left foot, between her and the tent. A split second later, she heard the shot. Instinctively, Charlotte veered in the opposite direction.

Her mind screamed, *Wrong way!*

She started toward the mess again and another shot sent her reeling to the right. Charlotte slipped, fell to one knee. Pain sliced through her knee and up into her thigh. She lurched to her feet and went left again. From the corner of her eye she saw Wallace Meade emerge from the near darkness. He raised the gun.

Pulse pounding in her head, Charlotte darted sideways, angling toward the dark. Toward the ice.

Moving target, her brain shouted as she zigzagged. *Don't stop.*

How many shots? Three? Four? Had he reloaded the bullets after shooting Burrows?

Oh God, Burrows. Was he dead?

Behind her, shouting. Not Meade, but she didn't dare turn. Didn't dare stop.

The ice sloped upward, worn smooth in places where the crew had trekked over the last several days. Wind biting into her face, she slipped and slid. She was getting closer to the crevasses. Meade was somewhere behind her in the dark. She couldn't stop.

The crew had marked the dangerous spots. Would she be able to see the marks before she fell to her death?

Something hit the back of her leg. She stumbled and fell, sprawling onto the ice. She scrambled forward. Her right leg collapsed beneath her.

Don't stop.

Using her hands, her left foot, and her right knee, she managed an awkward gait for a short distance, then sprawled again. Quickly, she rolled onto her back and sat up, hands braced on the ice behind her. Meade was on his knees holding the gun straight out toward her with both hands.

A fast-limping shadow loomed over Meade. It dropped onto him, shoving him forward.

Bang! Pain lanced through Charlotte's left shoulder. The impact knocked her back; her head smacked into the ice.

Help. Get up. Get away.

Shouts. Another shot. Loud enough to be heard over her pounding heart and ragged breathing.

Charlotte lifted her head. The shadowed figure rolled off Meade. He touched the producer's neck, then lurched toward her.

"Miss Brody," Roger Markham said kneeling beside her. "Charlotte. Where are you hurt?"

"Leg." A wave of pain and nausea rippled through her. "Shoulder. Caleb Burrows. In the prop shed. Meade shot him and killed Stanley."

Markham started unbuttoning her coat. He shouted toward camp, where Charlotte heard excited voices coming closer when the wind allowed. "Billy, go check the prop shed. Burrows is in there, shot. Take someone with you and do what you can. Someone go get my medical kit. Hurry. She's losing blood."

Cold. It was so cold on the ice.

"I was a medic during the war." Markham gently opened her coat. "Let me . . ."

His voice was swallowed by a roar in her head as she passed out.

Charlotte woke up long enough to realize she was no longer outside but lying on her cot. Paige and Elaine were getting Charlotte out of her coat and clothes. According to Paige, Markham had gone to check on Caleb Burrows and would be back as soon as possible.

Even with their help and moving as little as possible as they removed her garments, Charlotte could only bite her lip so long before the pain reduced her to tears. Elaine held a folded wad of linen to her shoulder. Paige tended to her leg.

"I played a nurse once," the actress said as she gently swathed Charlotte's calf. "This ain't so bad at all."

Charlotte was shaking and trying to control her breathing when Markham returned with his medical kit in hand.

Kneeling on the floor beside her, he withdrew a syringe and a small glass bottle from the leather and canvas bag. "Burrows is in his tent resting. Lucky for him, Meade was a damn awful shot. Bullet hit his right hip. Wound's not too bad, but I think it chipped or cracked the bone. Can't do much for him at the moment but keep him sedated."

Charlotte wished Meade had been less lucky when he'd taken aim at her, but it could have been worse, she reckoned.

"What is that?" she asked Markham as he consulted the bottle.

"Morphine. Bullet's still in your shoulder. We need to get it out, and it's gonna hurt like hell." He met her gaze and gave a rare smile. "Don't worry. I've done it before under worse circumstances."

"Morphine makes me deathly ill and I can't breathe," she said. His reassuring smile faded. "Can you use something else or get me a drink?"

Surely someone in the company had a bottle. Alcohol would numb her some or maybe knock her out.

Markham turned to Paige, who stood behind him with Elaine. "Go see if anyone has a stash. I need to sterilize the needle and wound anyway." He put away the morphine and syringe. "Glad you were able to tell me. I've seen guys with bad reactions. It ain't pretty."

Charlotte tried to relax on the cot, now that she knew she wouldn't stop breathing while Markham fixed her up. "When I was a little girl, I tried to see how far I could go when I jumped off a swing. Landed wrong and broke my leg. Doctor gave me morphine while he set it. It felt like I was trying to breathe through water."

"Lucky you didn't die," Markham said while he set out what he needed.

Charlotte chuckled at his lack of a bedside manner. He was a soldier-turned-cameraman, not a doctor. Though she had met doctors with less charm.

"Meade's dead, isn't he?"

Markham nodded, his lips pressed together. "I won't bother you for your side of the story now, but I have a feeling it's a doozy."

"Thank you for saving me."

He shrugged, as if embarrassed that she was making something of the act.

Paige came back into the tent. She pulled off her gloves with her teeth and retrieved a small brown bottle from her pocket. "Carmen gave me this. Stanley had a couple of bottles with him for the trip up that she'd forgotten were in her case. She promised it's safe."

Markham took the bottle and read the label by the light of the lantern. "Thirty percent alcohol, among other things. Can't hurt."

He uncorked the bottle and helped Charlotte take a generous swig. Almost too sweet at first, with the distinct tang of alcohol and a slightly bitter aftertaste. As she lay back down, Elaine returned holding a larger bottle.

"From one of the set guys," she said, passing it to Markham. "Not much left."

"It'll do for the wound and needle."

He opened the bottle and carefully poured some of the liquid over Charlotte's shoulder. Burning pain radiated out along her arm and up her neck. He stopped, gave her more of Welsh's medicine as well as a swallow of whatever was in the bottle. After several minutes, Charlotte started feeling woozy. She closed her eyes.

"There you go," Markham said. "Just go to sleep. We'll be done here soon."

For the next twelve or so hours, Charlotte floated in and out of consciousness. Markham didn't think her wounds were imminently life-threatening, but she heard him say he'd feel better once they were back in Cordova and at a hospital.

A fitful night of Paige or Elaine getting her a drink of water or giving her a dose of Welsh's medicine was followed by a morning sled ride to the train. After getting her and Caleb Burrows settled on beds fashioned from several cot mattresses, Charlotte went back to sleep. The train trip was a blur of vague pain and concerned faces.

"Stay with me, Charlie." Michael's voice was thick with emotion.

Back in Cordova already? At least she hoped that was the case, and not that she was having some sort of auditory hallucination.

Charlotte wanted to tell him she was fine, but neither her mouth nor her eyes would cooperate. Maybe she had taken a few too many doses. At least she didn't hurt much.

Chapter 16

Slowly, Charlotte opened her eyes. They felt gummy and gritty, the lids so heavy she considered going back to sleep.

You've slept enough.

She rubbed at her eyes with her right hand, the left refusing to move. All she saw was white and a slightly darker gray. Blinking her vision clear, she realized her head was turned toward a white wall and a white-curtained window. It was dark outside. Morning dark or evening dark? How long had she been out?

Charlotte turned her head, feeling the lumpiness of the pillow beneath it. Her left cheek touched the cool linen pillowcase. She smelled bleach and sweat. A second bed, unoccupied and crisply made, and a straight-back chair were on that side. A closed door interrupted another white wall.

Hospital. Semiprivate room, not in the ten-bed ward. The advantage of being the doctor's sister, she figured.

The door opened and her brother came in as if she'd somehow managed to mentally summon him. His face was pale beneath the dark blond beard and mustache, but when he saw Charlotte looking back at him, he smiled.

"Good morning." His shirt collar was open and his normally neatly knotted tie loose and askew beneath his suit coat. He bent down and pressed his lips to her forehead, perhaps as much in greeting as to check for fever, as their mother had when they were children. "How are you feeling?"

Charlotte tried to sit up, but a sharp ache cut through her shoulder. Her right leg throbbed in sympathy. She sucked in a breath.

"Lie still," Michael said. "Here, let me get you some water." He poured out a glass from a pitcher on the table between the two beds and helped her drink some. "Better?"

"Yes, thank you." Her voice sounded low and rough in her own ears. "Which morning is it? I've lost track."

He dragged the chair closer and sat. "I'm not surprised. You returned to Cordova yesterday. I looked at your wounds, but Markham did a fine job, considering what he had to work with. You woke up last night and spoke to me for a minute. Don't you remember?"

Charlotte shook her head, but only slightly, to avoid wooziness. "Not at all. Last thing I really remember is being on the train, then hearing you call me Charlie."

She must have been in bad shape if Michael had resorted to her childhood nickname.

He smiled, but there was concern behind it. "That was right before I examined you. The mixture you were taking did its job. I don't think you felt me poking and prodding."

"No, thank goodness." She asked for more water and after having her fill inquired about Caleb Burrows.

"He should make a good recovery," Michael said. "Might limp for a bit, but he'll be back in the courtroom in no time."

"He and Roger Markham both saved my life the other night." She owed the two men and had no idea how she might repay them.

"So I heard from the piecemeal story the film people were able to provide. Are you up to telling me what happened, or do you want to wait for Eddington?" Michael consulted his pocket watch. "I expect him to be here any minute."

Chances were good James had prepared a lecture on putting herself in danger after he explicitly told her to just watch and listen while he was gone. He had a point, of course, but he also knew saying such a thing to her was as good as telling her not to breathe. He'd be mad and concerned, as Michael was.

"I think I'll wait for James, if it's all right with you. That way, as my doctor, you can tell him not to aggravate my condition by yelling at me."

Michael gently tugged a lock of her hair. "Even if you do deserve it. I swear, Charlotte, if you don't start watching out for yourself . . . You had us scared to death, especially Becca."

Charlotte clutched at his arm, guilt and concern adding to her aches. "You didn't tell her I was bad off or anything, did you?"

He covered her hand with his and squeezed her fingers. "I told her you were young and strong and the wounds weren't critical. You did lose a lot of blood, though. But your injuries themselves aren't all that scared us."

She knew what he meant, and figured it would be the main topic of James's lecture. "I know. Truly, I don't intend to put myself in harm's way, but trying to figure out the identity of a killer comes with a certain risk."

"It does, but it's not your job to do so." A triple knock sounded on the door, interrupting Michael. He rose to open it, still talking to her. "What you have to remember is that you have people here who care about you, who wish you to be with them for as long as possible."

Like him and Becca. Charlotte had agreed to take care of the girl, was thrilled to be part of her life. But there was more to their relationship than guardian and ward, more than simple friendship.

Michael opened the door and Becca hurried in. Behind her, hesitating in the doorway, James caught Charlotte's eye. He was as pale and weary looking as Michael.

More than just Michael and Becca want you around.

"You're okay," Becca said, bending over Charlotte and giving her a gentle hug. Charlotte's shoulder throbbed sharply even with the minimal contact and she started. Becca straightened, her face full of concern. "I'm sorry. I didn't mean to hurt you."

Charlotte smiled at her and took her hand. "It's fine. I'm so glad to see you. Are you all right?"

"Me?" Becca asked with a laugh. "I'm not the one who got shot."

Thank God. If Becca had been on location with the company, and Meade hadn't been stopped from sabotaging the film, who knows what might have happened to whom when the gun went off "accidentally." Any of the actors or crew could have been hurt, including Becca.

"I'll be out of here soon," Charlotte said, looking at Michael. Her brother quirked an eyebrow at her in a skeptical manner. She didn't amend her statement. "In the meantime, let Esther's family know I deeply appreciate their generosity in letting you stay on with them."

"I will." Becca smiled, but within moments her chin was quivering and tears welled. She squeezed Charlotte's hand.

"Oh, honey." Charlotte wrapped her good arm around the girl's slender shoulders and drew her close. Becca pressed her face to Charlotte's neck. She felt Becca's hot tears, but heard no sound. What had she put her through? "I'm sorry," Charlotte whispered, emotion tightening her throat. "I didn't think . . . I shouldn't have . . . I'm sorry."

She laid her cheek on Becca's head and closed her eyes, fighting back her own tears. Michael had warned her that Becca was upset, but seeing the poor child like this, after all she'd been through with her family, hit Charlotte in the chest like a ton of bricks. While Charlotte had no intention of trying to replace Becca's mother, she realized just how close the two of them had become in the last few months.

Becca shifted and Charlotte moved her arm to allow her to straighten. She sat on the edge of the bed, holding Charlotte's hand while wiping away tears with the other. "I was so worried."

"I know, sweetheart, and I'm sorry I put you through that. Never again. I promise."

Becca nodded, then frowned. "What if there's a really important story and you have to help someone?"

Charlotte cupped the girl's cheek in her palm. "Nothing is more important than you."

She had promised to take care of Becca, but she hadn't expected to feel so protective of her, even against her own actions.

"You like doing that, don't you? Figuring out who did bad things?" Becca's brow wrinkled with confusion. Charlotte had often told her stories of how she'd helped expose a crooked politician or a cheating business owner. She'd led an exciting life. Perhaps too exciting.

She couldn't lie now. "I do, but I shouldn't do dangerous things for a story."

"I second that," James said. He and Michael had stood quietly by the door. Charlotte had almost forgotten they were in the room. She caught the deputy's eye. There was no glint of amusement or any sense he was trying to lighten the mood.

Michael glanced between the two of them, then cleared his throat. "Come on, Becca, I'll walk you to school."

"Do I have to?"

Charlotte smiled at her and squeezed her hand. "All I'm going to do is rest and give Michael a hard time. Go to school and come back at the end of the day, all right?"

"Visiting hours will be just ending," Michael said. "I'll make a note so you can stay."

Becca gave Charlotte a gentle hug and pecked her on the cheek.

Charlotte returned the kiss. "Have a good day, honey."

She sighed dramatically. "I'll be distracted all day with worry, but okay."

Becca slid off the bed to allow Michael to come over and give Charlotte a hug and kiss. "Be back in a bit, Sis. We'll talk then."

He and Becca said good-bye to James, who still hadn't smiled since arriving. Once the two of them were out of the room, James tossed his hat on the empty bed and sat in the chair beside her bed. He laid his hands flat on his thighs and stared down at the floor.

Several moments passed in silence.

"Hello, Charlotte, how are you feeling?" Charlotte said, deepening her voice in a poor imitation of his.

Slowly, James lifted his head. Dark circles bruised the skin beneath his bloodshot eyes. It appeared as if he'd been drinking too much, but Charlotte knew the man better than that.

She reached across her body with her right hand, offering it to him. He laced his fingers with hers. "I *am* going to be all right, you know."

"This time," he said, his voice rough. "I should have been there."

Charlotte squeezed his hand. "You had to go back and had no way of knowing what would happen. In a way, it may have been better that you weren't there. I think Meade might have been more reluctant to try something if you'd been around. Then he might not have been caught."

"And you wouldn't have been hurt."

She shrugged, wincing when the movement made her left shoulder pulse with pain. "There's no guarantee I wouldn't have done the same thing had you been there. Not likely, but you know me."

He rose suddenly, releasing her hand and stalking the room like a caged jungle cat. "I do know you. What I don't know is how the hell I'm supposed to protect you, mostly from yourself."

A heated rush of what she could only describe as resentment

burned in her gut. "I'm a grown woman, James. You don't have to protect me from myself, thank you."

He stopped midstride and faced her, blue eyes blazing. "As deputy marshal, it's my job to keep you from getting involved in dangerous situations. And as the man who—"

He cut himself off, jaws clamped tight.

"As the man who what?" she asked. He looked down at the floor again, breathing hard, his hands fisted at his sides. "As the man who slept with me? Do you think that gives you say over how I behave, some sort of special right?"

He took a deep breath and slowly released it, preparing to reply.

Don't say it. Please, don't say it.

"I can't do this, Charlotte."

She had hoped he wouldn't forbid her from following dangerous stories. Well, he hadn't done that, but she had no idea what he meant.

"Can't do what? Allow me to do my job?"

Charlotte's entire being ached. She had thought James was different. She knew her involvement in cases and stories pushed him to his wit's end, that he'd prefer she not put herself in harm's way. She'd prefer it as well. They'd spoken of consequences plenty of times. She knew what she was doing, usually, and accepted the outcome.

James walked back to the chair and sat down heavily, head bowed. Without looking, he reached for her hand. She took it. The ache inside eased some but didn't completely disappear.

He lifted his head, the redness in his eyes more pronounced. "I can't pretend that being intimate with you hasn't changed things between us, because it has."

"I liked what we had before," she said. "Adding physical acts doesn't have to change anything. I'm not asking that of you, and I don't think you should ask it of me."

"I'm gonna be honest with you. I've been with other women."

Charlotte opened her eyes wide in mock horror. "Scandalous."

A small smile curved his lips, then, staring into her eyes, he spoke again with a sincerity Charlotte had rarely heard from a lover. "There have been women I've slept with and said good-bye to the next day without a second thought. There have been women I had longer relationships with and was disappointed when it ended, but got over it." He swallowed hard, still holding her gaze. "But I can count on two fingers the number of women whom I've cared for deeply. So deeply, that when I became angry or terrified by situations involving them it felt like I couldn't breathe."

James had an ex-wife. He'd admitted beating a man when he'd suspected she was stepping out on him. The rage he'd felt then had scared him and precipitated their divorce.

"Stella," Charlotte said.

"And you," he replied, his voice cracking.

Her heart and stomach seemed to momentarily switch places. A lump formed in her throat. What was he saying?

"When I saw you yesterday, being wheeled down the corridor to the exam room, a bloody bandage on your shoulder, and your face so pale—" James shook his head. "I thought I'd lost you."

The lump in her throat grew, cutting off her air. Her pulse pounded in her ears.

"I'll apologize for my ham-handed ways that make you think I'm trying to force you to do something you don't want to, to be something you aren't." He half-rose and leaned over to kiss her. Just a light press of his mouth on hers. "But I won't ever apologize for wanting to protect you, or for the feelings I have."

He released her hand and turned to pick up his hat.

"James?" His name came out in a rough whisper. He set his hat on his head and faced her. "You don't ever need to apologize for that. Or for being ham-handed."

He smiled. "Appreciate that, 'cuz I reckon it'll happen again. Get some rest. I have to talk to those film people some more."

He started to walk toward the door, stopped, about-faced, and strode back to her bedside. Sweeping his hat off his head, he leaned down and kissed her on the mouth. Harder this time, but still more chaste than usual. Everything tingled. When he moved to break the kiss, Charlotte pressed her palm to the side of his warm neck, holding him in place for an extra second or two.

She tried to raise her left arm to draw him closer. A twinge of pain grabbed her shoulder. "Ouch."

James straightened, and she lowered both hands. His brow wrinkled with concern. "You all right?"

Charlotte managed a shaky smile. "I will be."

He studied her for a moment, then nodded. "I'll be by later. Good morning, Miss Brody."

"Good morning, Deputy."

He tugged the brim of his hat, then left the room, gently closing the door behind him.

She settled back against the pillow, and her smile faded. The pain in her shoulder had subsided to a dull ache. But that wasn't what had her worried.

Charlotte had a pretty clear idea how James felt. Her own feelings were equally obvious.

And they scared the hell out of her.

Later that morning, after a fitful attempt to sleep, Charlotte gave up trying. She asked the nurse, who had come in to check on her, where Caleb Burrows's room was located.

The nurse, an older woman wearing a white dress, white apron, and a starched white cap over her tightly pinned bun of hair, pressed her lips together. "Now why would you want to go see the likes of him? A proper young woman like yourself shouldn't be concerned with his sort. You need your rest."

The likes of him? His sort? What did she mean by that?

Irritation prickled at the back of Charlotte's neck. "Mr. Burrows is a friend, and I would like to talk to him, if he's up to visitors."

The nurse didn't waver in her determination to keep Charlotte still. "You lost a lot of blood, young lady, and I'm sure the doctor would be angry with both of us if you were to get out of bed."

"The doctor is used to me doing things against his wishes." Charlotte flipped the covers back with her good arm and carefully eased her legs over the side of the bed. Not bad, as far as pain went. That was a good sign. The simple cotton gown she wore covered her neck to ankles. A dressing gown hung on the back of the door. "Mr. Burrows's room? Or do you want me wandering up and down the hall calling his name?"

The nurse's lips came together again, so tightly they practically disappeared. "He's down the other hall, in B ward."

Steadying herself with her hand on the bed, Charlotte set her feet on the floor. The cold tile sent a chill through her. Her wounded leg protested but seemed willing to hold her up. It had only been a flesh wound, Michael had said, though it would likely scar.

To her credit, the nurse walked with Charlotte to the door and helped her with the dressing gown. She held it out while Charlotte threaded her right arm through the sleeve. The left side was draped over her injured shoulder and sling. The nurse tied the gown closed for her.

Shaking her head, the nurse said, "You have nothing on your feet."

Charlotte looked down at her bare toes. "I don't think anyone will care, do you?" That was met with a frown of disapproval, but Charlotte merely smiled. "Could you get the door, please?"

The nurse complied, and Charlotte limped into the hall. Another uniformed nurse walked past her, carrying a covered tray, her footfalls tapping softly in the quiet passage. Several other doors along the corridor marked the few private and semiprivate rooms. At the end of the hall to the left was A ward, with ten or twelve beds. Charlotte heard low conversations, though she couldn't make out words. She gave her nurse a questioning look.

The woman sighed and pointed to the right. As Charlotte started off, slow but steady, the nurse walked with her.

"I think I can manage," Charlotte said.

"There should be another nurse down there somewhere." She seemed somewhat relieved not to have to accompany Charlotte, yet still perturbed. "Call out if you need any help."

"Thank you."

Periodically using the white wall for support, Charlotte made her way down the hall and around the corner. The carbolic acid-bleach aroma was just as strong here, the hall lined with gurneys and a few buckets. A young woman in the same white uniform as the other sat on a chair near an open window smoking a cigarette and reading a magazine. The faint acrid bite of the smoke tinged the air when the wind blew the wrong way. The nurse glanced up as Charlotte limped past. From the open ward at the end of the hall, she heard moans and people talking.

B ward was larger than A ward, with over a dozen beds. Its windows were curtained, keeping the room dim and, dare she say, depressing.

Caleb Burrows was lying in the first bed on the right, and he had a visitor. His normally slicked-back hair was mussed, and his complexion on the gray side. Three of the other beds were occupied, the patients all Native men apparently asleep.

Charlotte considered turning around and coming back later, but she was already there, and the effort to make it down the hall had her sweating and hurting some.

Jonas Smith turned, surprised to find her there by the look on his face. He gave her a quick once-over. "Miss Brody. How are you?"

"Not terrible, considering," she said, smiling. "I don't want to interrupt."

"I was just on my way out," Smith said.

"Are you up to seeing me for a minute, Mr. Burrows?" She didn't want to tax the man. "I can come back later."

Burrows raised his hand to beckon her over. "Of course, Miss Brody."

Charlotte made her way to a hard-backed chair beside his bed. As she lowered herself down, Jonas Smith retrieved his coat and hat from a coat tree near the doorway.

"I'll leave you two to chat," he said, slipping the coat on. "Nice to see you up and about, Miss Brody."

"Thanks to Mr. Burrows," she said. "And Mr. Markham."

Smith offered his right hand. Charlotte took it, and the AEC president covered both with his other hand. "God bless you, Miss Brody. Take care."

Warmth filled Charlotte's chest. "Thank you, Mr. Smith. You too."

Smith smiled and released her hand. He nodded to Burrows. "I'll bring you some of Emma's fry bread tomorrow, Caleb."

"I should have gotten shot sooner if that's how you treat folks here."

The two men laughed quietly and said good-bye.

When Smith had gone, Burrows turned to her. "Your brother came by earlier to let me know how you were doing. I'm very glad you're all right."

"I definitely have you to thank for that fact," Charlotte said. "You saved my life."

Burrows's cheeks darkened. "Anyone would have done it."

"Maybe." She reached out and laid her hand on his arm. "But you did. I can't ever repay you for putting yourself in harm's way for me."

A hint of the shrewdness Charlotte had come to recognize lit his dark eyes. "Actually, there is something you can do for me."

"Anything." Taking heed of her journalist's instinct, she added, "Within reason."

Burrows glanced at the others in their beds. His ward-mates seemed to be asleep, but it was difficult to say for sure. "About what I told you and Meade that night," he said, his voice low.

It took Charlotte a few moments to recall the content of that conversation. A bribe that was later refused. Political ambition that might be thwarted before it could even begin.

"What about it?" she asked.

The lawyer laced his fingers together and rested his hands on his abdomen. "I would appreciate that exchange and any reference to the interactions I had with Mr. Welsh be forgotten."

For her own sense of having a complete story, Charlotte asked, "Was your tête-à-tête with Welsh near the rubbish bins before or after he made his offer?"

Burrows's dark eyes widened. "How—?" He clamped his lips together.

"The way Stanley was acting, I'd guess after."

The lawyer wasn't about to say anything more, so Charlotte let it go. In the grand scheme of things, the timing of that conversation probably didn't matter.

Burrows was asking for something that could set a dangerous precedent. The journalist in her fought against withholding information on a story. Under normal circumstances, she would have probably laughed at his request. But these weren't normal circumstances. He had saved her life, and the bribe money had been returned after he thought better of the conditions. Granted, the act was not completely unselfish, and it gave Charlotte good reason to be suspicious of Burrows in the future, which she certainly would be.

"Once I write up the events of the last few days and put it all together, I'm sure I'll be able to manage to leave that bit out."

Relief softened the tension in his shoulders and face, and Burrows smiled humbly. "Thank you."

"Though I can't guarantee such editorial restraint if there are any further shenanigans, Mr. Burrows." There was only so much she was willing to do.

"Understood, Miss Brody. Should I save your life again, however, I expect a bit of quid pro quo."

Charlotte laughed, as did Burrows, and both winced as their injuries were taxed by their movements.

When they recovered, Charlotte asked him something that had been bugging her since that night. "How did you come to be in the prop shed at just the right time?"

Burrows's dusky cheeks darkened. "Honestly?"

"That would be preferable, yes," she said, grinning.

"I was headed to the latrine and saw you go into the shed. Wondered who was sneaking about. Just my natural curiosity getting the better of me."

She leaned forward slightly. "I tend to do that too."

"I'll keep that in mind."

"What about the AEC and the film?" Without a real legal leg to stand on, Charlotte wondered what sort of action they might take should *North of Fortune* turn out to disappoint.

Burrows shifted slightly on the bed, more physically uncomfortable, she thought, than in regard to the question. "We'll give Miss Welsh a chance to keep her promise. There are enough well-placed Alaskans down there that we'll hear about any . . . shenanigans." They both grinned. "If she lets us down, we'll make a stink. It's not a legal maneuver, but we'll be sure to let folks know how we feel."

"And if she keeps her promise?"

"Then we'll sing her praises as an example for all to follow."

"I'm sure she'd appreciate that."

They spoke about the film, then other issues regarding Native Alaskans, particularly land, employment, education, and voting rights. Charlotte hadn't realized the vast and terrible history that had shaped the current underpinning of inequity and distrust. There were wrongdoings on both sides, but the fist of the federal government was squeezing hard where it could.

"I think the *Times* needs to do more," she said, taking a mental account of the varied topics pertinent to her new home that she knew little to nothing about.

"I'm certain Jonas—" One of the men in the room began to moan and thrash about in his bed. Charlotte started to rise, but Burrows stopped her. "He gets restless for a minute or two, then settles. It'll pass."

The man called out as if in pain, bringing her to her feet again.

"I'll get the nurse," she said. "Time I headed back to my room anyway. Let's talk again before you return to Juneau, Mr. Burrows."

She offered her hand to shake his. He took it, smiling, but Charlotte could see that he was tired and needed rest as much as she did.

"Absolutely," he said, "and please call me Caleb. If that's all right with you?"

"It is, if you'll call me Charlotte. Thank you again. Heal quickly, Caleb."

"You too, Charlotte."

With a last glance at the distraught man in the far bed, she limped back into the hallway. The same nurse was sitting near the window, writing on a sheet of flowery stationery.

"Excuse me," Charlotte said as she approached. "There's a patient who needs some help."

The nurse didn't so much as look up from her page. "Yeah, I'll be right there."

Charlotte continued past, the man's moans loud enough to hear from down the hall. She stopped and turned around. "I think he's in pain. This is a hospital, isn't it?"

The nurse glared at her, set her pen down hard, and then stalked off to the ward.

Dismayed and incensed by the shameless attitude of the nurse, Charlotte moved as quickly as she was able, anxious to ask the other nurse for a pen and paper.

*   *   *

Two more days in the hospital was two too many, as far as Charlotte was concerned, but Michael had insisted. She'd been able to negotiate a reduction in her stay down from the week he had originally ordered. The rest of her convalescence was spent at home, being nursed in turn by Brigit and Becca. James stopped in between runs to the glacier to gather the final details of the case.

When he came to visit, James relayed what he could to Charlotte. The film company had been given permission to continue, and did so, though they didn't stay at the site for the week Cicely had planned. Despite some of the crew grumbling suggestions to rename the film *Fortune's Curse*, she was determined to shoot as much footage as possible. Of course the weather finally decided to cooperate on their last day on-site, but all in all, Cicely Welsh and the *Fortune* crew were satisfied with what they'd accomplished.

During James's questioning, most of the company had been terribly shocked at the circumstances surrounding Stanley's death and the attacks on Charlotte and Caleb. The fact that Meade had considered framing Burrows for Stanley's murder, as well as her own, defied their assessments of the producer. "Meade seemed like a decent sort," was a common refrain. Charlotte had heard that all too often regarding the personality of a killer.

The morning of the company's departure, James picked up Charlotte at her house and drove her down to the steamship dock. She expected him to bring up their earlier conversation about consequences and why they mattered more now, but when he didn't she realized what he was doing. He had said his piece, had made his feelings known, more or less. It was up to her to decide what happened next. He'd waited her out before, allowing her to decide when their relationship would move on to the next stage. But how long would his patience last? It wasn't fair to keep him dangling.

Their arrival at the ocean dock put a hold on those thoughts for the moment. The crowd seeing the company off was considerably smaller than the one who had greeted them. Had the deaths and troubles that had plagued the production scared off the fans? For the sake of the people involved with the film, Charlotte hoped that wasn't the case, and that it wasn't a shade of things to come for audience attendance once *North to Fortune* was released. With any luck, when news about Welsh and Meade became public, people would be morbidly intrigued and ticket sales would soar.

James parked the car, then came around to open her door. Charlotte was still achy and tired quickly. She thanked him as he helped her out of the vehicle.

"My pleasure," he said, smiling as he held her good arm.

"I don't want you to treat me like I'm going to break, though," she reminded him.

He shook his head. "Oh, no no no. Never. In fact, I'm gonna have you walk back to town."

Charlotte would have swatted him if her left arm wasn't being held in the sling. Instead, she bumped his hip with hers and they both laughed.

The aroma of salt and tar filled the blustery air. The main storm had passed, but in Alaska Mother Nature was very good at reminding you winter wasn't over until she said it was over.

"Miss Brody," Cicely Welsh called out. She, Mrs. Welsh, and Roslyn came toward them, leaving the others in the crew chatting with fans and the locals who had been part of the production. "I'm so glad to see you up and about."

"Thank you," Charlotte said. "We just wanted to come down and say good-bye."

"It's been quite the time up here." Roslyn looped her arm through Cicely's and Carmen's. "Wouldn't mind coming back someday."

Cicely gave her friend, then Charlotte and James, a warm,

sad smile. "It's been bittersweet. When *Fortune* is finished, I'd like to arrange for a screening here. We'll come back up for that."

"A marvelous idea." Charlotte was surprised at her own anticipation. Perhaps seeing the final production would be the best way to prove to everyone that the film wasn't cursed. "I'm sure it'll get rave reviews here."

"I hope so," Cicely said. "I have enough footage to put together stunning exterior scenes. With some artful cutting, I think it will be as close to Papa's vision as I can get it and still have a story everyone will enjoy."

"We'll ask Nan if she can recommend someone," Roslyn said.

Charlotte had no idea who Nan was or what she did in the film business, but Cicely thought the idea a good one.

Carmen caught Charlotte's eye. She was a tragic figure, swathed in dark wool and fur, her face pale beneath powder and rouge. "I want to thank you for finding out what happened to my husband. It was a terrible thing, but knowing helps."

Charlotte eased her arm from James's and gently grasped Carmen's hand. "I'm sorry you and your daughter had to go through this at all."

The older woman nodded, blinking rapidly. "We'll have a memorial back home and lay him to rest with his parents."

"Did Norse Brothers take care of Mr. Welsh to your satisfaction?" James asked. Once Michael had released the body, despite several routine test results still pending, the undertakers had been tasked with preparing Mr. Welsh's body for transport.

"They were very kind and understanding, even when Mama asked to have Papa cremated." Cicely wiped away an escaped tear.

Roslyn hugged her arm closer, shared pain on her face.

"I couldn't bear to have him traveling in the storage hold of the ship," Carmen said, daubing her nose and eyes. "They gave us a lovely urn."

James's brow furrowed, and Charlotte knew there was something else on his mind. "I'm glad they were able to accommodate your wishes."

The ship's horn blew three times, calling passengers aboard.

"We'd better get settled," Roslyn said. She smiled at Charlotte and James. "Thank you both again."

The three women crossed the dock together. Cicely held on to her mother's arm as they climbed the gangplank. Roslyn followed close behind.

Others came over to say good-bye to Charlotte and James. Peter York was as cheerful as ever, his own continued recovery evident by the greenish yellow bruises on his face. Paige Carmichael held his arm, a new light in her eyes. Had she and the actor become more than friends? Charlotte hoped they were sincere, or at least mutually agreed upon in what the publicity of their new relationship might accomplish.

Roger Markham limped over and shook Charlotte's hand. "Take care of yourself, young lady."

"I appreciate the chance to do so, Mr. Markham," she said, squeezing his hand warmly. "I wouldn't be here if it wasn't for you."

"An old soldier like me needs to throw himself into the action now and again," he said with a crooked smile. "Keeps us from getting soft."

James and Markham shook hands, then the cameraman headed to the ship.

Arm in arm, Charlotte and James watched the passengers board for several minutes, until the wind came in over the water, sending chills through her. Charlotte shifted on her feet and grimaced when her right leg throbbed.

"Let's get you home," James said, turning her toward the car. He helped her settle in the passenger seat, then cranked the engine and climbed in.

"It'll be nice to see them come back for the film premiere." Charlotte decided talking about something—anything—was better than thinking about her aches or what personal topics might fill the ride home.

"Give you a chance to dress up again," he said, maneuvering the car back onto the road to town. "You enjoy that."

"And you don't," she said with a laugh.

"No, but I like looking at you when you're dressed up. Or not." He kept his eyes on the road, but she knew he was watching her in his peripheral vision.

Charlotte stared at his profile, the crooked nose and bearded chin, and the smirk that revealed the sense of humor he didn't share with many.

"Very funny."

"What?" His voice went up with feigned innocence.

She shook her head and rolled her eyes at his antics.

In the lull, Charlotte's mind grasped at more to talk about. Not that she minded companionable silence. She just didn't want it to inadvertently become filled with things she wasn't prepared to address. The case seemed to be a safe topic, and something that had been bothering her thankfully popped into her head.

"Did you find anything interesting in Meade's belongings?"

James shook his head. "Nothing to speak of." He frowned. "Why? What did you expect to be found?"

The money Meade had taken back from Welsh, but Charlotte couldn't say anything about that without explaining where it had come from and how she knew about it. That would break her promise to Caleb regarding the bribery attempt. If that amount of cash had been among Meade's things, she was sure James would have mentioned it.

Which meant someone else had gotten to it first. There had been an awful lot of excitement and confusion after she and Caleb had been shot. It wouldn't have taken much effort for someone to get into Meade's tent and go through his things. Perhaps the mob thug who'd been sent to keep an eye on Meade? There was no way to know.

"Just curious," she said. She'd tell him the whole story someday, but not yet.

"Uh-huh." James sighed. Maybe he was getting used to her not sharing everything.

Within a few minutes, they were turning up the hill toward her little greenhouse. Fatigue dragged at her limbs as she climbed out of the car. James helped her up the stairs. Just as they reached the door, she heard Michael call out to them from the corner. They waited for him to come up.

"You have to stop the ship," Michael said, huffing and puffing. He must have run all the way from his office.

"Why?" James asked.

"I finally got the results of those tests on Stanley Welsh's stomach contents." Michael followed them into the entry, and she and James proceeded to remove their coats and boots. "There was arsenic in him."

"His medicine had arsenic in it," Charlotte said.

"A lot of medicines do," Michael said, "but the results suggest elevated levels."

"Stanley Welsh was being poisoned." James's eyebrows met over his nose as he frowned.

"Possibly. Probably. I'd need to run more tests on the body. That's why you need to stop the ship and get him back here." Michael looked at James, perhaps expecting him to head back out to relay the order from the telegraph station.

Charlotte and James paused, looking at each other. He shook his head slowly as he hung up their hats and coats.

"What?" Michael asked. "If you can't bring the ship back, have them detained in Juneau, or at least contact the California authorities. Someone there can run the exact same tests. Probably more exact ones, as I'm sure their laboratories are better equipped."

"You released the body. Carmen had him cremated," Charlotte said, leading the way into the parlor. She sat on the divan, suddenly weary. "Norse's even gave her a lovely urn."

"Cremated?" Michael followed them in, forgetting to remove his wet shoes and outerwear. "Ashes can't be tested as effectively." He appealed to James. "She was probably poisoning him."

Via the medicine Carmen Welsh had given Paige for Charlotte? But Carmen had said the bottle was safe. Had she meant that it hadn't been tainted or that it was fairly innocuous as prescribed?

"That's not what killed him," James said. He sat to Charlotte's right, though not so close as to be inappropriate. Was he keeping space between them to keep their current relationship from Michael or to tell her she still had the reins as far as where they were going?

"Well, no." Her brother seemed rather disappointed in that. "But if she was trying to kill him, that's still a crime."

"True." James crossed his legs and leaned back. He seemed almost as weary as she was. "Though not necessarily one that can be proven, let alone prosecuted, at this point. If the medicine wasn't the source, or the only source, what else could have been?"

"Typically, poisoners use food or drink."

Charlotte remembered her conversations with Paige Carmichael and Smitty, the film company's cook and supply man. "Carmen cooked almost every meal for Stanley. Insisted on it. And when Smitty the cook tried to make him something, Smitty couldn't understand why Stanley said he didn't like garlic when he smelled of it."

Michael nodded eagerly. "Garlic, yes. His body had that aroma."

"I'll wire the California authorities," James said, "but I don't expect they'll be able to do a hell of a lot."

Michael's shoulders slumped. "Can't you exert your authority as marshal?"

"I'm not the marshal yet."

Marshal Blaine hadn't officially retired, though his wife was strongly suggesting it after his heart attack. If he decided to leave Cordova, then James would be his likely successor. Though whether James would be promoted to marshal was up to others, not Blaine.

"I'll do what I can from here, Doc."

"For a woman who was possibly poisoning her husband," Charlotte said, "Carmen was convincing in her grief. She even fainted when we first discovered Stanley in the crevasse."

"Well, she was an actress, wasn't she?" Michael unwound his scarf and tossed his hat on a nearby chair. Since there was no reason to run back out again, it looked like he'd decided to stay for a bit.

"I never suspected her to be anything but a grieving widow when I interviewed her," James said, shaking his head. "And I look for that sort of odd behavior."

Charlotte settled back against the cushion. "Maybe there should be some sort of award for that kind of talent."

James and Michael stared at her as if she'd grown another head.

"An award?" James asked, incredulous. "For acting?"

"Sure," she said, warming up to the idea, though she suspected pain and fatigue were playing tricks with her thoughts. "They could throw a big party and hand out medals or statues."

"You have some odd ideas, Sis." Michael headed to the kitchen.

"You wouldn't want me any other way."

"True," James said. His head rested against the back of the sofa, eyes closed, and his long legs stretched out. He was comfortable there in her house, with her.

And damn it, she was comfortable with him as well. Perhaps more than comfortable.

Charlotte nudged his leg and laid her right hand palm up on the cushion between them. His eyes barely opened, but she saw him glance down at her offered hand. He smiled and covered her palm with his, entwining their fingers.

"Staying for supper?" she asked.

"Sure. I'll even wash the dishes." James squeezed her fingers. "Whatever you want, Miss Brody. You just let me know."

Charlotte scooted closer and rested her head on his shoulder. "Oh, I will, Deputy. You can count on it."

Connect with Us

Visit us online at
KensingtonBooks.com
to read more from your favorite authors, see books
by series, view reading group guides, and more.

Join us on social media

for sneak peeks, chances to win books and prize packs,
and to share your thoughts with other readers.

facebook.com/kensingtonpublishing
twitter.com/kensingtonbooks

Tell us what you think!

To share your thoughts, submit a review,
or sign up for our eNewsletters, please visit:
KensingtonBooks.com/TellUs.